This time she'd listen to her broken heart, and not her hormones, even though her heart jumped at the sight of him.

He had never been there for her before, and certainly wasn't staying now.

Lacey managed to find her voice. "I hope this is a bad dream and I'll wake up and find you gone."

Her ex-husband pulled out a chair, turned it around and straddled it. "Well, darling, it seems your nightmare isn't going away. Neither am I."

She managed to conceal her trembling hands by wrapping her fingers tight around the beer bottle. Lacey took a deep drink, relishing the cool wash of liquid sliding down her throat. It reminded her of that time after they'd consumed several beers and then he'd kissed her and they had...

Not. Going. There.

"Go away, Jarrett. If you're here on a mission, aren't you supposed to be invisible in your invincibility?"

He did not smile. Flickering candlelight on the table revealed the sharp angles and planes of his lean face. Jarrett looked all business.

"You're my mission. I'm taking you out of here."

* * *

We hope you en̲_____but in

If y̲_____u
think ̲_____se!
̲_____ spense

Dear Reader,

Navy SEAL Seduction began on a warm February evening in a country I often visited for twenty-two years in my work as a humanitarian writer. I sat outside the hotel where I was staying and a group of the president's security guards crossed the terrace. Suddenly Jarrett, the hero, came to mind as clear as the guns the men carried. I could see Jarrett dining with Lacey, his ex-wife, and feel his worry and fear as Lacey shrugs off the impending violence simmering in the background.

Jarrett is a strong, sexy Navy SEAL who still loves his ex-wife, though he has fought these feelings since the divorce. He is determined to protect Lacey and keep her safe from all harm. Lacey still feels the old passion kindling when she sees Jarrett, but when he was deployed after she miscarried their baby, she felt abandoned. Although he makes her feel alive, and cherished and safe, she can't risk falling in love with him all over again. But when it becomes clear that someone is targeting Lacey and sabotaging the charity she runs, she realizes Jarrett is the only one she can trust to protect her and her adopted daughter.

Jarrett and Lacey are two people who need a second chance at love. Theirs is a story of passion and love, strength in the face of adversity, and having the courage to do what is right, not what is easy.

I hope you enjoy *Navy SEAL Seduction*.

Happy reading!

Bonnie Vanak

NAVY SEAL SEDUCTION

Bonnie Vanak

HARLEQUIN® ROMANTIC SUSPENSE

Recycling programs
for this product may
not exist in your area.

ISBN-13: 978-0-373-27997-5

Navy SEAL Seduction

Printed in U.S.A.

New York Times and *USA TODAY* bestselling author **Bonnie Vanak** is passionate about romance novels and telling stories. A former newspaper reporter, she worked as a journalist for a large international charity for several years, traveling to countries such as Haiti to report on the sufferings of the poor. Bonnie lives in Florida with her husband, Frank, and is a member of Romance Writers of America. She loves to hear from readers. She can be reached through her website, bonnievanak.com.

Books by Bonnie Vanak

Harlequin Nocturne

Phoenix Force
The Shadow Wolf
The Covert Wolf
Phantom Wolf
Demon Wolf

The Empath
Enemy Lover
Immortal Wolf

In memory of my uncle, Donald Fischer, who flew B-24s as a bombardier during WWII and was shot and injured on his 13th mission over German-occupied territory. Thanks for all the memories and the stories you shared.

Chapter 1

Everything was going to be all right, even if he had to resort to using his pistol on his ex-wife.

Cold sweat trickled down his back. US Navy SEAL Lt. Jarrett "Iceman" Adler rolled up the cuffs of his white shirt, tucked his loaded Sig Sauer P226 into the leather holster hanging on the belt of his black trousers and prepared for the most challenging mission of his life: dragging his ex-wife back to the United States, where she'd be safe from a country about to explode into violence and from the terrorist interested in donating to her nongovernmental organization.

He walked out onto the balcony of his hotel room, taking a deep breath as he studied the sweep of sagging tin hovels dotting the mountainside. Here in the rich enclaves of the capital, poverty snuggled side by side with the wealthy, who hid behind massive stone fences decorated with colorful pink-and-purple bougainvillea. In the distance sirens bleated as three floors below on the streets, horns blared, dogs barked and people shouted in French in the rhythm of the city at rush hour.

He'd listened all day to the radio. The reports were scattered, a volley of excited French talking about protests downtown regarding the elections in two days. The city was hot, and before long, violence would spill out all over the city, a stream leaking onto the streets like gasoline waiting for a lit match. His instincts warned the tiny island nation of St. Marc was a pressure cooker about to explode.

And Lacey was square in the middle of it.

His chest felt hollow as he stared for the tenth time at the old photo of Lacey he still carried in his wallet. Her large blue eyes sparkled with life, and her wide mouth was open in a delighted laugh. He'd dreamed of her two nights ago and tossed and turned in his bed, remembering the good times they had shared.

His CO had ordered him to take leave, so Jarrett decided to head to St. Marc to visit his good friend and SEAL buddy Kyle "Ace" Taylor, who was recuperating at a posh beachside resort managed by his widowed sister. Upon his arrival, Ace warned him Lacey was in deep.

No matter what it took, he'd get her home safely.

He dedicated his life to fighting for his country. But after the last mission he'd led nearly turned into a royal goat fluster, Jarrett wondered if it was time to step aside. Being a SEAL meant spinning the roulette wheel of broken bones, banged knees, gunshot wounds and worse. On the last mission, the team's communications expert, Cooper, narrowly missed coming home in a body bag. As the mission's leader, Jarrett felt responsible.

Jarrett ran a hand through his dark hair, then headed

out toward the third-floor elevators. What would Lacey say when she saw him? Would she be delighted? Appalled? Horrified? Turned on?

Sex had never been a problem with them.

His mouth twisting in a wry grin, he punched the elevator button and went downstairs.

Soft amber lamps hanging on the wall lit the hotel lobby, casting shadows on the white-bricked walls. The marble lobby flowed down to a bar, where three men sat on stools nursing bottles of beer. Jarrett chose the stool overlooking the courtyard, his back to the wall.

He ordered a Jameson neat and sipped the drink. Two minutes later his target walked past, a spring in her step, a smile on her face, her long blond hair swinging in a ponytail tied back with a tortoiseshell clip. Black trousers covered her legs, and a white peasant blouse displayed her curves. Jarrett's gut clenched with longing. Hell, he hadn't expected this kind of reaction. *Stay cool.* Lowering his head, he pretended to be absorbed in his drink. But deep inside he felt the old, familiar pain, the sense of loss and, worse, the yearning that squeezed him from the inside out.

Hips gently swaying with feminine grace he knew was totally natural, she walked outside to a metal table in the courtyard. A man in a black business suit greeted her French-style, a kiss on each cheek. He looked older, stylish and wealthy, with looks women swooned over. Jarrett recognized him from the newspaper clipping Ace had provided—Paul Lawrence, the vice president of the board of directors for Lacey's NGO.

Jarrett dragged in a deep, calming breath and willed away his jealousy. Steady. He focused on the mission. Always the mission.

Target: Lacey Stewart. Only child of Senator Alexander Stewart, retired corporate scion who'd made millions by opening outlets of exclusive espresso coffee shops across the United States and then chose to enter politics. Lacey Stewart, president of Marlee's Mangoes, a nongovernmental organization operating in St. Marc for four years.

Ives, the friendly waiter whom he'd tipped liberally these past two nights to find out about the meeting Lacey had arranged at this hotel, came over to greet him with a wide smile.

"Everything is going according to your plan," Ives told him.

Jarrett slipped Ives a US fifty-dollar bill to tell the dreamboat with Lacey the important client he awaited was out front and something was wrong.

As soon as the dreamboat left the table, Jarrett downed his whiskey and wiped his mouth with the back of one hand. With a long-legged stride, silent as if he glided through water and not walked on tile, he walked out of the hotel onto the courtyard, shaded by several sprawling mahogany and palm trees.

Busy peeling the label off her beer bottle—had anything changed? She still had that nervous habit—she didn't notice. Jarrett planted his size twelves square in her line of sight. Now she did finally look up and her rosebud mouth parted in a shocked gasp. But there was no mistaking the flare of heat in her gaze and the same quiet longing he'd harbored.

He nodded.

"Hello, Lacey. Nice to see you again."

A tall, muscled pirate in a clean white shirt and black trousers stood before her in the courtyard of Le Soleil Hotel. Scowling to hide her emotions, she stared, her heart racing as if she'd run a mile up and down the nearby mountain. Black hair cropped short, he wore a pressed white shirt, the cuffs rolled up to display tanned, muscled forearms. Smooth cheeks, strong jaw and a nose that had been broken at least once. Rugged, tough and those eyes, green as the ocean water he navigated on a mission.

Those eyes had turned smoky and dark with passion as they'd made love, and cold as the Arctic the day she'd announced she'd hired a lawyer to initiate divorce proceedings. Whoa, he still had it. Hot, hot, hot, as the locals said. Bad boy to the extreme, who made her female parts say *Why, hello there!*

Her female parts needed to stay quiet. This time she'd listen to her broken heart and not her hormones, even though her heart jumped at the sight of him.

He had never been there for her before, and certainly wasn't staying now.

Lacey managed to find her voice. "I hope this is a bad dream and I'll wake up and find you gone."

Her ex-husband pulled out a chair, turned it around and straddled it. "Well, darling, it seems your nightmare isn't going away. Neither am I."

She managed to conceal her trembling hands by wrapping her fingers tight around the beer bottle. Lacey took a deep drink, relishing the cool wash of liquid sliding down her throat. It reminded her of that time after they'd consumed several beers and then he'd kissed her and they had...

Not. Going. There.

"Go away, Jarrett. If you're here on a mission, aren't you supposed to be invisible in your invincibility?"

He did not smile. Flickering candlelight on the table

revealed the sharp angles and planes of his lean face. Jarrett looked all business.

"You're my mission. I'm taking you out of here. I booked us on tomorrow's early-morning flight." He glanced around. "Before the elections and before this place blows to hell."

Jarrett, trying to be funny, except his expression was dead serious. Had he heard about the mysterious vandalism plaguing her compound? It had been a few minor incidents she'd written off as a nuisance caused by locals who didn't like how she helped women, until last week's truck fire.

That fire had not been a nuisance. It had destroyed her best working vehicle.

She glanced around at the two other occupied tables and lowered her voice.

"Are you insane? I'm not going anywhere with you."

"St. Marc is teetering on a coup and I'm taking you back to the States."

She knew St. Marc intimately, shied away from the hot spots and knew how to handle herself. "Elections are in two days. I know about the violence and know how to avoid it. As soon as elections are over, things will cool down. Stop wasting your time."

"You're at risk of getting shot, kidnapped or both."

"The media exaggerates about a few protests downtown. It's not violent here."

Jarrett turned his head as six men carrying sinister-looking guns trotted out onto the courtyard, racing off toward the hotel disco. His mouth curved in a knowing smile.

"The president is here with his friends. He likes the disco," she snapped.

"Do all his friends carry assault rifles?"

"It's the latest fashion craze. Goes well with the Guayabera shirts. We do like to accessorize here on St. Marc."

The smile dropped, replaced with a dark stare. The Look. How many times had he aimed it at her in the past? The man had a stubborn streak bigger than a US Navy destroyer. Jarrett leaned forward. "This country is eroding into civil unrest, Lace, elections or no elections. You need to get out. How many State Department warnings does it take before you'll listen?"

Anger fisted in her stomach. "Those warnings are for the tourists who come here to do poverty tours or sun themselves on the beaches. Not for ex-pats like me or Paul. And who the hell are you to tell me what to do? We're no longer married."

She was twenty-nine, no longer that wide-eyed girl who'd fallen hard and fast for the handsome Navy sailor with a wicked smile, husky laugh and skilled hands. Marlee's Mangoes was her dream now, not a life of domestic bliss with a SEAL who was gone more than he'd been home.

Gone, too, when she needed him the most. Lacey clenched her beer bottle again and pushed away thoughts of the baby they'd lost. That was the past, and St. Marc was her future.

Jarrett Adler belonged to those ghosts she'd exorcised out of her life.

"Paul." Jarrett's gaze narrowed. "That simpering metrosexual who's with you?"

Blinking, she struggled to leash her temper. "Paul Lawrence is the vice president of the board for Marlee's Mangoes and my business partner."

The realization hit her. "Where is he? Did you do

something to him, Jarrett? We're supposed to be meeting a very important donor."

"The very important donor driving a late-model
white Montero SUV? He was unavoidably detained in
the parking lot. Your vice president went to help him."

More interference. But this time he messed with her
livelihood. "Damn, Jarrett, this is my life. You're not
part of it anymore, so go home and get out of here."

"Not without you. Darling, I'm sticking to your side
until I deliver you home."

She studied him with a keen eye. "Get used to disappointment. I'm not leaving."

Jarrett reached out, touched her hand. "Don't argue
with me, Lacey. We haven't seen each other in a long
time, and I'd rather spend what little time we have together catching up. Or engaged in more pleasurable
activities."

A shiver of awareness raced down her spine as he
slowly stroked his thumb over the back of her hand. His
smug smile dropped, replaced with a burning intensity
that could melt steel. When Jarrett aimed that look at
her, she'd wanted to do whatever he wanted. Usually
it had involved getting naked in very inventive places.

"Our days of getting horizontal are over," she
warned, drawing away her hand.

He considered, and scratched the bristles on his dim-
pled chin. "Vertical's always fun, too. Or we could try
those swinging chairs down by the pool."

Impish grin, a promise of pleasure in those dark
green eyes. Lacey's mouth twitched as she struggled
not to smile. Sex had always been great between them.

It was the other things that got in the way.

Her cell phone quietly chimed. Paul. She answered.
"Where are you?"

"Lacey, I'm sorry," her VP said in his singsong accent. "I went to the parking lot and Mr. Augustin was by his new SUV. Someone threw red paint all over his windshield as he pulled into the lot! He was infuriated and to calm him down, I took him home. We're here, drinking a nice rum. His cook is making an excellent grilled salmon and once we are done with dinner, I'll drive him back to the hotel and we all can have a drink there. Don't worry, *ma petite*, we'll be there in about an hour or so."

Her spirits sank. Damn, she had counted on Augustin's goodwill and money to pay for the houses she'd planned to build on her compound. He'd wanted to meet with her in person to arrange a tour of Marlee's Mangoes. And "an hour or so" on St. Marc time usually meant no less than two hours. She was stuck here until then. "Do your best to rush through dinner."

Jarrett quietly studied her as she thumbed off the phone and placed it into her backpack. "You don't do anything by half measures, Adler. Red paint? That man was a prime donor poised to fund housing I need for the women I employ." All her pent-up emotions tumbled out. "You don't care about anything, do you? Just like before."

Something flickered in his gaze. "You don't want him as a donor. I do care. I care about hustling you out of here."

She searched his face, the grim set of his jaw. Something was going on and he wasn't about to tell her. Jarrett was a SEAL accustomed to secrecy. But her life was transparent now and she hated secrets.

"Joseph Augustin is a respected member of the upper class here in St. Marc. Why wouldn't I want him as a donor?"

His gaze flicked around the courtyard. "Not here. We need to talk someplace where we won't be overheard."

Fine. "The hotel has a walkway around the gardens."

As she reached down to grab her backpack, a staccato burst of gunfire exploded in the streets below the hotel. Jarrett leaped to his feet and pushed her down to the ground, covering her body with his own. His muscled weight pinned her down. She heard a handgun's slide being racked, and looked up to see Jarrett, weapon in hand, crouching low. Screams and shouts erupted around her, and heavy footfalls pounded against the concrete courtyard.

Jarrett spoke into her ear, his deep voice rumbling. "I told you, this country isn't safe. Now do you believe me?"

Chapter 2

"Those shots were in the neighborhood below the hotel. It's nothing, Jarrett."

Twenty minutes after the gunfire, after the hotel manager had walked around and assured everyone there was "nothing" to worry about, Jarrett perched on the edge of his chair. His Sig Sauer tucked back into his holster, he stared at Lacey. His ex-wife's words didn't comfort him. "Nothing? With the president of the country dining within bullet range? Don't think so."

Lace shook her head, pushed back at the long fall of her hair. "I'm starved. I hope their griot is good here. It's expensive enough."

Hungry. She wanted fried pork and he wanted the hell out of here.

But he'd talked her into having dinner with him while she waited for her donor to arrive at the hotel for drinks later. And that particular donor wasn't getting within ten yards of Lacey.

He'd make sure of it.

He should have left her pinned to the ground, then tied her up with the linen tablecloth and carried her to his hotel room, trapping her there until morning.

Jarrett grunted as he sipped the bottled water the cheerful Ives delivered to their table. Lace had been in St. Marc far too long. Too easily dismissive of gunshots. He partly admired her cool aplomb under pressure when everyone else had run off screaming, and partly wanted to shake sense into her.

All those tours he did in the Middle East, despite the strain on his marriage, he'd never worried about Lace. Lace was safe, back in the United States. No one could hurt her. The marriage had died, but his protective streak and his feelings had not. Now she was in this place, with riots popping up like sniper fire, and he'd be damned if he turned his back and left her.

He'd feed her and stall her leaving the hotel. What if she'd driven off, headed down that same street where the gunfire erupted? A stray bullet could have hit her...

The grim image of Lacey slumped over the steering wheel, blood streaming down her head, turned his stomach into ground glass. Forget the danger Ace had mentioned. There were hot spots all around that could kill her.

Jarrett gave the menu another glance and as Ives returned, ordered in fluent French one order of griot with rice and beans, an order of broiled grouper for himself and a bottle of Bordeaux. Beaming, Ives walked off.

Lacey seemed paler at the order of French wine than she did at the gunshots. "I really don't need to drink and I'm really not that hungry after all..."

"My treat."

She sat straighter. "I have money."

"No worries. I'll pay for dinner. Call it a peace offering."

"Why are you here, Jarrett? You didn't just come to this hotel and find me because you have nothing better to do with your vacation. What's the deal?"

"I have leave and came here to visit Ace." At her confused look, he added, "Kyle Taylor. He's staying with his sister Aimee at the resort she runs on Paix Beach."

"I didn't know Kyle was here. I see Aimee from time to time."

"He's on medical leave. Busted his knee on his last deployment so he came here to visit Aimee and her kids." Jarrett's jaw tensed. "And keep an eye on her because of the increasing violence." He looked around. "When is Augustin getting here?"

"Paul said he'd phone and let me know. What's going on, Jarrett? Why all the secrecy? Does this have to do with my dad?"

Jarrett nearly laughed. The venerable Senator Alexander Stewart had refused to speak to Jarrett after they'd announced their elopement years ago. Her old man still blamed Jarrett for the marriage and the eventual breakup, calling him an "adrenaline-seeking hot dog."

"Your father doesn't know I'm in St. Marc. But he'd agree with me that it's not safe for you here, Lace." Jarrett leaned on the table and locked gazes with her.

"I'm not part of your life anymore, Jarrett. You never cared what happened to me before."

The accusation stung. "You were once part of my life, and I did care," he said quietly. "I care what happens to you now, Lace."

She looked troubled at the thought. "You really think

the country is headed toward another civil war? Everyone is hopeful that the elections will change that."

"If the current regime, and the military, allows a new president to take over."

Lacey gnawed at her lower lip. Jarrett watched, both sorely tempted by her lush mouth and worried as hell. He hoped she realized what he didn't say was more important than the information he offered. The White House had been closely watching the sitch here and was prepared to order US military intervention if a military junta seized control of St. Marc. It had happened in the past, so the possibility was quite real.

One reason he'd chosen St. Marc as his destination. He wanted to check on Ace and nudge Lacey into leaving before the country exploded and it became harder to hustle her pretty rear end off the island.

"What have you heard from your sources?"

Jarrett drew in a deep breath, not daring to say more. "Things are heating up a little too much."

"This is the city. The countryside is different. Quiet, peaceful, where I live."

He knew the stubborn line between her two silky eyebrows. Hell, he should have tied her up and carried her away.

Jarrett sipped his water, studying his ex. Her hair was longer now, and she had shadows beneath her eyes, and looked too thin, but she was still lovely. She no longer wore floral perfume, but he could smell the apple shampoo she used when he'd tackled her to the ground.

She smelled like home, and it amplified his sense of loss.

"You've changed. No more designer outfits?" He eyed her worn khaki backpack. "Or purses?"

"My priorities changed." Her mouth lifted slightly.

"But I still have my pink Michael Kors bag. It's in storage. Doesn't go well with T-shirts and worn denim jeans."

"I remember that bag," he mused. "You bought it shopping the day I returned from Iraq."

His body tightened as he remembered. He'd returned from a grueling deployment, drained and numb, the images of what he'd done haunting him. Jarrett had showered twice, scrubbing his body until the hot water ran out, still feeling the sand between his toes, the grit in his teeth. And then he'd sat in the living room, staring at the walls.

Lacey had walked into the house, the pink Michael Kors bag hanging from one slender shoulder, her lithe body covered in the sweetest pink sundress, her feet stuffed into pink designer sandals. Even her toenails were painted pink. She looked so cute, sexy and so *American* that all the pressure in his chest finally eased, morphing into pure sexual interest.

She'd dropped the bag in the living room, run into his arms. And then she'd looked into his eyes, really looked at him, and saying nothing, led him straight into the bedroom. The sex had been hard and rough, a purging of every damn thing he'd seen and done. Then they'd showered together, and had sex again, and afterward, they'd grilled burgers and she sat on his lap as they finished a bottle of white wine, and before they'd fallen asleep, they'd made love three more times.

Six weeks later the little white stick she'd taken into the bathroom showed two pink lines. They had conceived their baby that day...

Jarrett squeezed his beer bottle so tight his knuckles whitened. Didn't want to think of the time after that, how glowing and happy Lacey had been, and then growing paler and sicker, and worried at the bleeding the doctor assured her was normal, just spotting...

The past was the past.

Ives brought the wine and uncorked it with a flourish. As they ate, Lacey asked him about his work. He made noncommittal answers, as he always had, and turned the conversation to her life here in St. Marc. Maybe if he could discover why she was so determined to stay, he could coax her into leaving and finding something better back home.

"How the hell did you end up here in this part of the world?"

She sipped her wine and nodded. "Not bad. Remember how I told you I spent time here in high school when Dad was appointed the US ambassador to St. Marc? I developed an affinity for the people and learning the culture."

Odd. He'd forgotten her time abroad. She'd seldom mentioned it during their marriage, maybe because she knew her father disliked Jarrett intensely. He blamed Jarrett for Lacey's dropping out of college and getting married, no matter how much she insisted it was her idea.

Enthusiasm lit up her face as she described Marlee's Mangoes, the NGO she'd formed to help poor women and children. She'd started the charity from her share of profits from a coffee plantation in St. Marc. Marlee's Mangoes operated out of a twenty-five-acre farm a good two-hour drive from the city. She harvested fruit from mango trees, and her staff prepared a popular mango jam and salsa she hoped to start exporting.

Lacey waved her hands, illustrating the operation. He studied those hands with curiosity. Once she'd never failed to go without her weekly manicure. Now those nails were unpainted and filed down to the quick.

"The marmalade is well-known around the island. I have contracts with several high-end restaurants that cater to tourists who come here from the cruise ships or vacation at the beachside resorts."

"How did you get started?"

"I came here four years ago when Paul offered me an opportunity with his coffee business. He owns the plantation and factory where they process the beans. And I fell in love with the people, and the culture, and realized there was a need I could fulfill for poor women who had no place else to go. So I bought a small farm to start Marlee's Mangoes."

Four years ago, shortly after their divorce. He shoved his hands into the pockets of his jeans. "Buying a farm is a huge step. Isn't land expensive here?"

"Outrageous, but I bought the farm from the son who inherited the land after his dad died. I went to school with him here in St. Marc and got the land cheap, even before it went on the market." She grinned and his heart gave a little jump. Once she had grinned like that at him, and he fell hard and fast.

"Paul needed the capital for his coffee business and he needed help. I enlisted my dad's help to set up a new processing factory to wash the coffee beans and sun dry them. We sell those beans to companies in the States."

Jarrett was deeply impressed.

"Not bad for a college dropout, huh? With my share of profits from the coffee business I funded Marlee's Mangoes. But..." She leaned forward, her gaze sparking with life. "I'm very happy to announce that our NGO is now fully self-sufficient and no longer operating in the red. This is a huge deal for me because I'm teaching the women to be empowered, to learn skills that will grow their futures."

Candlelight flickering on the table showed the pink flush on her cheeks. "It may sound idealistic, but I believe in these women and their potential. Some lost their husbands to violence, but many were victims of abuse. They'll do anything for their children, and just want a chance for their kids to have a better life."

Admiration filled him. Lacey always had a tender heart for the underprivileged. "It sounds like a terrific project. How did you come up with the name?"

Her expression fell. She toyed with the stem of her wineglass. "That's private. I can't talk about it."

He let it slide. Jarrett noticed she drank very little wine. He lifted the bottle out of its silver bucket. "It's very good. Would you like more?"

She shook her head. "One glass is my limit. I have to drive."

Plan A out the window. She wasn't going to get drunk and spend the night here. Time to put Plan B into action.

"Excuse me," he murmured.

A pass of a few twenties to Ives, and he found himself in the hotel parking lot standing before Lacey's older and somewhat battered SUV. It didn't take long. Jarrett returned to the hotel, washed the grease off his hands in the men's room and went to their table.

Their food arrived and as he picked up his fork, Lacey handed him the hot sauce without asking. Amused, he shook the sauce over his broiled fish. Marriage did that to you. You had habits that your spouse knew, and those habits were hard to break. But he was quietly pleased she'd remembered his preferences.

She ate quickly, keeping her gaze focused toward the

hotel's front. As the hour passed, her animated conversation grew quieter.

Lacey realized her donor was not going to show up. She dug out her cell and excused herself.

Jarrett polished off his meal and waited, nodding at Ives as he came to check on their wine. He'd slipped Ives money earlier to pass a bottle of the hotel's finest rum to Augustin in apology for the thrown paint incident. If Ace's intel proved right, and Ace's intel always proved right, the bastard was drunk as hell right now on his favorite liquor. He didn't want him anywhere near Lace.

Sure enough, Lacey returned, palming her cell phone, her expression dejected as she resumed her seat. "He's not coming. Paul said Monsieur Augustin is inebriated and doesn't want to go anywhere. Paul is staying with a friend tonight and said he'd call him tomorrow."

And by tomorrow you'll be gone. The man's bad news, Lace. Will you trust me on this for once?

He signaled for the waiter. "Would you like dessert?"

She stood and he stood, as well. "I have to leave, Jarrett." She stuck out her hand. "Thank you for dinner. It was nice to see you again. I hope you enjoy your stay in St. Marc."

Instead of shaking her palm, he lifted her knuckles to his mouth. The kiss was a bare brush of his lips, but she turned pink. Desire and recognition flared between them, and her breathing hitched.

Then she pulled away, picked up her backpack and walked off, hurrying as if she wanted to get away from him fast.

He sat down, sipped more wine to quell his raging hormones, which urged him to run after her, sweep her into his arms and carry her upstairs to his room.

Straight into his bed, where they could get reacquainted in a much more pleasant way.

He waited.

Ten minutes later she stormed back to the table. "My car's dead."

Jarrett tilted his head. "Oh?"

"The battery is gone. Damn it, Jarrett, why did you do this? I need to get back home."

"Yes, you do." He leaned forward. "Home to the United States of America. That's your home."

Lacey dumped her backpack. "You bribed someone."

He shrugged. "Money talks in these countries. Think, Lacey. I paid cash for someone to point out your car so I could remove the battery. What if I wanted to blow up your car instead?"

"Will you stop being so paranoid."

"It's my job to be paranoid and protect citizens like you. You're not going anywhere. You're spending the night here."

Then he added in a gentler tone, "You couldn't drive all the way back to your home this late, anyway. It's too far and too dark on these roads. Stay here, and things will work out."

Her mouth trembled as she sat. "I can't stay here. This is an expensive hotel. I'd planned to go to the L'Étoile d'Amour."

Recognizing the name as a place one of his teammates had visited during a deployment here, Jarrett choked on his sip of wine. "The Star of Love? Lace, that's a place where you pay by the hour and you bring your own sheets!"

"It's inexpensive and only for one night. And I know the owner."

Jealousy wormed through him. "How do you know the owner?"

"He's donated to my NGO."

Long as the man didn't donate anything else, like his DNA. Jarrett inwardly swore. Why was he reacting like this? He'd thought his feelings for her had died. Obviously not.

Hands on hips, she glared at him. "I'll hire a taxi and go there. You can't keep me here."

Think fast. Don't let her get away. If he lost her for the night, he lost her for good.

Jarrett went to her, clasping her shoulders, feeling delicate bones beneath her soft skin, feeling her quiver beneath his touch. "You're right. I can't. Don't go, Lacey. I'll make you a deal. Stay the night here and I'll give you a ride back to your compound tomorrow. You can make arrangements to return your truck."

Anger faded from her expression, replaced with wariness. "Spend the night with you, in your room?"

Oh, the possibilities, but Jarrett forced away the temptation. "I'll pay for your room tonight. Tomorrow we'll leave. I want to see this place you've talked so much about."

Lacey bit her lower lip, and it made him hard all over again. Such a sweet, lush mouth. "C'mon, Lace. I wouldn't let you stay at a fleabag motel, and I do want to see your NGO's compound while I'm here. It sounds amazing. I'd like to visit and see all the work you've done."

Finally, she nodded. "All right. But I'm paying you back for the room and the dinner when we get to my home. And I'm not getting on a plane with you, Jarrett. No matter what you say."

"Fine. Come with me and I'll reserve you a room."

As she walked with him into the hotel, he felt a sense of relief more than jubilation. Lacey was safe here tonight, with him. And tomorrow he'd see the compound she had worked hard to establish.

He just had to convince her to leave it all behind.

Chapter 3

Much as he'd wanted to head out at first light, for Jarrett didn't want to take chances of running into protestors, they didn't get on the road until nearly noon. Lacey had business in the city, and Jarrett drove her to various stores and did shopping of his own.

They were safe enough for now. She'd monitored the radio, heard reports of burning tires and roadblocks planned for later this afternoon.

Riding shotgun as he steered the rented Montero SUV through the city streets, Lacey fisted her hands atop her backpack. She'd spent a restless night thinking of Jarrett and their past. Once they had deeply loved each other. But life changed her. She wasn't the naive, sheltered senator's daughter who thought the sun rose and set on Jarrett. Her horizons had broadened and she wanted more. No longer did she want to sit and wait for him to come home. Sit and worry he would never come home, for he was a SEAL and his missions were dangerous.

Being a military wife hadn't suited her. She'd spent her time indulging in silly pastimes like manicures and shopping to ease the constant worries about his welfare. And in between remained glued to the twenty-four-hour television news channels to glean the slightest information about volatile parts of the world where Jarrett might be.

No, she didn't need Jarrett in her life anymore.

Unfortunately, her libido remembered well the pleasure he'd given her in bed and begged her to draw closer. She hadn't had sex since her last relationship two years ago. Francis Monroe was a great guy, son of a wealthy independent contractor, and exciting.

All the men she'd dated since Jarrett had been dull and safe, except for Francis, who was on the board of directors of her charity. Francis was both wealthy and charming, and his family was connected. Their dads were friends and Lacey knew her father was grooming Alastair Monroe to become the next US ambassador to St. Marc. But as responsible as his dad was, Francis was not. He was more interested in playing the field than a stable relationship.

Lacey was determined to never again get involved with a man who would desert her, both emotionally and physically.

Unfortunately, Jarrett now seemed determined to stick by her side. How could she shake him? And why was he so worried about Augustin?

Maybe when he saw her compound, he'd change his mind and leave. Some people shied away from her charity and the terrible reality of what the women had suffered.

Lacey stole a sideways look. With his long legs encased in blue jeans, gray T-shirt molded to his muscled torso and chest, and his jaw set in a determined line, Jarrett made an imposing figure as he navigated through the tight streets where vendors lined the sidewalks and paraded their wares. Driving through downtown had always frayed her nerves, even after living here. She hated the tight spaces in this most dangerous part of the city one had to drive through to get to the main road leading south to her home.

There was always that element about Jarrett that hinted at calm confidence. Once his overprotective streak had annoyed her. Funny how it didn't anger her now, but made her feel safe. Maybe because she'd finally found a life of her own, and the confidence she'd lacked when they were married.

She didn't need designer handbags or dresses to prove her self-worth. Her purpose rested between the concrete walls of her compound with the women who relied on her.

Finally, they cleared the city and accessed the national road hugging the turquoise bay that flanked the capital.

A few abandoned homes that had been bombed years ago during a coup faced the bay, their broken windows looking like sad eyes. "Nice homes. Terrific view of the water. Needs a little work. Perfect for a do-it-yourself," he murmured.

"Comes complete with running water, when it rains. Air-conditioning when there's a breeze," she joked back.

He glanced over and grinned, and the power of that smile made her toes curl. Lacey scolded her raging libido. Sex was on the back burner. She had other priorities.

"We're in your car and no one can hear us. Can you tell me now why I don't want Monsieur Augustin as a donor? He's a very wealthy philanthropist."

Jarrett checked out his rearview mirror. "He's wealthy, but his idea of philanthropy isn't charitable. And his real name isn't Augustin."

He shot her a hard look. "It's Robert Destin. He's an illegal arms trader who found refuge here. He isn't interested in your NGO for a tax deduction."

Lacey's heart dropped to her stomach. That was news. Jarrett might be overprotective, but he had excellent information. "He's known around the country as a philanthropist. He donates to several NGOs."

Jarrett eyed her. "He's rich because he sold weapons to terror groups, Lace. Intelligence chatter has it that he's looking to finance a new op out of this country."

His face tightened. "Perfect place to plan an attack. St. Marc is a Third World country already balancing on chaos, where money can buy a lot of new friends in low places. His cover is doling out money to international charities with global operations."

It didn't make sense. "Why would Augustin want to donate cash for my NGO's irrigation system? I'm a small operation."

"You have something he wants. I don't know what. But he's not interested because he's a nice guy."

"Or he needs a tax deduction." She reached for her cell. "I have to warn Paul."

"Don't." Jarrett stayed her hand. "Tell him not to meet with him, but don't share what I told you. That's for your ears only."

The fact that Jarrett shared such information warned he was deadly serious. In their years of marriage, he never told her anything about his work, his missions or the scumbags he encountered.

Lacey called Paul, telling him she'd handle Monsieur Augustin. As she hung up, wished she could light a fire beneath the bottoms of the State Department workers who were processing the paperwork. *I need more time...*

The car radio blasted out the news. In St. Marc, Lacey always listened to the radio to get reports of possible protests or roadblocks. But today seemed peaceful, and even more so as they drove farther south.

They entered a small town where a man led a donkey through traffic, ignoring the red light on the main road. A parade of motorcycles streamed past their vehicle like water. Bright red umbrellas with a local phone company's logo lined the sidewalks, shading the vendors who sold mangoes, breadfruit, candy, gum and other wares. The mountains rose to their left, dotted with trees.

They got stuck behind a tangerine-colored bus. A goat and a man perched on top of the bus, enjoying the view. Two men jumped onto the bus as it pulled into a small town. One held a clear plastic bag filled with bread. The other clutched plastic baggies of water.

Jarrett navigated through a local market, people milling in the street as they examined fruit for sale. Behind his shades, he seemed to study the mood of the street. Outside the city it was peaceful and normal. No torqued crowds. No danger.

Please let it stay that way. Last week someone had firebombed her best truck when she'd parked outside the compound to check out property she'd thought of purchasing. Lacey was doing all she could to expedite the paperwork, but it hadn't come through yet. Damn red tape...

"See how peaceful it is here?" She needed to assure

him she was fine, and he could leave her once he'd driven her home.

"It's deceptive. The radio said there are strikes planned for Monday. The president is planning to raise fuel prices again and the people are going to march." Jarrett peered over the top of his shades. "Marching people usually equates to violence, Lace."

"In the city."

"There's been a few protests in the country, as well, along this road."

She knew it and had taken great care to monitor reports to avoid roadblocks. "Not recently."

"And that will change when the president raises fuel prices if he's reelected. The poor are desperate and things are getting worse. I don't like it. Everything in this country points to another coup and it'll turn into a royal goat fluster. You really want to take a chance with your life?"

"You're as bad as my father. He wants me to come home, as well."

But she couldn't leave, even if he paid her. Frustration bit her because she suspected Jarrett was right, but she was trapped here. Lacey fished her mobile out of her backpack and thumbed it on. "You don't like it here? You need to book the next flight out for yourself? Use my credit card."

He ignored the jab. "Tell me what's been going on with the locals where you live. Any hot spots?" He lifted his right hand and pantomimed a gun and trigger. "*Bang bang* much?"

"There's been hot spots in Danton, the city closest to us, but there's always hot spots flaring up."

Mango and palm trees flanked the road as they drove south, past hand-painted signs advertising auto part repairs, billboards in French for local hotels, past the small concrete "banks" where lottery tickets were sold. They passed a herd of motorcycles, their riders waiting for passengers. He glanced to the right and noticed the gas station with its bright yellow-and-green sign remained open.

Calm. So calm. But she knew the peace could shatter as quickly as a fired shot.

Jarrett glanced at her. "Why don't you get some shut-eye while I drive? You're nodding off."

She didn't want to admit he was right, but he was. Lacey closed her eyes and dozed off.

When she opened her eyes, he was turning onto the unpaved road leading to her compound lined with dusty mango trees. A few dump trucks loaded with rocks rumbled past.

Sitting up straight, struggling to snap to attention, she pointed to a turnoff. "Turn at the sign that says Mangoes For Sale. There's a quarry not far from here. Reason why the road is so bad. But we got the land very cheap, and it's right off the main highway to make it easier to find us."

The vehicle bounced up and down as he drove. "Bounce factor," he mused. "Makes you feel like a bobble-head doll."

"You get used to it."

He gave her an amused grin, pushed down his sunglasses to peer at her. An impish look of mischief and sex gleamed in his green eyes. "I give great massages to work out the kinks in your body."

A shiver raced down her spine. Jarrett did give great massages, and the smooth glide of his big hands over her naked skin had always been so arousing, leading to him getting naked, as well, and then…

"I have a vibrator," she shot back and then flushed as his grin widened.

"A BOB doesn't substitute for the real thing, Lace."

"I didn't mean a battery-operated boyfriend kind of vibrator. I meant a massager. For my neck."

"Still," he murmured.

He drove toward the handmade sign, passing several mango and palm trees. Small wood houses peeked through the trees, as goats grazed in the scrub. An abandoned building came into view. Painted on the building was a mural of rows of corn, with happy children peeking out among the stalks.

"Originally that wall had a mural of a young woman being led on a chain before the devil. The man leading her clutched her beating heart." She sighed, remembering all her hard work to convince the locals she was committed to staying and helping them. "I found the artist, paid him to paint the cornfield because the mural kept spooking people. This farm kept spooking people. They said hoodoo rituals were conducted here, ones where a man cut out a woman's heart for good luck. We've managed to overcome some of the tainted superstition, but it's been a long process, with lots of patience and working with the locals."

"You always did have a lot of patience." His hands tightened on the steering wheel. "You did with me, especially when I was gone so much. Maybe if I hadn't been gone all those times, we'd still be together."

Lacey had wondered the same at times, wondered if he had stayed that one time and given her the support she needed, would they have worked out their problems? But she'd vowed to not regret the past.

"Maybe. Or not. You can't go back, Jarrett. We've both changed and moved on."

Jarrett drove until reaching a tall concrete wall with an imposing red gate. Lacey's heart went still. Panic clogged her throat as she stared at the gate.

"You were saying something about hoodoo?" Jarrett turned to her, his expression grim. She'd been gone only a day, and this was bad news. Lacey had thought the other little things that had happened, like the graffiti warnings, were just some kids fooling around. Not this.

The white, hand-painted sign reading Marlee's Mangoes had been obscured with a splatter of crimson paint. But it wasn't the vandalism that worried her.

It was the dead chicken impaled on the iron spikes of the gate. The bloody entrails were draped over another spike, along with a clear warning painted on the gate in French.

American, go home before you end up like this.

Lacey swallowed the bile rising in her throat. She beeped the horn and a man in gray trousers and a blue shirt came out, opened the gate. Pierre waved at her, twirling the shotgun in his hands as if it was a baton.

"That's your security?"

She bit her lip. "I told you, it's peaceful out here."

"And that dead chicken and the sign are a welcome home?"

Ignoring him, she rolled down the window and spoke in rapid French to the guard, who stared at the dead chicken. "Pierre, when did this happen? Did you see anything? Hear anything?"

He shook his head, his eyes wide in his face. "Nothing, miss. I was here all night."

She nodded. "Get some help and clean this up right now. I want it all gone before the kids come home from school."

Jarrett drove through the opened gate, and looked into the rearview mirror as Pierre shut the gate behind them.

"How long has he worked for you?"

"He's the cousin of one of the women I'm helping. He's been here about two months. I don't pay him much."

Her budget had already been strained with fixing the outdated irrigation system and the other unexpected expenses.

"It shows. Your security sucks, Lace. He doesn't even look old enough to shave, damn it."

The thinly disguised anger in his deep voice fueled her own anger. "My compound is respected by locals. They know the farm provides jobs and teaches skills to women."

Jarrett snorted. "You call a dead chicken respect?"

"It was probably a prank." Lacey's stomach tightened. If he found out about the other incidents, she'd never shake him loose. She couldn't be certain it was locals causing trouble, or worse.

Jarrett drove into the loose gravel drive, flanked by tall mango trees and colorful hibiscus bushes. He parked before a turquoise two-story house. The white, one-story guesthouse was a short walk away down a gravel pathway.

Lacey jumped out, relieved to see everything looked normal.

He nodded at the solid concrete building. "At least your personal living space looks secure. From a distance, anyway."

Fumbling in her backpack for her key, she walked up the steps to the front door. "Thanks to Paul. He helped me find the right construction team to expand the house and put in a water system. He's well connected."

The compound held acres of corn and a clearing near the cornfield. Construction equipment and stacks of concrete blocks sat in the clearing. Jarrett adjusted his sunglasses and pointed to them. "What's going on there?"

"Houses. I'm going to build them for twenty-five single moms helped by my charity. I'm in the process of subdividing the land so each woman will have the land and the house in her name and never have to worry about hooking up with a man just to have a place to stay for her and her children. Paul thinks I'm crazy for building homes, though he agreed to try to find funding."

Jarrett peered over the top of his shades. "Pity the man. He doesn't know your stubborn streak."

She smiled and pushed back a stray lock of hair. "I had a lot of opposition. Some of my friends said the women would bolt soon as they found a man. It was tough at first. I couldn't find funding, so I used alternative sources."

"You used your trust fund."

Heat suffused her face. "I needed start-up capital."

Jarrett reached out and stroked a knuckle down her cheek. The bare caress filled her with yearning. "You have a real heart. Always knew you'd use that fund for something other than designer bags and shoes."

Lacey turned away, her emotions churning. How could she even share with him that she'd wanted to make some kind of contribution? Jarrett chose the Navy and dedicated his life to serving his country. Her father had entered the diplomatic corps and then became a US senator to serve, as well. And all she'd done was contribute to the United States economy with her shopping sprees, which left her feeling cold and empty afterward.

If she hadn't lost the baby, maybe then her life would

have taken a different turn. But no use agonizing over the past...

"Come inside. I'll get us some cold water."

Jarrett followed her into the living room. She flicked the light switch, but nothing happened. Sighing, she dumped her backpack on the orange sofa.

"The electric's out. One of the biggest drawbacks to living here outside the capital. I'll have to use the generator to power the water pump if you need to use the bathroom until the inverter kicks in tonight. I have solar-powered batteries as a backup power system."

"I'm fine." He removed his sunglasses and placed them on his shirt.

She grabbed two bottles of cold water from the fridge and gulped down half of one. Jarrett didn't touch his, but rubbed his bristled jaw. He looked so sexy with the dark beard shadowing his face, but the sexiness was tamped down by his grim expression.

"Why are you so determined to remain here, Lace? Why not return to the States and work with wealthy donors to fund your project?"

She gave him a calm, assessing look as she set down her bottle. "There's a certain satisfaction in personally cultivating hope among people who have little of it. I don't grow mangoes, Jarrett. I grow lives. I give a hand up to women who want a better life for their children, and all they need is a fresh start. They need someone to believe in them before they can begin to believe in themselves. But because some nasty ass of a man decided to kick them or beat them, they don't think they're worth much. They have no real job skills and I give them the chance to learn self-worth."

Jarrett's gaze softened. "You're something else, Lace."

She didn't know what to make of his comment, but

knew it was important to show him she was safe and had no intentions of leaving.

"Let me give you the ten-cent tour. This is where I live. The real action is in the outbuildings where the women work."

Tugging his hand, feeling his calloused fingers beneath hers, she felt a thrill of excitement. Jarrett was the first person from her past to see what she'd done. As they walked down the dirt pathway to a large concrete building, she talked about the coffee company she half owned.

"Paul is my dad's old friend from the days when we lived on the island, and the CEO of Coffee from the Heart. I got a contract to sell the beans to Dad's competitors, the local upscale cafés in Washington. They love the fact they're getting a good deal from the daughter of the man who is their biggest competition."

"I bet that hurts the old man's pride."

"A little."

At his understanding grin, she remembered the old times, when she and Jarrett boldly made their own way, refusing to take money from her wealthy parents. It was only after his assignments as a SEAL took him away from her so much that she turned to her trust fund for shopping and other empty pursuits to pass the time.

Sometimes she wondered if the extreme measures she'd taken after the divorce—moving here and starting her own nonprofit, had been to prove herself. Prove she was capable of being successful on her own. Prove she wasn't a failure, like her marriage had been.

They reached the building and she couldn't help a tinge of pride. Solar cells powered the lights, and the hot water heater was a black plastic tank. Efficient and economical. Jarrett looked impressed as she took him into the processing room. The women washed mangoes at a long sink and looked up and said a shy hello. A tall woman with dark-colored skin in her late thirties came over. She wore low heels, a blue dress and had a white apron tied around her waist.

Lacey introduced Jarrett to Collette March, the manager of the mango marmalade project. Educated in the States and extremely efficient, Collette was a hard worker and good at motivating the women.

"Are those jars of jam ready for shipping yet?" she asked.

Collette nodded. "Yes, Miss Lacey. And the two you want shipped to the US to your father, as well. They're all in the storehouse."

As Collette hurried back over to supervise the women cutting the fruit, Lacey tossed Jarrett a mango. He bit into it, juice running down his chin. She grinned at his surprised look.

"It's better than the mangoes I've had in the States. Tastes like a tropical drink without the alcohol."

"That's the special appeal of these mangoes, and what makes the jam so tasty. We buy from local farmers, though we grow our own, as well, on the property."

As he finished the fruit, she took him into a room where women sat at long tables, hand-peeling the fruit and then slicing it into sections.

"It's pretty easy to convert this into a large-scale operation because I have the labor. I hire women from the community and I pay them more than they'd make at the local sweat shops. I employ mainly women, and as a condition of employment, they have to attend classes here on Saturdays in reading and writing if they are illiterate."

At another table women were putting the mango

slices into big pots with pectin, the main ingredient needed to make the jelly. Jarrett gave a friendly nod to the women as she showed him the area where the fruit was prepared and cooked.

"The pectin keeps the jam from getting too runny. Next we cook the fruit with the sugar. And we boil the jars to sanitize them before they're filled and then after they're filled. Boiling after keeps the fruit from spoiling. We have to set the jars overnight to cool them and then in about ten days the mixture is ready to eat. We ship it out immediately because it lasts a little over a year."

"How the hell did you learn so much about making jam?" he asked. "You could barely cook."

"I wasn't that bad!"

"Sweetheart, you made eggs so hard-boiled they could pound nails."

At his wicked grin, heat suffused her face. Lace wasn't certain if the blush was from his teasing or the endearing *sweetheart*.

"I'm learning, though I have Rose. She's the best cook in the region. She's the one who gave me the recipe for the marmalade. The local women I employ have given me new ideas, too. They wanted jobs and they had skills. I learned a lot from them."

"And I'm sure they're learning a lot from you," he murmured.

She shrugged, embarrassed at the praise as they moved outside to the sunshine.

"It's a lot of work and I can't do it all, so I appointed one of the women as the manager. Collette is good at motivating the staff. I'm the director who tries to let them alone and give guidance as they need it."

"This is real nice, Lace. You've done a lot."

Pride filled her at his acknowledgment. She had taken an abandoned farm and turned it into a thriving charity. Jarrett gazed around the compound, but she could tell his mind was working. Quiet, efficient. The man never stopped working, either at home or on the job. Always looking out for threats.

She glanced at her watch. "School's out and the compound's children will be home soon. I want to be here to greet them."

Lacey hurried down the stairs of the building, back to her house and the porch with its pots of colorful tropical flowers. The sun burned bright overhead in the brilliant blue sky. Even though it was February, it was warm.

She only hoped the heat would remain with the weather, and not with the people growing tired of a president who ignored their plight.

Jarrett followed her and stood on the porch. "You always greet the children when they come home?"

Her chest tightened with emotion. "I try to, if I'm not working."

A door beside the compound gate opened, admitting three little girls, all dressed in red-checked uniforms and carrying backpacks. Two waved at Lacey and called greetings, skipping past them to the mango processing building. But the third child headed for them.

She was tiny, her skin the color of coffee with cream poured into it. Lemon-yellow ribbons were tied into her braided hair. Her bright yellow jumper and white short-sleeved shirt with its Peter Pan collar seemed almost too big on her small frame. The pink backpack she carried was nearly as big as her body. Her black shoes were patent leather and her white socks were cuffed.

She was so tiny and sweet, with a heart-shaped face. But she did not smile.

Lacey put a hand on the girl's thin shoulders. "This is Fleur."

Jarrett squatted down and smiled. "Hello, Fleur," he said in French.

The child's large, dark eyes regarded him. She said nothing. Jarrett glanced up.

"One of your charges here on the compound?"

Her insides squeezed tight at his words. "Fleur isn't one of my charges. She's the reason I can't leave St. Marc. She's my daughter."

Chapter 4

If his ex-wife had punched him in the stomach, Jarrett knew he couldn't have felt more shocked. He stared at the little girl, her solemn dark eyes too big for her face. His throat tightened and his chest hurt.

He'd always wanted a little girl. A daughter in pigtails, with a cheeky smile who'd giggle when he tickled her stomach or swung her around. A little girl who looked like Lace. When Lacey lost the baby, part of him died, as well. But he had learned to hide his emotions.

Get a grip, he told himself. Jarrett forced a smile, sensing the child's unease. "It is very nice to meet you," he said in French.

She said nothing, only kept staring at him. Lacey wrapped her arms around the child, holding her tight. Jarrett straightened, anger surfacing at his ex. Had to control it, didn't want to frighten the child. There was a story here in the little girl's dark eyes and solemn expression.

He'd seen the same ancient weariness in the eyes of children he'd met overseas. Adults with a kid's skin, a kid's body and the experiences no human being should ever endure...

Lacey hugged the child. "Fleur, this is Mr. Jarrett Adler. He's an American. I used to be married to him."

Her expression wary, the little girl looked up at Lacey. Lacey smiled and spoke in French. "It's okay. He's a good guy."

Jarrett felt his throat tighten more. At least the child had a safe place to live, and he could tell from the way Lacey hugged her that Fleur meant everything to Lace.

"That's a pretty name. Fleur. It means flower," he said in French.

Still, the child said nothing.

"Fleur, go into the house and change into your play clothing. You can play for an hour before starting on your homework," she said in French.

The little girl nodded, took another look at Jarret and ran inside as if the hounds of hell pursued her. Lacey sighed. "I think she's afraid of you. You're a big guy, like the man we suspect killed her mother. It may take a little while for her to get used to you."

Okay, more surprises. He was used to surprises; hell, it was his job to be prepared and adapt on the turn of a dime, but from his ex-wife?

He could easily handle an enemy tossing unexpected small arms fire, but a bombshell like this? His temper rose.

"Why the hell didn't you tell me about Fleur?" he snapped.

Lace didn't even blink. "You've been out of my life for a long time now, Jarrett. You don't know anything about me. And I certainly wasn't expecting you to drop by for afternoon coffee."

Dragging in a deep breath, he struggled to leash his temper. "Your daughter. You're adopting her."

"If we're going to talk, let's work. I have to get these crates ready for shipping the marmalade."

Lacey went over to a stack of crates and began packing them. He picked up a hammer and helped. *Bang, bang.* Felt good to slam the hammer down against the nail, get his emotions under control.

After a few minutes he wiped the sweat off his forehead. "Talk to me."

Lacey stopped stacking large empty sacks near the crates. "Fleur is five years old. She's lived with me for the past year. I already adopted her in this country. What happened to Fleur's mother is one reason Marlee's Mangoes is important to me. I met Jacqueline about a year ago. She was a single mother, only nineteen, trying to sell Fleur to me because I was a wealthy American."

Jarrett's jaw clenched. "I've heard of that happening."

"Her mother had kicked her out of the house because Jackie had an illegitimate child. Jackie was staying at a friend's guesthouse, but it was only temporary. She begged me to take her daughter because Fleur's father refused to give Jacqueline child support. He was a wealthy man and they had a brief affair.

"I gave her a job. I tried to find out who the father was, so I could pressure him, but Jackie refused to tell me. One day she showed up with terrible bruises on her face. She told me Fleur's father had shown up the previous night, drunk, and then beat her because she refused to have sex with him."

The hammer trembled in her hands as she picked it up and turned it over. "I was renovating my guesthouse and promised to give her a safe place to live, but I didn't act soon enough. When Jacqueline didn't arrive for work the following morning, I had this terrible feeling. I went to her home. Fleur was sitting on the floor by her mother's body. Fleur's bastard father had beaten Jackie to death...and Fleur saw everything."

Jarrett's stomach pitched and roiled as he imagined the horror witnessed by the little girl. "What about the cops?"

Lacey shook her head. "No one knew the name of the father, because Jackie kept the affair secret. All we know is he was a very big man and Jackie called him *Chou Chou*. Fleur was too traumatized to say anything other than she saw *Chou Chou* kill her mother."

French for "my favorite." Not much to go on.

"I wanted to take Fleur home with me, but she got embroiled in a mass of red tape. The police took her to an orphanage. I spent two months trying to find her because the admission paperwork was misfiled. When I finally found her, she refused to speak. I legally adopted her here. I have her passport and I'm just waiting on the damn visa to get her into the States."

She threw down the hammer. "I want to go back home to my parents and give Fleur the opportunity to heal and receive a quality education. Get her far away from the memories that give her nightmares each night. Only in the States can I find her a psychologist who will help her recover."

"And you're stuck here until the visa comes through."

"This is why I can't leave with you, Jarrett. Can't leave and won't. I am not leaving my little girl behind."

Her lush lower lip wobbled a little. "I've already lost one child. I'm not losing another."

"I'm sorry, Lace," he said gently. And he was sorry,

for many things. He pushed aside the surging guilt. Now was not the time to examine how he'd screwed up in their marriage.

He had run into unexpected trouble before, and gotten his team out of a royal goat fluster when they'd been pinned down by enemy fire. Nearly lost one of the guys, too. He could figure out a way around this.

"Did State give you an ETA?"

"No. You know bureaucracy, and now with the unrest, it's not looking great. Even my father can't pull that many strings. I have to wait until after elections."

Assess and then action. "What else do you need to tell me, Lace? If there are any other surprises, I need to know. Now."

Disclosure would allow him to plan and strategize. And action was a hell of a lot better than the guilt squeezing his guts right now. *I've already lost one child.*

The ghost words that weren't uttered hovered in the air all the same. *Lost one child and you ran off, away to some foreign country, leaving me to deal with the loss on my own.*

He had a job to do. Jarrett kept telling himself that over and over, a soothing balm that assuaged his conscience. But this time, faced with his ex-wife and old hurts, the balm wasn't as effective. Deep inside, he found a tiny sign flashing over and over, taunting him:

All your fault she left you. All your fault. You failed.

He was not failing her this time. Not leaving her here with her little girl to face a country toppling around her like a house of cards and a terrorist who wanted access to her NGO.

And that dead chicken on the gate...

"Why do you need to know about my life, Jarrett? You're not part of it anymore. I can handle myself. Unless you have a way of pushing the adoption papers through faster."

"I can't. But your father could."

She shook her head. "He's already tried. He wants me to come home as much as you do. I'm here until the papers come through, Jarrett."

A breeze lifted stray locks that escaped her ponytail. Jarrett folded his arms across his chest and looked over the compound. It seemed peaceful, and the broken glass atop the tall wall would deter trespassers, the ordinary type. But he'd witnessed what kind of damage a grenade lobbed at a wall could do, and worse, what a grenade thrown at a person could do to a human being.

Why was Augustin interested in her compound? He held up a finger. "Give me a minute."

Jarrett walked away as she kept working on the crates. When Ace answered on the first ring, he lowered his voice. "Ace man, got a problem. I'm here at Lacey's house. She has a daughter she's adopting and wants to bring to the States. But her visa is stalled."

His friend groaned. "She never told me and neither did Aimee. Your ex plays it close to the chest, Ice."

"Yeah, don't I know it. If that visa comes through soon, I can hustle her out of here. She won't budge until then." He gripped the phone. "Any word on what Augustin wants with her farm and the donation?"

"Dude, the man's an octopus, not a snake. He has tentacles all over the island with NGOs and parades around as a do-gooder. But word is he's supplying guns to the drug gangs that are causing all this *bang bang* before elections. He's a quiet supporter of the current regime, although the president would never admit to controlling these gangs. He just throws up his hands and says the police can handle it.

"They've burned homes in the slum in the capital and executed two people. One was a radio journalist who talked extensively about ousting the current president. The guy kept advocating a candidate who is gaining more popularity, a candidate the US supports."

Ace paused. "A candidate that Congressman Alexander H. Stewart himself backs."

Jarrett's blood ran cold. "I didn't know Stewart was involved in supporting political parties here."

"His daughter's living here, and he still maintains business interests in St. Marc. He wants her home as soon as possible."

Quickly he told his friend about the threats at Lacey's compound.

"Maybe the threats are politically motivated. Lacey is well connected. But back in the States, not here."

"Or maybe Monsieur Augustin doesn't want to build homes. Maybe he wants to kidnap your ex and wave that over her dad's head as a threat."

Ace had vocalized the deep fear Jarrett harbored. Still, his gut warned it was something else the man wanted. "Kidnapping is too messy."

"I'll say. Two weeks ago the gangs kidnapped a local and held him for ransom, and his family paid the money, but it was no use. They found his head in the local garbage dump. These guys are slick, Ice. And someone is funding them. Augustin may have the money, but someone else is directing them. Someone very quiet, a real shadow."

"Let me know what else you find out." He clicked off the phone and shoved it into his pocket then felt in the back of his jeans for his sidearm. Damn, life had just got a whole lot more complicated.

He knew how to maneuver around complicated. But not with a woman and a child's lives at risk.

As he joined Lacey at the crates, she straightened. Despite the relative coolness of the day and the refreshing mountain breeze, sweat dampened her temples. It partly soaked her shirt, making the white fabric stick to her torso and breasts. She'd unbuttoned the shirt, and he could clearly see the tempting valley between her breasts.

Male interest surged, but he grimly ignored it. Sex would only complicate things a lot more.

"If you're ready to leave, you can go now. I'm staying."

The past was behind them. No going back. But he'd be damned if he got into the SUV and turned around and hopped a plane for home. He was a SEAL and the only easy day was yesterday.

Even when it came to dragging his ex-wife back to the States.

"Got a spare room? I don't take up much space."

Lacey's eyes widened. "No, Jarrett."

"I can sleep on the floor."

"You're not staying. You saw my compound, met my daughter. Goodbye."

He walked over to her, stroked a finger down her cheek. Lacey quivered. They still had it. The chemistry between them was combustible.

He dropped his hand with a grimace. Nearly as flammable as this country.

"I'll camp by a mango tree if I must."

Lacey shook her head. "No. We're not married anymore, Jarrett. You have no authority over me."

"Dead chickens on the gate and a known arms dealer showing interest in your charity give me the authority.

I'm staying until I find out who's behind it, whether I sleep on the floor, in a bed or on the ground. Get used to the idea."

"Jarrett…"

"Try to drag me out of here, Lace. There's a child involved now and what threatens you also threatens her. That changes everything. I'm not budging. Not until I know you're safe back in the States with Fleur."

Or without her, but that option was too terrible to entertain.

He softened his tone. "If not for your sake, then think of Fleur. She's already lost one mother."

Her lower lip trembled. "Damn you, Jarrett. That's a sucker punch and you know it."

"Show me where I'll bunk. My gear is in the back of the truck."

After he grabbed his duffel bag, she led him upstairs to a small hallway. Four bedrooms and a bathroom were at the landing. Lacey unlocked the bedroom door on the left corner and stepped inside.

The room had a double bed with a plain white bedspread, a small desk and chair, scuffed wood bureau and a closet. Jarrett opened the closet, walked over to the window and tested the lock.

At his inquiring look, she sighed. "I haven't had time to fix it yet. It's safe out here in the country."

"Safe as dead chickens with their guts ripped out."

She folded her arms over her chest. "If you're staying here, you work. No one gets a free ride."

"I like hard work." If he had to camp out by that damn gate, he would.

"Fresh towels are in the bathroom. Unpack and be downstairs and ready to work. You have twenty minutes."

"Yes, ma'am."

At his lazy grin, she frowned. "And Jarrett? We're all women here, so remember to shut the bathroom door and for goodness' sake, leave the toilet seat down."

His deep chuckle followed her out of the room.

Jarrett stopped laughing and slung his duffel bag onto the bed, then he checked his weapon and then his wallet. He had no idea why Lacey was being threatened or what Augustin wanted with her charity.

But he sure as hell was going to find out.

The dead chicken bothered Lacey more than she admitted.

After checking on Fleur and giving her a reassuring hug, she talked with Rose, her cook, and Collette. Neither had seen anything unusual.

Pierre, the guard at the gate, finally admitted he had been dozing off last night. He wasn't certain how long he'd slept.

Yelling at him did no good. Part of her challenge in running operations at the coffee plantation was hiring good help. Pierre was the son of a factory worker who begged her to hire him. He was a decent employee, and when her regular security guard took two weeks to visit his family in New York, she put Pierre in charge.

She had a bad feeling her security guard wasn't returning.

Lacey told Pierre she was withholding his wages for the day and told him to go home. She called a friend about hiring a new guard. That was life here in this country. One must constantly improvise.

But the dead chicken was a new twist. Ever since she'd fired some of the local single men for laziness, replacing them with women, there had been grumblings in town. She did have enemies. Because of this, she'd made friends, as well, and hired four older, more muscled and trustworthy men, brothers and fathers to the women she hired, as caretakers to work in the cornfield and keep the grass cut around the property. Some slept in small storage sheds on the property, glad to have a place to bunk. Lacey reasoned if they stayed on the property, they could keep a close eye on things.

But it was a large piece of land, and the caretakers couldn't oversee everything at all times, especially at night.

Fifteen minutes later, after a quick check of the outside of the house, she went into the kitchen. Jarrett was inside. Straddling a chair, he rested his muscled arms upon the back and chatted with Rose as she chopped carrots.

He flashed Lacey a warm smile as she entered the room, which she ignored, despite her rapidly beating heart. She couldn't fully ignore him, though. A subtle tendril of scent threaded through the air as he neared—the spicy scent of his cologne. Jarrett still wore the same cologne and it opened a floodgate of memories. The smell of him, delicious and spicy, on his pillow the mornings after they'd made love. For months after the divorce, every time she smelled that particular aftershave, she wanted to cry, because it reminded her so vividly of Jarrett.

Sometimes when he'd deploy she would roll over at night and hug his pillow, breathing in his scent so she'd feel a little less lonely.

And then when he came home, the sex between them was good, so very good. Jarrett had been insistent on spoiling her, feeding her breakfast in bed, making sure she was covered and warm. Sometimes they spent two days in bed, exploring each others' bodies, getting re-acquainted in the most delightful of ways.

Now, staring at her ex, the old desire surfaced. Jarrett was solid muscle, all grace and strength. It showed in the way his powerful biceps flexed as he talked with Rose, but more than that, the man gave her cook his undivided attention. When he centered that emerald-green gaze at you, a woman couldn't help but melt. Do anything he asked. And if the anything involved getting naked, even better.

Down, girl.

So what if she hadn't had sex in more than two years?

It didn't mean she was going to entertain thoughts of getting cozy with her ex, no matter how much her body said *Go for it.*

She had a compound to run, a daughter to adopt and someone trying to hustle her out of her compound. At least she could rely upon her staff's discretion.

"Rose and I have been having a delightful little chat. She told me last week someone set fire to your best truck," Jarrett said softly in English.

So much for discretion.

"It was an accident, I'm certain." Lacey picked up a bright orange carrot piece and chewed it. "Someone probably tossed a lit cigarette into the cab, which I was foolish enough to leave open. It was extinguished in minutes."

"Rose also told me that the women have been spooked by things left hanging from the gate. This is not the first dead chicken."

Jarrett's even gaze met hers. She shrugged, hiding her thoughts. The man could smell anxiety from miles away.

"She's only upset because it was the waste of a good chicken for dinner."

He did not smile at her little joke. She walked over to the counter to peer out the window. Fleur was outside, playing jump rope with the two other little girls who had accompanied her into the compound. Their mothers worked at the mango factory.

Lacey turned, studying her ex. Her gaze fell to the curve of his spine against the tight white T-shirt, the muscles on his back, down to the pistol tucked into the leather holster.

Jarrett was walking, talking security. He wouldn't have fallen asleep at the gate. He'd have tracked down the trespasser and squeezed out the information about who wanted to scare her.

He rose off the chair, all six feet, three inches of muscled male. Her heart pounded faster.

"I think I'll have a look around your house before I start on whatever manual labor you have assigned to me."

For a big man, he had a quiet, graceful stride. She supposed it came from the nature of his work. And he was very security conscious. Lacey watched him check all the downstairs windows. Funny, she'd always felt safe when he was home.

When being the operative word.

But before he'd left for a mission, Jarrett had always ensured that the house was tight and secure, the alarm system working and emergency contacts within easy reach.

Jarrett went to the front door and ran a hand over the edge then jiggled the lock.

He turned, dusting off his hands.

"One well-placed kick could knock down this door."

"We've never had anyone try. Usually they're more polite and open the door." She tried to hide the worry he'd put into words. When she'd been alone with Rose, she never worried about sleeping here. Now that she had Fleur, she constantly worried.

"Lacey, I don't like it," Jarrett began.

She held up a finger as her cell phone rang. Lacey's heart sank as she answered and heard the news. Frightened by the spreading violence in the city, one of her best donors was packing his bags and heading back to France.

More and more wealthy donors were pulling out. Her chest constricted. She had to ship out jam and make good on her new contract or she'd lose all her profits.

She crooked a finger at Jarrett. "Come on. I have work for you."

They walked outside, down the dirt path that led to a large, wood-frame shed where she packed the marmalade. Lacey fished a key out of her pocket and unlocked the door.

He picked up a jar of jam with the labels she'd made on her computer. Lacey took it from his hands.

"This one's crooked. I'll save it for the house."

"You always were a perfectionist." Jarrett smiled at her and the power in his smile made her weak. That smile...it was what attracted her to him long ago. Not his great, killer bod or his quiet intellect. That 10,000-watt smile. When he turned it on her, giving her his full attention, she felt like the center of his universe. She, who had been ignored by a father more interested in his business and a mother more concerned with her society parties, mattered the most to this man.

Lacey set the jar on the shelf among those she'd intended to keep, her heart squeezing painfully. Jarrett had another lady who came first—the Navy.

Duty before love.

They walked into the room. Jarrett's gaze went from

the stacks of crates and packing to a bottle sitting by the table. He went to the empty bottle, turned it upside down. There was a set of keys beside the bottle.

Her temper rose as she grabbed the keys. "Now I know why Pierre didn't see anything."

Jarrett sniffed the bottle. "Doesn't help when your security guard has been drinking all night."

"Job hazard in this country. I'll have to fire Pierre. Total security fail. Damn it."

He raised a dark brow, and the cynical expression on his face kicked in all her defenses. Maybe he perceived this as evidence she couldn't hold her own out here, even though she had done it for years.

"One bad call in giving a guy a chance doesn't make it a total failure."

She blinked in surprise at his understanding and sought to regain her lost composure. "I'm not upset about that. I'm mad because that was a damn fine bottle of wine I'd been saving."

His full mouth quirked in a sexy little grin. "That's the spirit. I'll find you a new security guard, screen him and have him start right away. I'm sure there are guys Ace can recommend on the island."

Her mind zipped through the figures it would cost. The type of security Ace would recommend would strain her already screaming budget. "Things are a little tight in the pocket…"

"I'll pay for his salary."

"I don't need your help," she started. Jarrett raised a brow and she sighed. "All right. But I'll pay you back after I get the check from the restaurants that ordered the mango marmalade."

"Deal." He whipped out his cell phone and sent a text. As he tucked the phone away, his relief was obvious.

"You'll be doing me a favor, Lace. If you had someone on that front gate who knew how to hold a weapon, a trained professional, I could sleep at night."

"Me, too. Maybe. Lately that's a challenge, even with a glass of red wine."

Jarrett smiled, looking lost in thought.

"Remember when we made the wine after I came home from the tour of Iraq?" He stepped closer, ran a hand down her arm. She shivered with pleasure at the contact.

"I remember how drunk you got me." Her voice dropped. "I remember…what we did afterward."

Jarrett's gaze grew heated. "Every time I cracked open a bottle of wine, I remember what I did with you. Every single moment."

Lacey hurried through the room, her body tingling. She had to put him at a distance. So many memories, and here he was before her, like a gift she never asked for.

A gift that could lead to heartache all over. She didn't need this heartache.

And even if Jarrett Adler meant to stay for the fore-seeable future, it didn't matter. She couldn't risk falling in love with him and ruining her life again.

This time it would be different. He wasn't going to stick around, anyway. He'd get the call to return to base, and return to being a SEAL. Men like Jarrett Adler never did stick around.

Chapter 5

This time it would be different. Jarrett planned to stick to her side until she screamed.

Once he'd made her scream a different way…in bed. That memory had his blood surging hot and thick. He remembered her blue gaze dazed with pleasure as he'd slowly thrust into her, their naked bodies achieving a mutual rhythm and pleasure that sent him sailing into the stratosphere. Sex with Lace had been the glue in their relationship.

But now he needed more to get her back into his life. He needed to give her a safe haven where she could raise her daughter without either of them harboring the fear of someone tossing a firebomb into their car or shooting at them on the street.

Until Ace got back to him with more intel, he would try to glean as much information as possible around her compound. Good thing he was fluent in French.

She pointed to the wooden crates and neatly stacked boxes by a table topped with glass jars filled with jam. "Help me get these ready for packing. Each wood box can hold four containers of jam. Seal them with the staple gun."

As she picked up the gun, he gently took it from her. "I know how to handle one of these. I'm the weapons expert, remember?"

"Yeah, Mr. Weapons Expert. I remember how you spent a whole weekend trying to fix the gate and the first time you used the nail gun you ended up in the ER with a nail sticking out of your hand."

He laughed. "It almost ended up in my ass. That would have been special."

A ripple of sensual appreciation passed over her face as she glanced at his bottom. "A real shame to hurt that part of your body," she murmured.

Pleased he still had that effect on her, he loaded up the staple gun.

They worked in companionable silence for a few minutes. Lacey wiped the sweat off her brow.

"Most of the jam goes across the country to restaurants, but I'm shipping a box to Mom as she and Dad love the stuff." She pointed to the box he worked on. "Set that one aside. I'm going to ship it via air freight."

Her face fell and her lower lip wobbled a little. "I was planning to hand-carry them when I took Fleur with me back home as a welcome home gift. Now I don't know when I'll get her home."

He knew she was fighting emotions. Knew how she tried to hide it, because she'd always tried to be brave in the past, but that little wobble in her pretty mouth gave it away.

Jarrett set down the staple gun, making sure to

switch it off. He put his hands on her shoulders, feeling delicate bone beneath the soft skin. Lace wasn't frail, but she had a soft heart and it had to kill her to be put into this position.

"Hey," he said gently. "Everything's going to be all right, Lace. Have faith."

Have faith in me. I won't let you down. Have faith in the job I do. It comes first. But I'll always be there for you.

In the end he wasn't there when she truly needed him. Jarrett gave her shoulders a reassuring squeeze, fighting the urge to kiss her senseless as he had in the past. Kiss her and lead her into the bedroom where he'd made all her woes fall away.

When the last staple secured the last box of jam, they stacked them inside the shed, making certain to set apart the four jars destined for sending to Lacey's father. Tomorrow a truck would collect the crates to distribute to restaurants.

After they stacked the boxes, she wiped off the sweat from her glistening forehead with the back of one hand. "Thanks. You really helped. Now I have one less chore."

He brushed off his jeans. Lacey gave him a friendly smile as she pointed to her soaked shirt.

"How do you do it, Jarrett? You never break a sweat. Not even that day when you nailed your hand. Do you even have sweat glands?"

Oh yeah, he had plenty of times on ops. Down range, he sweated quite a bit, waiting in hiding for the moment to move in and take down the enemy. Sweating profusely while sitting in a plane at 30,000, waiting to do a HALO jump.

Sweating as he waited in a courtroom for the judge to declare the divorce final...

But he'd never let on, because he was tough. A man's man who never showed his emotions. Emotions killed you in the field; they slipped beneath your collar and taunted you, distracting you from the mission, the target…

Had to steer this disturbing thread of conversation in another direction. He eyed her shirt and the curve of her full breasts.

"You've made me sweat plenty, babe."

Lacey didn't return his grin. "Don't call me that. I hate that word."

She turned and left and he inwardly cursed. Any inroads he'd made with her in packing the boxes had been lost.

He could regain that ground. Had to, because she needed to trust him again, this time with her life.

His cell phone quietly buzzed. Ace. His friend recommended a private firm he worked for on occasion when wealthy islanders held private parties.

Guy by the name of Marcus. We did a few details together. Knows the business end of a shotgun, but prefers to work with more reliable firepower.

Jarrett called the firm, who promised to send over a security detail in an hour.

Near the house he spied Lacey's daughter skipping rope with two other girls. Jarrett didn't follow his ex into the house. Deciding to give her time to cool down, both emotionally and physically, he headed for the girls.

Wearing blue shorts, blue tennis shoes and a white T-shirt with the logo of Marlee's Mangoes, Fleur skipped rope. She did not smile, even as the other girls laughed and sang a song in French.

He wondered if she ever smiled.

Such a thin little girl. He rubbed his chest. Jarrett imagined how terrified the child had been to seen such violence and lose her mother. And how brave Lacey had been to step out and adopt her, give her a home instead of losing her to an orphanage where Fleur might not receive the help she needed.

He pointed to the jump rope the girls were twirling. "Mind if I join?" he asked in French.

The three girls stared at him as if he'd lost his mind. Jarrett smiled. "I'm good, but I bet you can teach me a thing or two."

That started the two twirling the rope to giggle. But little Fleur, with her skinny shoulders and solemn eyes, did not react. She stepped aside.

The two on either end of the rope moved closer to accommodate his height. Jarrett stood at the center and nodded. "I'm ready."

They began turning the rope and he made a big exhibit out of bending over to accommodate the twirling rope, jumping slow and stomping on the ground. Every loud *whomp* evoked a giggle from the girls. Finally, he turned and stepped aside.

"This is tough," he complained. "Fleur, can you show me how it's done?"

Fleur still stared, but took his place. She began to jump rope and he nodded. "You're fast. Let's see how fast when I take over."

Beckoning to one of the girls, he took the rope from her and began to twirl it. Fleur jumped harder and faster to the shouts of the girls.

And then he stopped and grinned at her. "You're pretty good," he told her. "You're faster than me."

Fleur blinked, but not before he caught a glimpse

of something faint and precious in her dark eyes. Connection.

As he started to turn, Fleur saw the handle of the pistol tucked into his waistband. Her eyes widened.

He turned and saw Lacey standing on the porch, a smile on her face. "Fleur! Time for homework. Tell Michelle and Catherine you'll see them tomorrow," she called.

The two little girls ran away toward the mango factory, where a stream of women had begun to leave the shop.

Jarrett had a sudden memory. Touring Iraq, teamed with the marines. They'd infiltrated a nest of insurgents. He'd done his duty, but the kills that day had haunted him. And then he'd called home and heard Lacey's voice, her low, sweet dulcet tones, and the tightness in his chest had eased a little. She'd told him the baby was doing fine, and she expected him at the sonogram when he got home in three weeks...

The thought of seeing their baby, making it real, had carried him through the next three weeks through blood and death and everything bad...

He turned to Fleur, struggling to regain his composure. "Hey, little one," he said in perfect French. "Thanks for letting me play with you."

She pointed to his jeans and said in a small voice, "Gun."

He squatted down. "Yes. It's my pistol. I keep it close."

"To hurt people?"

Damn, this was not the way he'd anticipated conversing with his ex's daughter. He'd wanted to talk about playing games, what classes she liked, not firearms.

"Yes, but only bad people who want to hurt you and your mom." Awkwardly, he patted her shoulder. "Go do as your mom says."

Fleur gave him a shy smile then skipped away toward the house.

Do as your mom says.

How he'd dreamed of saying those words to their son or daughter. He fisted his hands and turned away from the house, staring at the distant fields. Then his gaze swung to the gate, that gate with the dead chicken.

He couldn't return to the past and change things. But he could help Lacey now, and her daughter.

While waiting for the security detail to arrive, he went to the front gate and did a thorough check. The eight-foot gate was solid steel and required someone to open it by hand, like typical front gates in St. Marc that guarded private homes and businesses and schools. Effective, if you had the right person standing guard.

The man at the gate right now had a careworn face and gray hair. There was a spark to his dark gaze as he greeted Jarrett. He didn't carry a firearm, but the sun glinted off the polished steel machete he held in a firm grip.

"Afternoon," Jarrett greeted him in French. "I'm Jarrett Adler, friend of Lacey's."

"Joseph." The man shifted the machete to his left hand and shook Jarrett's outstretched palm. "I work in the fields for Miss Lacey. She asked me to take over guard duty for now."

He nodded at the gleaming blade. "Know how to use that thing for something other than cutting corn?"

White teeth flashed at him in a knowing grin. Joseph picked up a coconut fallen from a nearby palm tree and placed it near him. The machete whistled through the air and two halves of the nut spilled to the ground as he cut it.

"Don't you worry, Mr. Jarrett. Anyone try to hang

dead chickens on this gate I go *chop chop* with my big knife," Joseph told him. "I'm not that young fool Pierre. He had no respect for the job. Miss Lacey's good people. She deserves better."

He liked him. Joseph had years on him, and the kind of wisdom and experience that indicated he wasn't about to put up with anything.

They made small talk for a few minutes. Joseph was a wealth of information. Most of the locals liked Lacey and were grateful she saved the coffee factory from closing—news to him—and gave the community much-needed jobs. And many were appreciative of her charity.

A few "big talkers" dissed Lacey and didn't like her because they saw her as a rich American, but those were the men she'd fired for laziness.

A car honked at the gate and he and Joseph stepped through the door at the side of the gate. It was the security detail Ace had recommended. Joseph let the car through. They parked inside and all four men got out. Marcus, the leader, was all muscled bulk, tall and dressed in neatly pressed trousers and a tan shirt with the firm's logo on it.

Jarrett talked with him, liking his quiet intelligence, and his alertness. He really liked the M45C handgun he carried. "Nice piece," he told Marcus.

"Gift from Ace from the last job we did together," Marcus replied in his singsong accent. "I have a suppressor, but for jobs like this I need to make loud *bang bang* to let intruders know I mean business."

Between Marcus and his security detail, and Joseph, any perp trying to get through the front gate would be toast.

Marcus knew the area, too, and had been born and

raised here, which was an additional bonus. If trouble flared in town, he'd hear about it.

After extensive interviewing of Marcus and his men, with additional questions by a sharp-eyed Joseph, Jarrett agreed to let them to work out details of guarding the gate around the clock.

Of course, it was the gate and this was a big compound, which worried him. He needed to check for weaknesses in the wall ringing the complex. Not for the first time that day he itched to have his regular weapons. The Sig was a constant friend, but more firepower would come in handy if things got rough and the violence spilled from the capital to the countryside.

Satisfied with the gate security, he headed toward the house. Lacey met him inside.

He told her about Marcus and added his praise of Joseph.

"Joseph is a loyal employee, like most of my staff. He lives here on the compound and he's a very hard worker, typical of most men in St. Marc. The ones like the men who beat the women in my compound are outnumbered by the good ones in my book," she said.

He wondered if he'd ever rank as a *good one* in her book again.

"Thanks for taking care of that for me," she told him. "Have a drink with me. I've got a bottle of the finest island rum. Dinner won't be ready for another hour. Rose is making chicken and gravy and rice."

Sounded good. The smells of chicken coming from the kitchen smelled good, too. But never pleasure before business. "Want to check the place first."

He went to the guest room, changed into running clothes and tucked his pistol into a special jogging holster around his waist and pulled his gray T-shirt over it. After lacing up his running shoes and grabbing dark sunglasses, he headed outside.

He chose the perimeter near the gate and broke into his normal stride, his gaze sharpened as he scanned the compound. Feet pounding against the hard earth, Jarrett fell into an easy rhythm, relishing the pull of his muscles and the burn of his lungs. Sweat dripped down his back and temples.

Jarrett finished his run without incident and went into the house.

Lacey sat in the living room, a glass half-filled with dark liquid. She carried her drink as she followed him into the kitchen as he fetched a bottle of cold water from the refrigerator. Rose stirred a big pot at the stove and then vanished into the next room.

Standing at the sink, he drank deeply, sensing Lacey's gaze. Jarrett finished the bottle and turned, amused to see her staring and licking her lips.

Oh yeah, sweetheart, you feel it, too.

Flushing a little at being caught ogling him, she looked away. "Enjoy your run?"

He set down the bottle, wiped his face with the corner of his shirt. "As you can see, I do sweat."

A flash of heat entered her gaze.

She sipped her cocktail. He reached over, took the glass from her and drank.

"Hey!" Lacey protested.

Jarrett nodded in appreciation. She'd cut it with cola, but the taste was quite potent. "Very fine dark rum. Smooth as a baby's bottom. Too much cola, though. Rum like that should be drunk neat."

"Do you mind? You're drinking out of my glass."

He handed her back the glass and their fingers touched. Heat blazed through him at the gentle touch.

Once those fingers had explored every inch of his body, dug into his shoulders as she clung to him and cried out as he moved inside her.

"Sweetheart, we've shared more than backwash... and swapped body fluid a lot more interesting."

At his drawled words, she flushed. They went into the living room as Lacey carried her glass and then set it on the coffee table.

"It wasn't only jogging, Lace. I checked out your compound. You're too vulnerable here. Too many places open to intruders."

"I have an eight-foot wall topped with broken glass. No one is going to break inside my house. You see shadows in shadows."

"The world can be a very bad place. I'd rather see the shadows than have them surprise me."

Lacey sighed and the move lifted her generous breasts. He tried not to stare, but he was only human. *Focus.*

"Do any of the women ever bring in visitors to the compound?" he asked.

"No. One of the conditions of working here is that I screen all visitors. I don't want strangers inside who might hurt one of them."

Jarrett laced his fingers gently around her wrist, feeling her soft skin. Touch. Contact. She'd survived out here on her own without him, but his protective streak surged hard. "Lace, is there any chance the dead chicken incidents and the car on fire have anything to do with any of the women you hired? Are there angry husbands, boyfriends, who are threatening you?"

He almost wished this were so. It would make it easier to pinpoint the threat.

"Not outright, but a few men in town have disliked

what I'm doing for the local women." She studied his fingers around her wrist and put her hand over his. "A few have made vague threats, but nothing concrete."

Jarrett's blood ran cold at the thought of someone hurting her. He inhaled a shaky breath as Rose came into the living room to announce dinner was ready.

Throughout the meal as Lacey talked with Fleur about school, asking questions about her teachers, how she was doing studying for upcoming exams, Jarrett could not get the burning image out of his mind. Lacey, injured and unable to summon help. She was too vulnerable here.

He helped her wash the dishes as Fleur cleaned off the table. They went into the living room and Lacey read Fleur a story as thoughts raced through his mind. Then Lacey took Fleur away to get her ready for bed.

Jarrett checked the downstairs area again, testing the locks.

When Fleur came into the living room in pajamas to shyly bid him good-night, he hugged the girl a little harder than intended. Jarrett followed Lacey into her bedroom. As Lacey tucked her daughter in, Fleur stared up at him.

"Are you staying here tonight?" she asked in French.

Jarrett squatted down by the bed and said in the same language. "Yes. I'm going to make sure you and your mom stay safe."

"Will you keep the bad man from coming to school?"

He exchanged looks with Lacey. "What bad man, honey?"

"The man who had a gun like you." She pointed to the waistband of his jeans. Lacey released a shaky breath.

"Fleur, sweetie, tell me everything," Lacey said. "Was this bad man in the schoolyard?"

"No, he was in the street."

"What did he look like? Was he white like me? Tall?" Jarrett asked.

"He had dark skin, like me. He was standing by the man who sells the plantain chips. Sally wanted to buy chips but when I saw him I got scared and didn't go."

"Good girl," Jarrett said softly. "Did Sally tell you anything about the bad man? Did they say anything?"

"He was looking for a flower and wanted to know if a flower went to our school. Sally said we have lots of flowers on the classroom blackboard."

He reached over and pressed a kiss on the little girl's forehead. "I'll be here all night, honey. No bad man will get you."

When they went into the living room, Lacey's shoulders trembled. She plopped into a chair. "She's not going to school tomorrow. Dear God, what is going on?"

"Hey." He flopped down beside her and began rubbing the tensed muscles in her shoulders. "Tell me about the school. Gated compound? Security?"

"It's the safest elementary school outside the capital. A few ex-pats who run missions in the country send their children there. They have a security guard, and no one gets in or out without clearance from the head office. But at recess the kids go outside to buy snacks from vendors on the street. They're locals who make a living and they've been cleared by the school. Bad men with guns. My daughter could have been hurt."

"You got a lucky break. But it's obvious someone is searching for her. How does Fleur get to school?"

"Usually I drive her. In the afternoon Sally's mom drops her off near the front gate."

"She'll go to school tomorrow." Jarrett locked gazes

with her, knowing she would protest. "With me. I'll drive her and check out that bad man."

"Jarrett, no…"

He gave her a pointed look. "If someone is threatening Fleur, I want to know who. She'll be safe, Lace. She's a smart little girl, too."

She buried her face into her hands. "If something happens to her…"

He squeezed her shoulder. "Nothing's going to happen to her. I promise."

Lacey lifted her head, her blue eyes bright. Not with tears, but glittering anger. "You made a lot of promises to me in the past, Jarrett. Am I supposed to believe you this time?"

Sucker punch. Damn. "That was a low blow, Lace. I never broke my promises to you."

"No, you only left. You didn't need me. You had your SEAL buddies and the Navy."

His temper started to uncoil like a rattlesnake. He struggled to leash it. "I had a job to do."

"You left me right after I lost our baby. I needed you and you left. You weren't there for me when I needed you most, so why should I trust you now?"

Ouch. Now guilt twined with the anger. "I was there for you at the hospital and when you were released. The doctor said you'd be fine."

"After, Jarrett! Not the physical part." She pressed a hand to her heart. "Here. Where it hurt the most. You were home five days and then you were deployed. You left me to deal with the loss of our baby by myself."

"I had a job to do, Lace."

"You could have asked for leave." Lacey's slender shoulders trembled. "I knew how important the teams were to you, and how important you were to them. I was so proud of you that you chose that path to serve, Jarrett. I hated it when you left, but I never complained because that was the life you had chosen, and the life I chose to share with you. But just that once, I really needed you to stay home, and you left, anyway."

She got him there. He could have. In fact, his CO asked if he was okay to take the mission. And dumbass he was, he told his CO, *yeah, I'm good to go, everything's a-okay, let me go eliminate some tangos, let me fight so I can forget this panic I felt when I thought I'd lose not just my baby, but Lace, as well.* He'd gone charging into the mission with a muddied mind, trying to push aside grief and acted recklessly, almost suicidal in the risks he took.

If not for Ace pulling him in, reminding him there was no *I* in team and he needed to get himself together, Jarrett could have lost it for good.

By the time he returned home six weeks later, his head was clearer, but Lacey was gone.

"Five days." She held up five fingers. "You were distant the whole time. You barely said a word to me."

"I waited on you hand and foot and hired a housekeeper to cook and clean…"

"But you never talked with me, Jarrett. We never talked about the baby. The nursery we'd planned, the first coat of paint, the crib my dad bought for us." Her voice cracked. "I was living at home with you, but I was already alone. No wonder they call you the Iceman. Because you were one cold bastard."

He sucked in a breath and his temper surged. "You left me, remember? You left me and all I had was an empty house when I came home."

"I left you to go to my parents' house because I needed someone other than a paid stranger to do housework and cook. And what was the point of trying to make it work out? The job always came first, Jarrett. Always. My dad told me not to marry you because you were a SEAL and the divorce rate among SEALs is very high. He wanted me to stay in college and get my degree and wait. But I loved you and didn't want to wait. I'd have done anything to make it work, Jarrett. I gave up my education, I gave up my friends to move with you onto base because I had faith that we could make it work."

She drew in a deep breath. "And I never complained, not once, not even when you'd come home and go quiet for days. I knew you were trying to get your head together because of the awful things you'd seen…"

"And done," he cut in.

"I didn't want to be one of those nagging wives who pestered you to communicate. I gave you space. I let you talk when you needed to, and let you party with your SEAL buddies because they were your family as much as I was. But the one time I asked you to stay, to talk with me after we lost our baby, you clammed up. You couldn't give me what I needed and I had no faith you'd change, Jarrett."

She fell back onto the sofa, wiping her forehead. Jarrett stared down at his hands, the scarred knuckles and the closely trimmed nails. Big hands, big heart, she'd teased him in the past. Hands that had pulled the trigger too many times to count, had snapped the necks of the enemy. Hands that had stroked and caressed Lacey in the dark of night, and held her as she'd sobbed in the hospital.

But they were the same hands that saluted his CO after Lacey's miscarriage and then hours later quietly turned the front doorknob in the gray hours of dawn as he picked up his duffel and left to go downrange yet again.

"I deserve that," he said quietly. "I'm sorry, Lace. I'm sorry I couldn't give you what you needed at the time."

Her lower lip wobbled again, that precarious little tremble hinting of her raging emotions. "It's in the past, Jarrett. I've made a new life here and I'm so damn scared for my daughter."

He covered her hand with his. "Then let me help you. I'll drive her to school tomorrow, check out this guy and we'll go together to pick her up in the afternoon."

Lacey rubbed circles on her knee, and he could see her mind working. "Fleur has a test tomorrow."

"In kindergarten?"

"The test is to put her into a higher level of learning class. I've been working with her on learning to read in French."

Bemused, he shook his head. Kids these days were brighter and learned quicker than he ever did. "At her age I was finger-painting and pulling little girls' pigtails." Playfully, he tugged on her ponytail, hoping to coax a smile to her solemn face.

She went to the window, pulling aside the curtains. He regarded his ex. She'd done well for herself and struck out on her own. He was mighty proud of her, but didn't quite know how to say it. Didn't quite know how to reconnect. Once sex had been the answer, and hell, he'd gladly pick her up, sling her over one shoulder and carry her into the bedroom to explore what they'd had in bed, but first he had to gain her trust.

She'd left him because he hadn't communicated in the past. Time to start talking.

"Lace, how about we…"

"I have an early day tomorrow. I'm going to bed."

Lacey tugged the band off her ponytail and her hair spilled around her. Loose, and wild, a little like her. He hungered to see her like that in bed once more, her silky locks spread out on the pillow as she lay back, naked, her body bared exclusively for him...

Stop thinking about sex. Yeah, right. Tell me to stop breathing. That would be easier around her.

Frowning, Lacey stared at the window.

"It's too quiet. Usually the roosters are crowing."

Instantly he pulled away, his body on full alert. He noticed the quiet, as well. Roosters, contrary to myth, crowed whenever they felt like it, not just in the morning. Jarrett snapped off the living room lamp. "Step away from the window."

Standing to one side, he lifted the curtain with the back of one hand. He peered into the blackness. Every cell in his body warned something was wrong. Jarrett spotted movement by the storage shed and heard glass breaking.

And then he heard a loud *pop*, like a firecracker going off. All the hairs on his nape saluted the air and his body went cold. Suddenly, an orange glow erupted inside the shed, followed by thick black tongues of smoke curling into the moonlit sky.

The shed was on fire and the flames were headed for the jam they'd packed this afternoon.

Chapter 6

Lacey saw the fire and her stomach clenched hard. But she knew how to handle this.

Her ex drew his pistol and started for the door. "Stay here. Call the fire department."

The fire department was twenty miles away and she wasn't certain they would even respond, as rumor had it the fire station had been shut down due to non-payment from the government. Jarrett ran outside with his sidearm drawn. That was her shed going up in flames!

She raced into the kitchen, told Rose to watch Fleur and grabbed a flashlight. On the porch, hanging from the building's side, was an old-fashioned school bell. She ran outside, rang it hard to alert the compound's caretakers and then headed toward the fire.

As she reached the shed, heat curled through the air, a living thing that licked at the wood shed with greedy tongues. But she'd planned well.

The hose, curled up by the building where they'd packed the jam, was attached to the water tower. In the afternoons on hot days, the kids sometimes used it to cool off. She grabbed the hose and it came off in her hands. One section. Then another.

It had been cut too short now to reach the shed. The men who stayed on property were running toward the fire, shouting as they ran.

Lacey ran toward the buckets used for hand-watering the garden near the building. "We have to use buckets. The hose is useless," she shouted in French. "Pierre, run to the garden shed and get the other hose!"

The five men who lived on the compound raced toward the scene, grabbing buckets and filling them, forming a line as they tossed water onto the flames.

The fire hadn't spread yet to the crates. She could still save a few. Lacey ran toward the burning shed. Tremendous heat baked her body. Smoke made her eyes sting and water. But she had to save some of her wares. She started inside when someone grabbed her from the waist.

"I told you to stay in the house," Jarrett's voice rumbled low and deep in her ear.

"Let me go," she protested. "I can get them."

"It's too late." He picked her up, slung her over one broad shoulder and headed away from the burning shed. As she bounced upside down, she could see her future going up in orange flames.

Finally, when they were several yards away, he set her down. The smell of burning fruit and sugar made her ill. She bent over and coughed, her eyes stinging.

"Deep breaths. You've got smoke in your lungs. Deep, easy breaths."

His voice was quiet and soothing, but as she stared

at the men trying to put out the fire, misery engulfed her. Jars in the crates began to explode from the heat as the flames reached the crates. The bucket brigade now concentrated on wetting down the grass and preventing the fire from spreading. Finally Pierre, the man she'd hired as a gardener and painter, arrived with the hose from the garden shed. But even as they sprayed the flames, she knew it was pointless.

All the hard work of the women was gone.

"That shed contained next month's salaries. They worked so hard on the jam. That's their livelihood," she said, coughing again.

"Better their livelihood than your life." His mouth tight, the fire casting flickering shadows across the hard lines of his face, Jarrett tucked his gun away. "I told you to stay put."

"Like I'm listening to you?"

"You should. What if someone wanted to smoke you out? Set the fire to lure you outside so they could hurt Fleur? Or take her away? Or hurt you?"

A flicker of fear raced down her spine. "Rose is watching her."

Seeing that the men had the fire under control she turned on her heels and headed for the house to check on her daughter.

"Rose is a middle-aged, nice lady who is a great cook. Not a bodyguard." Jarrett was on her heels, jogging behind her.

Ignoring him, she raced inside and headed for Fleur's bedroom. Rose stood outside, hovering, her dark, careworn face twisted with anxiety.

"Fleur?" she asked Rose.

"Sleeping. What is happening, Miss Lacey?" Rose asked in French.

"It's all right, Rose. A fire, and it's under control now." She opened the door to Fleur's bedroom, relieved to see the little girl slept through the chaos outside.

As Lacey turned, Jarrett peered past her. He gently shut the door and told Rose in French, "You can return to bed, Rose. I secured the house. I'm staying here now and will keep watch."

"Thank you, Mr. Jarrett."

He had barely been here a day and already he issued orders. But she was too miserable to care. Jarrett followed her upstairs into the hallway bathroom as Lacey splashed cold water on her face, breathing deeply and trying to calm her nerves. He handed her a towel and their eyes met in the mirror. Soot streaked his hard features, and there was a red stain on his white T-shirt.

She turned, her alarm growing. "You're hurt!"

"It's not blood. It's red paint that got on my shirt when I scaled the wall. Whoever set that fire left you a message. *American go home*."

Lacey shook her head, still stunned at the audacity. They were inside her compound, her sanctuary where she'd worked hard to make women feel safe. "That wall is topped with broken glass."

"Not anymore. Whoever set the fire removed the glass and used it as an entrance and exit point. They were damned determined to get inside, Lace. That was a fire set by an incendiary device, maybe with a timer. It's gone beyond dead chickens and someone is targeting your NGO. Will you listen to me for once?"

Her heart raced. Inside her compound! Someone had set the fire inside her compound. What if they had set fire to the house, as well?

Jarrett was experienced in security and flushing out bad guys. His SEAL training made him one of the best.

Along with arrogant and confident. Arrogant and confident he might be, but he was concerned for her safety. The dynamic changed the moment the arsonists had climbed over the wall to set the fire.

Then there was the matter of the men with the guys near Fleur's school...

"All right." She leaned against the sink, suddenly exhausted. "I'm listening."

Jarrett blinked in apparent surprise. "This is a first."

"It's getting dangerous and I won't have Fleur at risk. Tell me what you want."

"Downstairs, and we'll talk. I need to wash up first."

He pushed past her to the sink and peeled the dirty shirt over his head, dropping it on the floor. Fascination filled her as she stared at the muscles flexing smoothly over his tanned skin as he bent over the sink. His gun stuck out of his holster, a grim reminder of the lethal soldier.

Lacey swallowed against a sudden surge of lust as he straightened and wiped his face with the towel she had used. Sharing towels, sharing drinks, Jarrett didn't mind sharing when they were married.

Except secrets. She'd always tried to understand that was his job. He couldn't ever talk about it.

But he'd never talked about the important things between them, either. Instead, he'd clammed up and walked away. Jarrett had never been like that before. He'd shared himself, his dreams and his feelings, and when they got married, she thought she'd found her life's partner who'd regard her as the most important thing in his world.

Gradually, as he went on one deployment after another, sometimes back to back, she came to realize the teams were the most important thing in the world. He'd come home sometimes and barely speak.

He seemed willing to talk now and she'd listen, for Fleur's sake.

Lacey went to the bathroom adjoining her bedroom and quickly washed up, changing into a fresh T-shirt and sleep shorts. By the time she went downstairs to the kitchen, she felt in control.

When he joined her in the kitchen, Jarrett wore a clean gray T-shirt with a football logo. Her female hormones sighed with disappointment at the covering. He did have such a terrific physique.

She watched as Jarrett checked and rechecked the window. The orange glow from the fire was banked now, and smoke hovered in the air. He went into the kitchen, pulled a bottle of water from the refrigerator and drank, then handed it to her.

Sipping at the water, she watched warily as he sat at the table.

"Whoever did this knew you used the shed to store the jam and wanted to destroy your stock. Someone here on the compound must have helped them. The fire was professionally set."

A shiver raced down her spine. "Why would someone target me?"

"I don't know." He gave her an even look. "You tell me what's going on. Do you trust your staff?"

Lacey traced a circle on her knee. "If someone talked, I'm sure it wasn't intentional. Around here, people love to gossip and tell stories. They exaggerate, too. There's even a rumor circulating about a rich man who lives behind tall walls who lures women to his home and cuts out their hearts to use them in some black magic ritual. They say he was connected to this farm and the hoodoo that was conducted here. The original rumor had died out, but resurfaced after a local girl, Caroline Beaufort, went missing about two days ago, after I fired her."

"What happened?"

"She was one of my recruits for the mango project. I hired her because she needed a job, but she kept complaining the work was too hard. Collette caught her taking too many breaks. I gave her another chance, but in the end, had to let her go. She was setting a bad example for the women who wanted to work."

She hated firing Caroline, but the woman had ideas of grandeur and wanted to work as an assistant to a "rich man" who would end up falling in love with her and marrying her.

Jarrett raised his eyebrows. "And the locals started saying someone kidnapped her and cut out her heart after she left your project?"

"When you live in a community where many of the people are poor and resent those who have money, rumors like that are bound to happen."

His gaze sharpened. "And what about you, Lace? Any rumors about you? Locals who dislike you because you have money? Those who would like to see this place burn down?"

Despite the good she'd done for the community, she could not overcome the natural resentment, especially among men. "Some, but they just talk. No one has overtly threatened me."

Until they started leaving dead chickens on the gate and firebombing my truck.

"Is there anywhere you and Fleur can go until her visa comes through? A friend's house? A trusted friend you'd rather stay with than here with me?"

He wanted her to run. "Of course. But this is my

home, and Fleur needs the stability here. The women here need me. I'm not leaving. I won't run, Jarrett. And if someone is after me, sooner or later, I'll run out of places to hide."

A small smile touched his mouth. "Knew you'd say that, Lace. You and that stubborn streak. Tomorrow call your father and see if he can nudge the DC paper pushers into expediting the visa. Get him to throw his weight behind it. I'll drive Fleur to school tomorrow and check out those men."

"So that means you're staying?" She had mixed feelings about this. Relief he would hang around, for she trusted him with security.

And dread, because she didn't trust her raging hormones. Lacey didn't want to get involved with her exhusband, and having him sleep so close to her room.

She could put him in the guesthouse, but for Fleur's sake, liked the idea of him being in the same house as her daughter. Especially now.

He gave her a level look as she handed the bottle back to him. "When you planned to take Fleur to the States, who were you leaving in charge here? That metrosexual Paul?"

The faint note of jealousy in his deep voice amused her. "He has the coffee factory to run. Collette is the manager who oversees the women. She's the only one suitable until Clare returns. She's the daughter of a friend who graduated from university in Spain and is doing an internship with a large NGO in Europe. She'll be here in another month or two."

Jarrett finished the water and capped the bottle. "Here's what you need to do. Act as if you're leaving for the long-term and hint that Fleur's visa is coming through soon and you'll be boarding a plane to Miami with her and leaving with me. That will draw heat away from you, and make whoever is targeting you relax a little. Throw them off guard."

She began to see what he planned. "And while they are relaxed, you'll have time to ask questions. But no one will talk with you. You're a stranger and an American."

"But they will talk with Rose when she goes into town to buy paint to whitewash the wall. I have my own methods of interrogation. When I catch the bastard who did this, he'll talk."

The empty bottle crushed beneath his grip. Her stomach tightened at the grim look on his face. Jarrett had always been gentle with her, and when she'd seen him skipping rope this afternoon with Fleur, it made her melt. He'd been so good with her friend's children and he'd have made an excellent father. But he was a SEAL and a fighter, and this lethal side of him she'd seldom seen.

She needed to find a way to relax or she'd never sleep tonight, and tomorrow was an important day. Paul was meeting with her to go over the profit and loss statement of their shared business and she had a bad feeling about it.

Lacey tapped her fingers on the table. "I have some wicked peppers that would break the strongest man. You're welcome to use them."

He blinked in apparent surprise. "Oh you do, my little creampuff killer?"

Smiling at the nickname, she went into the little room that she'd made into a pantry and returned with a jar of ripe, red peppers. The tiny peppers looked like cherry tomatoes, but packed a punch. Rose loved to cook with them.

My little creampuff killer. The nickname came from

when he'd come home banged up and hospitalized, requiring surgery. She'd found out he hadn't received his morphine dose and railed at the hospital staff. Lacey had gone through the ranks until she made certain Jarrett received what he needed. Later he'd joked about overhearing an orderly shake his head and say, "Your wife may look like a creampuff, but she's a killer when it comes to your welfare."

Jarrett raised his dark brows when she emerged from the pantry with the jar of peppers.

"These will make a grown man cry. A friend from Guyana brought me some on his last trip there when he was with the Peace Corps. Wiri Wiri peppers are ten times more lethal than a jalapeño. Tasty, though. I bet you can't eat one whole."

At the challenge, he leaned forward. "You're on, sweetheart. I can eat five straight. I bet you can't eat two whole."

"Stakes?"

"If you win, I'll sleep alone."

"You're sleeping alone, anyway, buddy," she warned.

"And if I win, you give me a kiss."

Her mouth watered. Since the moment she'd seen him in the hotel, her body had tingled with memories of the hours they'd spent in bed, pleasuring each other. Jarrett was such a great kisser. Her female hormones sang out, "Lose, lose, lose!"

He watched her, his green gaze intent on her face. Lacey licked her lips, aware he tracked the move. She longed to kiss him. Seeing him this afternoon after his run around the compound had reminded her of what they once shared.

As she'd stared at him swigging down the water, she'd admired the curves of his muscled calves. Dusted

with dark hair, his legs were firm and trim. Not an
ounce of fat on the man, and seeing his wet gray shirt
plastered to his body reminded her of the time years
ago when he'd returned from a long run when they were
married and he was home from a recent deployment.

Sweat streaming down his temples, he had drunk a
bottle of water and wiped his face with the corner of
his shirt. She'd been standing behind him, staring at
his butt. Jarrett had a terrific butt, tight and smooth,
and then her gaze dropped to the curves of sinew and
muscle lining his long legs.

Her need had been so very great. Lacey had stolen
behind him, wrapped her arms around him, very glad
that he was hers.

The impromptu hug had led to him seating her on
the counter, pulling off her panties and thrusting deep
inside her. The sex had been quick, hot and very sat-
isfactory.

That was in the past. But one kiss now wouldn't
hurt. Wouldn't lead to other things. She could control
her raging libido. Oh, yeah.

"Do you have any milk handy?"

She went to the refrigerator and poured two glasses
and set them on the table, along with a loaf of French
bread. Milk and bread were essential for eating these
peppers raw.

On second thought, if she lost, she wouldn't want him
to taste pepper juice and get all turned off. Lacey found
a tin of butter mints and put those on the table, as well.

Clever guy. He grinned as he sampled a mint. "I play
to win, sweetheart."

"Oh? Get ready, tough guy. I have an immunity to
hot peppers." Lacey uncapped the jar and pushed it toward him. "You're on, Jarrett."

He shook his head. "Challenger goes first."

She bit into one and wheezed. Oh wow, that was bad, bad, bad. She managed to swallow and gasped.

Jarrett took one and didn't blink as he ate it. Of course. The man was forged from molten steel, despite his SEAL nickname of "Iceman."

After the second pepper, her eyes watered, and her throat felt on fire. Lacey gripped the table. "Holy crap."

She gulped down the milk and her stomach roiled, but then finally settled. Jarrett broke off a piece of bread. "Eat this. Helps with the burn."

As Lacey gulped down the white bread, and then more milk, he ate two more peppers and then leaned back in the chair. He took his glass of milk and sipped as if it was a cocktail and he hadn't eaten five raw peppers that could bring a grown man to his knees.

"I win."

"How the heck did you do that? Part of your SEAL training?"

He grinned, setting down the milk. Jarrett ate two mints. She ate three and wiped her eyes with a napkin. "Confess, mister. How did you eat those peppers?"

"I cheated. I didn't bite the pepper. Swallowed it whole."

Lacey sputtered. "You what?"

"Learned that from a buddy during a contest. You can do it with peppers that are small enough. Works every time." His grin dropped and heat smoldered in his eyes. Jarrett was all business. No more joking around. "Now, about that kiss."

Her mouth curled into a wicked smile. "On the forehead, like a good ex-husband."

"The hell with that," he growled. Jarrett pushed back his chair so quickly it nearly fell, pulled her upright. As she sagged against him with a startled whumph of air, he bent down and she had time to register his warm breath feathering against her trembling lips before he claimed her mouth.

He didn't kiss her like any other man ever did. He devoured her, his mouth moving hotly over hers, his tongue thrusting past her lips and licking the inside of her mouth. Jarrett kissed like the times when she knew he'd have her naked and in bed, her legs spread wide for him. He kissed with the arrogant confidence of knowing he'd have her screaming his name.

Then his mouth left hers and Jarrett kissed a fiery trail down to her ear, right behind the lobe where he knew she loved being kissed. Her knees buckled, but he held her up with one strong arm as he fisted a hand in her long hair.

Lacey slid her arms around his neck as he skimmed a hand down the curve of her spine. She wanted him inside her like he'd been before. Moving inside her, creating a dance that set her body humming like a live electrical wire. Making her feel sore and used and dazed with sweet pleasure. Claiming her so thoroughly, going into her body so deep that she'd feel him days later, after the front door had quietly shut and he'd gone off to yet another mission, and she'd wondered if he'd come home to her this time. The smell of his spicy aftershave lingering on his pillow, in her nostrils, the remembrance of sweat and the musk of sex.

He pressed her closer and she felt the rigid length of his erection. Awareness pushed aside the sensual heat licking through her body. This was Jarrett, determined and ruthless in his pursuit. The man had chased after her, determined to marry her and bring her home as his wife.

No longer his wife. And her life had changed. Lacey reluctantly pulled away. As he stepped back, his eyes darkened and grew stormy.

"You said a kiss," she whispered. "That wasn't a kiss. That was…a take-no-prisoners move. Why, Jarrett?"

"Had to do that. Like the first time I kissed you. I had to kiss you quickly, in case you changed your mind. Because if I didn't kiss you, damn it, I was gonna die."

Shaken by the intensity and her own reaction, she sank back into the chair. He pulled out his own chair and quietly regarded her. She touched her mouth, swollen by his kisses. "I remember our first kiss. And the first time we made love. That's in the past, Jarrett. I've changed. And so have you. We can't recapture what we once had."

Expecting denial, she was surprised to see him nod. "I know."

"Maybe things would have been different if…" Lacey stopped, not wanting to provoke an argument.

"If I wasn't a SEAL? If I hadn't been gone so much?"

She looked at him directly. "Yes. And I had issues, too. If I hadn't been so lost, maybe it could have worked out."

Two lines dented his dark brows. "Lost? You?"

"I always felt like I searched for my place in the world. While you were off fighting the bad guys, keeping the country safe for us, I was shopping and waiting for you to return home, trying to deal with the fear that one day you might not come home at all."

He stretched out his long legs and folded his arms across his broad chest. "There are bad people in this world, Lace. It's my job to protect civilians against them. The world is getting very dangerous."

"You don't need to lecture me about that."

"I didn't mean to sound condescending. Was just stating a fact I wish I could change."

She pushed at the jar of peppers. "I used to insulate myself from your world, your work, when we were married. I figured if I made you a safe little cocoon, far away from the nasty things you had to see, and do, it would protect us both. I guess it was a little self-centered, like the shopping I always enjoyed. And then I came here to live and there it was, in my face."

Silence draped between them, but for the dripping of water into the sink. She'd meant to fix that. Another thing she had needed to get done around here. So many little tasks left undone because there simply wasn't enough time.

"I want Fleur to have all the opportunities she can, get the help she needs to heal. But in a way, when I go back home it will be an adjustment like the one you always had to make after deployment. Even when I lived here as a teenager, I was insulated from the poverty and the misery. Now I'm not.

"My friends from the States don't understand. They want to discuss theater and fashion and how they beat the stock market and I've been helping a woman beaten so badly that she'll never walk correctly again. They worry about their kids not getting into a prep school that will guarantee them an Ivy League entrance and feeding them organic whole foods, and I'm worrying about women with kids who won't even live to see their fifth birthday because they don't eat, period."

She took a deep breath. The world was evil, but there were good men like Jarrett who fought the evil and pushed back the darkness a little.

Jarrett's expression softened. He started to reach for

her hand. "Lace, you were never self-centered. You were one of the most…"

A scream sounded from the hallway, cutting him off.

Chapter 7

"Fleur," his ex-wife breathed. "No, not again."

Jarrett followed her as Lacey ran into the hallway toward the back bedrooms. Was it a threat? Did someone break in? He'd checked the house twice, but damn, maybe he should have checked it again.

Pushing open her daughter's door, she raced into the room and flipped on a light.

The child thrashed on the bed, screaming pitifully, her arms waving. Lacey gathered her close and rocked Fleur back and forth in her arms. Fleur woke up and began to sob.

"The bad man, the bad man, he was hurting her! Chou Chou!"

Lacey's troubled gaze met Jarrett's as he entered the bedroom.

"Always the nightmares. I thought they were going away. I feel so damn helpless. She needs more than she can get here, Jarrett. And I can't get her home. I can't get her home where she'll be safe and I can really take care of her."

Jarrett's heart twisted as he looked at Lacey, her long hair tumbling down her back, her mouth swollen from his fierce, possessive kisses, her eyes wild with frustration and grief.

He sank to the bed. "Let me try."

Her lower lip wobbled, but she nodded and rose, standing near the bed.

Jarrett gathered the child into his arms and began to sing a lullaby in French he'd learned from babysitting one of his teammates's kids. At first Fleur stiffened and kept sobbing high-pitched cries like a frightened bird. And then as he kept singing and rubbing her back, she gradually relaxed.

Finally, he felt her little body grow slack and her breathing even.

He laid her gently back into the bed. Lacey tucked the covers around her. Tears glistened in her eyes as she studied her daughter.

For a full moment he looked at her, mother and child. The pain in his chest trebled. This should have been them. Both of them, sitting on their daughter's bed, soothing away the bad dreams, reassuring her that the bogeyman didn't live in the closet or under the bed. Singing to her songs that made her eyes close and the bad things go away.

But he knew from hard experiences that the bad things didn't go away so easily. And though children were resilient, no child should ever have to experience the horrors Fleur had.

Finally, he drew Lacey aside. They left the bedroom and she cracked the door open.

"Thank you, Jarrett. That's the first time she's fallen

asleep that quickly after a nightmare." Lacey's face tightened. "Usually it takes warm milk and lots of hugs, and even then…"

She turned and fled into the kitchen.

At the sink she braced her hands on the counter. "I try so hard, but some days I feel so damn overwhelmed. This place, the work, and all the attention Fleur needs. I'd give anything to make her feel normal again. To have a normal childhood. I love her so much, and she's starting to respond…it hurts to see the terror in her eyes, know she could have been her father's next victim…"

Jarrett said nothing. He pulled her into his arms and held her tightly against his chest. Stroking her hair, he rested his chin atop her head.

Lacey pulled away, and he inwardly swore. It felt so good, so right, to have her in his arms again. All those times after returning home from missions, he'd turned to her in bed and the release he'd found in sex had pushed the haunting images back a little further. Connection. Bonding. He found release in sex, and she found it in talk.

"Get some rest," he told her gently.

Jarrett watched as she climbed the stairs. He rubbed his tight chest and went outside to check the perimeter one last time. He'd find a way to bring Lacey and her little girl home.

In the morning he woke before dawn, jogging around the complex and scanning for new threats. Usually he loved this time of day, before the world awoke and the sky was leaden and gray. He found solace in running, listening to the sound of his lungs working hard, his feet slapping against the ground. Always he'd pushed himself harder and harder.

Maybe he should have pushed himself harder with Lace, too. He'd had a restless night, knowing she slept only footfalls away in the next room. His arms itched to hold her close once more.

Man, those were the things he'd missed the most after returning home after an op. Sex, yeah, the sex was mind-blowing, but he missed cuddling, one arm secured around her waist, listening to her breathe, feeling her warm, soft skin against his naked body. Curling up next to a pillow didn't cut it. It was Lacey, holding her close next to him, listening to her soft breaths as she slept, that fueled his purpose each time he went downrange on an op. He'd keep that memory close as he had to sleep at night in the field, remembering the reason why he fought to keep his country safe.

By the time he returned to the house from his run, showered and dressed and sent a few emails from his laptop, there was movement in the kitchen and the smells of frying bacon and peppers. Jarrett rubbed a hand over his clean-shaven face and grinned, knowing he would never eat another pepper without remembering the taste of Lacey beneath his tongue.

Fleur sat at the table, eating spaghetti. He joined her and poked at the bowl. "You like this stuff for breakfast?" he asked in French.

At her nod, he wrinkled his nose. "Looks like worms. Yuck. How can you eat that big, messy bowl of worms?"

She giggled. "It's paghetti," she said in English.

Surprised at her use of English, he tilted his head. "Spaghetti," he corrected.

Jarrett poured himself coffee and thanked Rose as she set a plate of eggs scrambled with bacon and peppers before him. As he dug into it, Lacey appeared in the doorway.

"I overslept. Why didn't anyone wake me up?"

He didn't reply. Too busy staring. Her blond hair rumpled, her eyes still dazed from sleep, she wore a gray sleep shirt and pink pajama bottoms. For a moment he stepped back into time, remembering those mornings when she'd rise like this, her hair tangled, her face smudged with sleep, her nightwear rumpled. And he'd think how beautiful she was, and how damn lucky he was because she was his.

No longer his.

Jarrett mumbled good morning and turned his attention to the eggs to hide his raging emotions.

Lacey's gaze met his when he finally looked up. She sat at the table sipping her coffee, and he noticed the smudges of fatigue shadowing her face. "Fleur's classes start at 0800. School lets out at 1400."

Two o'clock. She still used military time, a habit Lacey acquired while married to him. He set down his fork. "What are your plans for today?" he asked in English.

"Trying to salvage whatever's left from the fire, paperwork and then setting our plan in motion that we talked about last night. I'll drop hints at the packing house, gauge reactions. Those women are hard workers, but they adore good gossip. I have a meeting with Paul at 1300 here at the compound. He's having a driver bring back my SUV. You'll get to formally meet him."

At her stern look, he flicked out his hands. "What?"

"You know what. No paint on his car or tinkering with his battery. Be nice."

"I'm always nice." To those who deserved it.

Fleur picked up her empty bowl and carried it to the sink. He lowered his voice. "Call your dad. If anyone can expedite the visa, he can. Get the old man to pull whatever strings he can."

She nodded. Jarrett polished off his eggs and then stood. He dropped a hand on Lacey's shoulder. "I'll take care of her. Try not to worry. Worrying sucks out your energy."

This vehicle sucked.

Lacey's elderly pickup truck had a finicky clutch and rumbled like an old horse with colic. Used for transporting mangoes, it made a lousy passenger vehicle. As he navigated on the main road toward Fleur's school, he asked Fleur about her classes, careful to mask questions about the "bad men" so he wouldn't scare her.

The bad men hung outside the school. They were there each day before classes and remained through recess and lunch break. When she left, they were still there.

She had noticed them about four weeks ago.

Jarrett passed a small market, keeping his eyes open for threats. Vendors grilled corn on small charcoal stoves on the sidewalk. A woman clutched a little boy's hand as she walked him to school, his blue backpack hanging against his back. A girl in a red-and-white-checked uniform like Fleur's bit off the plastic to a bag of chips.

He reached the school, beeped the horn and the security guard opened the tall metal gate. Jarrett drove inside, noting the guard held a shotgun. Held it the right way, too, not like Lacey's guy who'd missed the dead chicken at the gate.

He parked the SUV in the yard and they hopped out. Jarrett straightened her backpack and stared at her solemn face. "I'll be right here when school lets out. Don't leave the yard. Rose packed you a nice lunch, so you're all set. If anyone or anything scares you, call me on this," he told her in French. "Do you know how to use a cell phone?"

"Yes."

Palming one of the local cell phones he'd bought in the city, he slipped it into her backpack. Fleur gave him a dubious look far too wise for a five-year-old. "We're not supposed to have cell phones."

"It's our secret. Only for emergencies. You call your mom and I'll be here before you can say 'paghetti.' Deal?"

The shy smile she gave him melted his heart. He reached down and hugged her. The child barely came to his thigh, and she felt all skin and bones.

"I'm going to keep you safe, Fleur. No one's going to hurt you or your mom. They have to go through me first."

"Promise?" she whispered.

He hugged her again, his throat closing tight. "Promise."

She nodded and hitched up her backpack. "And jump rope after school."

He laughed. "Deal."

Jarrett watched as she trudged off to class.

He went outside the gate, scanned the area and saw two men hovering near the school's front gate close to where men played dominoes. Both men had tell-tale bulges in their jeans he instantly recognized as sidearms. One was short and dark-skinned, but muscled like a bodybuilder. The other had dark blond hair, stood about six feet and was trim and athletic.

As Jarrett leaned against the wall, he pulled out his phone, pretending interest in checking his messages. A bystander watching the game had ten red plastic clothespins on his arm. So the man had lost. Bet he'd love to have the chance to make a little money.

Time to create a distraction.

He ambled up to the game and struck up a conversation with the clothespin man. Five minutes and two US twenties later, Clothespin Man began arguing in a loud voice with the players.

He knew from experience such arguments tended to be more boisterous than violent, for people in St. Marc loved to express themselves. But if these guys, Americans from the looks of them, didn't know much about the island, they would check it out. At least one of them.

Jarrett walked back to the gate, passing the men, ignoring them.

Sure enough Blond Guy walked toward the game, leaving his pal behind. But the dark-skinned man turned his attention to the game, watching his buddy. Jarrett stole toward the dark-skinned man and snuck up behind him. He pressed his Sig into the back of the shorter man's head.

"Talk to me. Who are you, why are you here? Talk fast unless you want a head full of lead," he said in English.

The man didn't budge. "What do you want?" he replied in the same language.

"Never question the man holding the gun. Why are you hanging out at a private school attended by ex-pats' kids?"

No answer. Jarrett pressed the gun barrel deeper. The man stiffened. "I'm only here to watch over Fleur."

Watch over her before hurting her? "What do you want with her?"

"Senator Stewart hired us to watch Fleur's school in case there was trouble."

"Hired you? Who are you?"

"Sam Pendleton. Her bodyguard. What do you want with Fleur?" To his credit the man didn't even flinch.

"I'll ask the questions. Why are you here? And why not tell her mother?"

"I'll answer when you tell me who you are."

"I'm her personal bodyguard. Why doesn't Lacey know about you?"

His quarry seemed to relax a little. "Her father didn't want her to know because she'd put up a fuss about him interfering."

That sounded like Lace. "ID?"

"My wallet and ID are in my back pocket. There's a white card with a phone number with the senator's private cell phone. Call the number and tell him who I am."

Training his weapon on the man, he fished out the wallet, flipped it open and saw the ID and the card. Sam Pendleton, Security. Flipping out his phone, he called the number.

His ex-father-in-law's gruff voice answered on the first ring. "Stewart speaking."

"Hello, Alex," Jarrett drawled. "Remember me? Your ex-son-in-law."

Sam turned his head and gave a slight guffaw. "Oh, shit."

"Adler! How the hell did you get this number?" Senator Stewart bellowed.

"Nice to talk to you again, too," he said. The man had never liked him, always resenting the fact that Jarrett, a kid from New England who'd joined the Navy as enlisted, had stolen away his only daughter. Nothing Jarrett had done was good enough. Not even the fact he'd gone to school and gotten his college degree and became an officer. Not the fact he was SEAL, certainly, because Stewart thought SEALs were "hot dogs."

"Got it from the man who said you hired him. Who is he?"

"He and Gene work for me. I hired them a month ago when Fleur's visa wasn't coming through."

"And you didn't think it was a good idea to tell Lace that armed men were watching her daughter's school?"

"That's my business," the man snapped. "Why are you there, Adler?"

"I'm here to take Lacey back to the States."

Silence on the other line. Finally, the man sighed. "She won't budge without Fleur."

"Then light a fire under the asses of those paper pushers. Use your clout and do something useful instead of hiring muscle and scaring her daughter and your daughter."

"Leave those men alone, Adler. They're employed directly by me."

"I will if they check out with my references." Jarrett flipped off the phone, tempted to give it a one-fingered salute.

He lowered his pistol but did not put it away as Blond Man jogged up to them. Blondie introduced himself as Gene Armstrong. He had a Southern drawl and cool green eyes. They gave their military creds and Jarrett made another phone call, this time to Ace.

"Ace. Need you check out two guys. Sam Pendleton. Company F, First Battalion, First Marine Division. And Gene Armstrong. He was with the 75th Ranger Regiment."

"Give me a few." Ace hung up.

Jarrett eyeballed the men, who stared back with equal hostility. He wasn't leaving his position, or trusting his ex-father-in-law until he heard from Ace. Alexander Stewart might think he had hired bodyguards, but he could be fooled. And this was Lacey's little girl.

His cell rang. "Yeah?"

"Both check out. Enlisted, both received honorable discharges. Armstrong was wounded in Ramadi. Took a bullet to the leg."

He thanked Ace and thumbed off the phone. Jarrett tucked his Sig back into his holster. "My friend says you're cleared. I'll leave you to your job. I'm picking Fleur up at 1400 hours."

Gene and Sam nodded.

He gave the dark-skinned Sam a scrutinizing look. "Were you hanging out, asking if a flower attended this school?"

Sam's brow wrinkled. "No. We knew she was here all day."

This was troubling. "Anyone else you've seen who has been asking questions about her?"

"Not me, but my French isn't that great," Sam admitted. "Gene's is better. We've been keeping an eagle eye on the place with all the growing unrest. There's a chance someone could have been here for a few minutes and we missed him."

A few minutes around recess, when children came outside to buy snacks from the vendors. Jarrett rubbed the nape of his aching neck. "This ices my balls. Someone's been asking about Fleur. Someone other than you two."

Quickly he gave a description. "If you see this guy again, get hold of him. I'd like to question him. My way."

"Would hate to go up against you in a fight, sir. You military?" Sam asked.

When Jarrett told them, Sam's face lit up. "Knew

you had to be a SEAL. Only a frogman could sneak up on me like that. Don't feel so bad now that you got the drop on me, sir."

"Where you boys from?" Jarrett asked.

"A little town near Houston, Texas," Gene said. "Best damn state in the USA."

"Don't mind him," Sam drawled. "He gets a little antsy when he's not within shooting range of the Alamo. I'm a Yankee. From New York City. You?"

"We're almost neighbors. I was born in New Hampshire. The old man was military so we moved a lot."

Gene gave him a look filled with respect. "Lt. Jarrett Adler. You're the Iceman. I heard about that op you did in Ramadi. You laid down enough fire in that neighborhood for our boys to beat it the hell out of there."

Uncomfortable with the praise, Jarrett gave a brusque nod. He didn't like talking about that op. Too many nightmarish images from that time, men who died with their legs blown off, screaming, the blood and the slick, coppery scent of it...

"You're the Iceman?" Sam asked. "Hooyah, sir. Semper Fi."

He relaxed a little and for a few minutes, talked with them about missions in Iraq and Afghanistan, the crummy food and American football. Gene had retired from the service only last year, and Sam had left six months ago.

"It was tough getting used to wearing civvies," Gene said. "Tougher finding work after being a Ranger for years. We were happy the senator gave us a detail. I speak French, but ole Sam here barely knows any words."

"I'm good at pointing and talking with my hands," Sam said, grinning.

Jarrett gave a gruff nod, for Gene had voiced a fear

he also felt. What life did he have upon leaving the teams? He was nearly thirty-five, and some days he didn't think he'd live long enough to celebrate his fortieth. Thirty-five was approaching senior citizen age in the teams.

These young kids coming into the teams with their snappy attitudes and do-or-die zeal… Yeah, they had respect for all he'd done, and more than often there was a quiet sense of almost hero worship. He'd lived for the adrenaline thrill, the sense of a job well-done, knowing he kept his country safe.

Jarrett didn't want to be pushed into retirement. He wished he could find something to replace the sense of purpose that had driven him all these years.

He could still serve. But how?

Gene handed him a white business card. "When you get back Stateside, look us up and we'll buy you a beer. Be honored to share a brew with a frogman who watched our six."

Jarrett thanked him, fished a card out of his wallet and scribbled down the number of his local cell phone. "Where are you two bunking?"

"Local hotel. It's not bad." Sam's voice was neutral.

"The fleas aren't as big as the sandfleas in Ramadi," Gene added.

Jarrett grinned. "Yeah, I know it. While you're here, keep an eye out for anything suspicious and call me at this number if you see anything."

He told them what happened with the shed and Gene's eyes narrowed. "This country's getting too many hot spots. I heard last week that the favored candidate might not win because the current regime could be targeting him."

He considered. These men, ex-military, might be

good resources. "Let's get together tonight at Lacey's place, dinner and drinks." He grinned at the hopeful look on Gene's face. "Lace has a great cook. I bet she can whip up a mean Texas-style chili that will melt your socks."

"Only Texans can do that, sir," Gene said.

"Yeah, Lace has a stash of peppers that would do you proud. Trust me. I'll scrounge up some cold brews, too." He rubbed his chin. "I know the senator is paying your bill, but it would be a huge relief to my ex to know the men hanging outside her kid's school are aboveboard."

He gave them the address. "Be there at 1800 hours."

"Be nice to hang with other Americans," Gene said.

"Honored, sir." Sam saluted him.

As he returned to Lacey's truck, feeling a little more relieved that Fleur was being guarded by professionals with weapons, Jarrett couldn't help but wonder if someday soon it might be him standing outside a school, keeping watch on someone else's dime. He loved his career in the Navy, but what came next?

When he returned to the compound, he did a thorough check of the property, riding along the narrow pathway of the wall's perimeter, looking for weaknesses in the wall or an easily penetrated spot.

At the field near the homes where the women lived, four men picked corn. He questioned them all, but none had seen or heard anything suspicious. The men worked in the compound during the day, but left before dusk fell. All four had worked for Lacey for two years and seemed loyal and grateful for the jobs she'd given them.

They promised to keep an eye out and report anything odd.

At the property's northwest corner, beneath the

shade of several mango trees, he saw a man leaning on a shovel near the garden. Dressed in dirt-stained jeans, a button-down shirt plastered to his sweating body, he appeared to be taking a break.

Except he wondered what the guy had been doing, for he didn't see evidence of holes dug or dirt piled up. Jarrett parked the truck and climbed out.

"Who are you?" he asked in French.

The man gave him a long look before answering. "I'm Jean. I work here."

He remembered him from last night. Pierre, the man Lacey had sent to fetch the hose from the gardening shed.

"For how long?" Jarrett asked.

"Miss Lacey hired me last week to take care of the garden."

He swept a critical eye over the tomato garden. "By weeding with a shovel?"

"I'm planting seeds. Over there." Jean waved at a spot closer to the compound's wall. "The sun is better there. More tomatoes to grow."

Jarrett wasn't a gardener, but it made sense. Except he didn't like the way he kept glancing nervously at the wooden shed near the garden.

"Do you live here?" he asked.

Jean pointed to the shed. "Miss Lacey lets me stay there. I live an hour away off the main road and visit my family on the weekend."

"Did you see anything last night before the storage shed started burning?" he asked.

Jean shook his head.

Following his instincts, he walked around the shed, with Jean following him. Two walls sported new coats of bright red paint.

"Odd color to paint a shed," he told Jean.

The gardener shrugged. "Miss Lacey had the paint donated. No choice."

Jarrett went to the shed's door and stepped inside. Jean followed him.

Inside he found nothing unusual. The shed was neatly organized, and in the back room with a narrow bed where Jean obviously slept, there was a small kerosene stove and a table with a few plates and pots.

The front room of the shed contained gardening tools, buckets, a few burlap bags that he opened, and found to contain chicken droppings. It could have been used to help start the fire, but it wasn't as effective as regular fertilizer when making a bomb.

"Guano is a good fertilizer. Natural," Jean said.

The man seemed eager to explain everything. Interesting.

Even more interesting were the two plastic buckets of paint and the still-damp paintbrushes. Jarrett picked one up and examined the bristles.

"The paint protects the wood when it rains," Jean told him.

"Do you keep the shed locked? Or can anyone walk inside?"

"Why would we lock it? No one steals from Miss Lacey."

Yeah, no one stole. They just set fire to her storehouse and left threats on the walls...in red paint. Jarrett didn't like it. He dropped the brush. He went outside and touched the red wall and his fingers came away stained crimson.

"I painted it this morning," Jean said.

Too convenient. He made a mental note to keep his

eye on the gardener as Jean returned to the garden and began to dig.

When Jarrett finished patrolling, he parked the truck in front of Lacey's house and went searching for his ex. Rose was in the kitchen and told him Lacey was talking with the women at the mango processing building.

"Miss Lacey said Fleur's visa is coming through. I'm happy for her, but sad to see my little Fleur leave," Rose said in French.

"Well, I have news that'll make you happy, Miss Rose. I have a challenge for you."

When he told her about dinner, her dark eyes gleamed.

"I have to go into town for paint Miss Lacey wants, and I'll get some beans from the grocery. I will make a chili that will have your American friend howling, Mr. Jarrett."

He grinned. "Go for it."

Leaving Rose to plan the meal, he headed for the remains of the storage shed. It still smoked, though the fire was long out. Jarrett rummaged through the remains of the shed. After an hour he found something that made his blood run cold.

Charred, enough of the mechanism still existed for him to ID it. A sophisticated incendiary device with a timer. Maybe even a cell phone.

He traced back the path he'd taken last night. The red painted words still stood out on the wall: *American go home*.

Beneath the red splatter of paint was a large footprint that stuck out like a black stone in white sand. He squatted down and analyzed it.

Jarrett brought a ladder over, scaled the wall and

jumped over. Lacey's property abutted a small stretch of forest that marched up the mountainside.

Another few feet, he saw the same kind of footprint. And then a few yards away, bingo. He picked up the cell phone. Cheap, throwaway type that were common here in St. Marc.

The detonator.

He imagined the owner standing here, safely far away from the compound, making a call to trigger the detonator.

His guts clenched. And Lacey could have been hit with this. Nightmarish images flicked through his mind, Lacey screaming as the device exploded...trapped in the shed, no way to get out...

Pocketing the cell phone so Ace could try to trace it, he returned to the compound.

He went into his room and put the cell phone on his bureau. His own phone rang. It was Ace with the full 411 on Paul Lawrence, Lace's business partner.

After, he found Lacey in the workshop, supervising the women peeling mangoes. She greeted him with a quick smile that had his whole day vastly improve. If he got a smile like that every morning, he'd be a happy man.

Jarrett nearly stopped in his tracks, dumbfounded. He was happy, right? Had a secure job with the teams, making sure his country was safe.

But ever since the divorce, there was a big, empty hole in his heart, not just his bed.

"Hey, sunshine," he told her, dropping a kiss on her cheek. She flushed beneath the touch of his lips.

Her skin was so warm and soft, and he had to fight the urge to keep kissing her and not stop.

"Fleur's safe in school." He explained about her bodyguards and how her father had hired them.

"I should be angry he didn't tell me. But he meant well. Thanks, Jarrett. That's one less thing I have to worry about, knowing they check out and they're keeping an eye on her."

"I invited them for dinner tonight, so you can meet them."

"Thanks."

The fact that she wasn't furious at her dad, and she seemed resigned, warned him she was under much more pressure than she'd alluded to.

She swept a hand over the workshop. "Though the fire took the mango marmalade that was ready for shipping, we still have plenty of stock to work with. Collette told me the women were quite worried that I'd shut down operations. I assured them I would not abandon this project. We've all worked too hard to let someone chase us away."

But clearly, Lacey was tense this morning, her body stiff and rigid. Jarrett stepped behind her and began massaging her shoulders. At first she tensed and then sighed as he kneaded the tension away.

"Wow, I miss this. You always did give great massages." She stole a peek over one shoulder. "And other things, as well."

"Still do." He finished and Lacey rolled her shoulders. "I have a report I have to complete before Paul gets here. Care to keep me company?"

"Let's go outside first. Away from all the ears." He glanced at the women.

When they were outside the building, he lowered his voice. "That man you recently hired, Jean. How well do you know him?"

"He's related to one of the women I'm helping. Jean is her cousin. Why?"

He explained his suspicions about the red paint and how it was the same color as the messages on the wall.

"Someone could have taken it from the shed. It isn't well guarded and sometimes they leave the paint outside. I've been after Jean to finish for two days."

"He seems more interested in planting a tomato garden. Did it occur to you that the red paint he's using for the shed has been used for the wall?"

Lacey sighed. "It couldn't have been Jean. He doesn't speak English, and he's illiterate. He wouldn't have done it, Jarrett. Why would he threaten me when I gave him a job?"

The arson indicated a professional. Still, he didn't trust the man.

"Don't let him sleep on the property anymore." He pushed a stray lock of blond hair out of her face. "You're a good manager, Lace, but you have a soft heart for the downtrodden. Keep that soft heart for the women."

She gave him a wry smile. "I'll tell him to find lodging in town. What else did you want to discuss?"

"Lace, have you seen anyone or heard anyone in the compound who stuck out like he didn't belong or was interested in your operations? Any guests you've given tours to lately?"

"I had a small group of donors from the States three weeks ago." She pursed her full lips. "There was one guy who was with them who seemed interested in the shed and how we pack the jam for shipping. But he's legit. Friend of a big donor. Why?"

"I found an incendiary device and the timer. Cell phone. Cell phone timers are popular with terrorists because they can remotely trigger bombs."

The floral scent of her shampoo tickled his nostrils as she leaned close and whispered to him. "That's crazy! Why would a terrorist be interested in my NGO?"

"Why would an illegal arms dealer be interested in donating?" He lightly clasped her shoulders. "Lacey, you're the daughter of a US senator and former ambassador to this country. Even if you aren't political, your father is. And I'm certain he made enemies here in St. Marc."

"There are lots of ex-pats more politically connected than me," she pointed out. "My friend Helen, Sally's mom, is married to a well-known UN diplomat. She's the one you'll meet this afternoon when you take Fleur to Sally's house. And sabotaging their businesses or their homes would make more of a statement, if this is political."

"Augustin could have sent someone to scout out the compound, target you where you were most vulnerable. It's gone beyond chickens and painted threats, sweetheart." Jarrett braced himself mentally for her protests. "After today you should leave and take Fleur someplace else."

"For Fleur's sake, I would. But what about Rose? And the women who live here? Work here?"

She folded her arms and stared at the building. "This is their world, Jarrett. They have no place else to go. They can't go back to their families. If something else happens around here and the compound shuts down, they'll be on the streets."

"If something bad happens to you, the compound will shut down and they *will* be on the streets."

"Collette can take over. But I have to let them know I'm strong and I won't let these vandals drive me away. I'm not only their director, Jarrett. I'm a role model."

He said nothing, only listened, sensing she needed to get this out.

"When they first came here, they were beaten, not just physically, but emotionally. I taught them to be confident, that their lives have worth after all they've heard for years that they aren't worth anything. I taught them that a real man doesn't hit a woman, ever."

Her gaze shining, she studied him. "I told them about you."

Stunned, he blinked at her. "Me?"

"We might be divorced, but you always treated me with respect, Jarrett. You taught me how to shoot a gun and defend myself from attackers, too. I told them how I was married to a man who could kill enemy soldiers with his bare hands, but he never raised a hand to me. Not during the times when we argued or any other time. He valued my opinion and he treated me like an equal. And that is what real men do."

At a loss for words, he pondered her words. He'd been seen as a role model, among the teams, among the men who accompanied him on missions, but as one for battered women? And to know Lace still held him in high regard...

"Real men stay married and stay committed," he said quietly, watching her face to gauge her reaction.

A shadow entered her eyes. "Divorce isn't one-sided, Jarrett. I'm the one who broke it off. But even that didn't change my opinion of you. Even what my father said never changed my opinion of you."

A tiny flicker of hope blinked on and off. Maybe they still could make it work. And then he remembered he wasn't here to patch things up with his ex. He was here to haul her out, get her home where he wouldn't have to worry about her anymore.

"You still remember those self-defense moves I taught you?"

Lacey nodded.

Her gaze softened. "You taught me a lot, Jarrett. I still know how to pick locks. That skill has come in handy a few times when I managed to lock myself out."

She grinned and his pulse kicked up a notch. Unable to resist, he cupped her face with his hand, rubbing his thumb across the smooth skin of her cheek. "I still have a few moves I could teach you."

Lacey's eyes closed as he kept stroking her face. Her long lashes feathered her cheeks and she made a little humming sound of pleasure he remembered well. She was enjoying this.

So was he.

Opening her eyes, she pulled away. "I have work to do before Paul gets here."

Watching her walk off toward her office, he rubbed a hand over his face. He was committed to staying with Lacey and safeguarding her and her daughter until he could hustle them out of here.

Unstable governments, risky missions, hell, he was a SEAL and used to danger. There was always a plan, and always his training to fall back upon.

But nothing in his military career ever prepared him for this—keeping his ex at a distance and not falling for her all over again, screwing up this relationship any more than it was already screwed up.

A while later Jarrett joined Lacey in the living room to meet her business partner, Paul Lawrence. The man hadn't impressed him when he'd seen him in the hotel. Up close, he was less impressive.

Jarrett stretched out his legs and gave the man a long,

cool look. Paul wore an Italian tailored gray business suit and had thinning brown hair and watery blue eyes. After listening to the man for ten minutes, he disliked him intensely. Paul was condescending and slick, the smooth oiliness of his voice grating on Jarrett's nerves as he talked about how his family had come from a long line of distinguished notables in St. Marc. Nothing against the guy's family tree, but Paul definitely had an attitude about Americans.

Odd that he'd agreed to partner with one.

When Jarrett asked him about it as Lacey went into her office to get papers, Paul shrugged. "Alex Stewart is a good friend and a good businessman. And when Lacey asked to partner with me, I felt I owed it to my friend."

Hmm. "I heard that your coffee business was running out of money and you were operating in the red, desperate for a cash influx. Odd, too. It was profitable for a long time and suddenly you owed money. Lots of money."

The man's gaze flicked to the left. Then Lawrence gave a philosophical shrug. "Times were hard. And I welcomed the opportunity to work with my friend's daughter and give her a head start on her charity. She has done much good in this region of St. Marc."

Right. "You like going to Île du Paradis?"

At the mention of the ritzy resort on St. Marc's northern coast, the man swallowed hard and tugged at his tie. "I have friends who live near there. It is a very nice resort when one wants to get away."

It was also a haven for gamblers. According to Ace, Lawrence had lost money at the roulette wheel. A lot of money.

Lawrence abruptly changed the subject. "Enough of me, Mr. Adler. I am worried for Lacey. I have told her for weeks that the country is not safe and she should leave."

Interesting. Why was the man concerned in Lacey leaving? Beads of sweat dotted Lawrence's upper lip. It was warm, but not that warm. Jarrett studied the way his jugular throbbed.

"It isn't safe here in the country or inside Lacey's compound?"

Lawrence's gaze darted away and he removed a neatly pressed handkerchief from his jacket pocket and mopped his perspiring brow. "Why are you here, Mr. Adler?"

A question to answer a question. Typical evasive tactic. "Take off your jacket. You seem warm," he suggested.

"I am fine. But I am worried for Lacey."

"Why do you want her to leave when her daughter is still here and can't yet emigrate to the United States? Isn't Lacey your business partner? Are you leaving, too?"

"So many questions. She is a woman, alone, living in this big compound without a man to protect her or help her run her charity."

"Lacey's done fine by herself. She doesn't need help."

"But women on this island are treated differently. They do not have the same respect as men, and men working for them will not listen to them. With the growing violence, how can she protect herself and her daughter?"

Jarrett didn't like the thread of this conversation.

"She's not alone. I'm here." He narrowed his eyes and sat up. "And anyone who thinks about hurting a hair on her head, or Fleur's, or anyone else living within the walls of this complex, has to deal with me."

Paul's gaze flicked down to the sidearm now holstered at Jarrett's right hip. "It is good Lacey has you to look after her."

Lacey returned with papers, and Paul signed them. As Lacey and Paul discussed exporting the coffee shipments to Miami, Jarrett watched Lacey's animated face. Wistfully he remembered when she used to light up like that around him, when they had one of their late-night conversations in the kitchen, sharing a glass of milk and a plate of cookies when he couldn't sleep, the haunting images of war flicking through his mind like a PowerPoint display.

Back then, every time he woke up, and no matter how quiet he'd been, she'd awaken, as well. She'd sit with him in the kitchen, encouraging him to sip warm milk and talking about everyday things he'd missed while on an op. Gradually, she'd get him to loosen up, come out of the semicoma state he'd retreated into for self-protection.

By the time Paul extended his hand for Jarrett to shake goodbye, he'd done his own sizing up.

"You believe in more than office work." Jarrett took his hand and turned it over, exposing the palm. "Your hands are rough, calloused, like a laborer."

When he glanced at the man's face, Lawrence was sweating again. But then he smiled. "I have an affinity for gardening. It keeps my mind off troubling matters these days, and I find it relaxing."

Jarrett flashed an equally chilling smile as the man jerked his hand away. "There are many troubling matters these days. I find it most troubling when someone puts up a front to hide what he truly is, like a snake hiding in the grass. But I'm very good at uncovering snakes."

Lawrence turned to Lacey. "Excuse me, my dear, but I must leave. First, I need to check on the mango factory and see how Marie is faring."

"Marie?" Jarrett tensed. "Why? Hasn't she been traumatized enough?"

"Paul has been very generous and he's letting Marie stay in a small house on a piece of property he owns near here. It's a house he rents out to coffee factory employees for a very low fee," Lacey said tightly.

"It is the least I can do. I wish to find houses for all the women since it's apparent we cannot find funding to build them homes here on the land you own, Lacey." Paul gave a very Gallic shrug.

When Paul left the house, Lacey turned to Jarrett, anger flashing on her face.

"You all but called him a snake! He's my business partner. Give it a rest, Jarrett. Not every single man is a threat. So he has rough hands. He told you, he likes to garden."

"That man hasn't held a spade or a fork a day in his life. And if he has gardened, it's not something as benign as growing tomatoes and cucumbers."

He wasn't sure what was wrong with Lawrence. But his well-honed instincts warned the man wasn't aboveboard. He might be cheating Lacey out of profits. Or worse...

Chapter 8

Jarrett's bald opinion of her business partner sent all Lacey's instincts on full alert. Her guard was already up, for Paul hadn't brought the latest profit and loss statements for her perusal.

He kept stalling, and that worried her, especially after the rumors she'd heard that wages were being cut at the factory.

She headed for the mango processing building, Jarrett trailing behind her.

"You don't have to tail me."

"Sweetheart, get used to it. While I'm here, consider me your shadow, especially after what happened last night." Jarrett reached the building and held the door open for her.

In the main room where the women sliced the mangoes, another worker sat by herself at a small table, using a hand press to squeeze out juice from the leftover pieces of fruit not good enough for canning. Lacey was disturbed to see it was Marie, the latest arrival. She lived in the house once inhabited by Jacqueline. Lacey had found Marie two weeks ago by the market, dirty, one eye swollen, begging for food. Marie's boyfriend had beaten her up and kicked her out of his house.

The woman was gradually beginning to open up. Lacey made a point of checking on her frequently, for although Marie was slower at cutting the fruit than the other women, she had determination and willingness to learn.

Lacey beckoned to Collette, who was supervising another woman. Her manager approached, her clipboard in hand and the ever-present yellow pencil she used to write notes.

"Why is Marie sitting by herself at the juicing table?" Lacey asked in French.

Collette shrugged. "She is nervous. I put her at a table by herself because she makes the others nervous, as well, and they are slower to produce."

"Put her back with the others. I don't want her isolated, even if they slow down. She needs to socialize and be with other women."

"We need to increase production since we lost the jam to the fire." With her pencil, Collette pointed to the piles of fruit. "And what about the orders you were supposed to fill?"

The restaurants had paid in advance for her product, but Lacey had already thought of that. "Use the crates I have stored in the guesthouse pantry. There's enough."

Surprise flicked in the other woman's eyes. "I did not know you have extras."

"Now you do. I always have backup in case an order needs to be expedited."

Collette nodded, but her gaze kept flicking to Jarrett. *Tap, tap, tap.* The pencil hit her clipboard with increasing intensity.

Jarrett moved away, making his way through the shop.

"He should not be here. He makes the women nervous, as well," Collette murmured.

The other women gave her ex quick glances, but in those looks she didn't see fear, only curiosity.

"They're not afraid of him. And there is nothing to fear. Jarrett is a good man," she told her manager.

Lacey headed for Jarrett, who reached Marie. She jumped up with a little cry and spilled the tub of mango juice.

"Oh no, I'm sorry, I'm so sorry," Marie wailed, righting the tub with hands that shook badly. "It's going to go all over the place!"

"Easy," Jarrett said in French. "It was an accident. My fault. I startled you."

Tugging his shirt over his head with one hand, he mopped up the spilled mango juice. "It's not a big deal."

"Miss Lacey will be so upset." Her breathing rapid and her pulse jumping, Marie wrung her hands. The fear in the woman's eyes broke Lacey's heart.

She touched Marie's arm. "Miss Lacey is not upset. Accidents happen. As long as you're all right. You okay?"

"Yes, Miss Lacey." Marie sat, her hands still trembling.

"Miss Collette is going to put you back with the other women cutting fruit."

"I'm not as fast as they are," Marie whispered. "I am too slow."

"I was slow once. But sometimes slow is good, because it allows you to learn. The important thing is to not give up," Jarrett told Marie.

She gave him a grateful look. "Thank you."

Collette rushed over. "Marie, go sit next to Paulette. She will show you how to select the fruit for canning."

The woman left, murmuring apologies all over again. Collette's pencil beat hard against the clipboard.

"I could have handled the spill," Collette said in English.

"I'm sure you could have, but it wasn't necessary, since I was closer. And I'm the one who startled her," Jarrett said.

Her ex was polite, but his tone frosty. And Collette's dislike of Jarrett seemed obvious. Was it because Collette resented a man taking charge?

She studied her manager. Collette never had an attitude problem. She had always been friendly and respectful, if not direct. But sometimes power, even a position of managing others, went to your head.

With a little nod, Collette headed toward her office.

Jarrett sighed as he held out the stained T-shirt. "Hope you have a laundry around here."

"Leave it here. One of the women will wash it better than I ever could." Desire curled through her body as she studied his naked chest. "We have to find you a new shirt. ASAP."

His gaze gleamed. "What's the hurry? I'm enjoying how you keep staring at me."

Heat suffused her face as they walked to her house. In the kitchen Jarrett opened the refrigerator as if he lived there, removed two bottles of water and handed her one. He opened his and took several long gulps.

Lacey uncapped hers and drank, amused to see beads

of sweat on his forehead. Maybe she was sweating because he was damn fine to look at, but he was, as well.

"Look at you, tough guy. I made you perspire."

He rolled the cold bottle over his forehead and didn't return her smile. "I've been in combat and faced tough sitches before, Lace. But seeing the look on Marie's face, damn. What happened to her?"

"Her boyfriend beat her up. And then he enjoyed using her to put out his cigarettes. Did you see the burns on her arm? I'm trying to make her feel comfortable and safe, and let her gain some confidence. She sorely needs it."

Everything she worked so hard for here on the compound was directed for these women. But it still scraped her raw, knowing what they had suffered.

"That kind of thing makes me mad as hell. You're doing a good job here. You're giving them hope for a better tomorrow."

His quiet praise and his intensity jolted her. Jarrett had always been intense, but this was a different side he'd seldom shown. "I'm trying with what little I have. It isn't enough."

"You're doing more than what most people would, Lace." He finished the water and braced his hands on the counter, staring at the cabinets. "There's a lot of evil in this world. Sometimes I wish I had been able to do more."

She could almost see the images dancing about in his mind of the nasty things he'd seen, and what he'd been forced to confront. She put a gentle hand on his arm.

"There are evil people in this world. And the good ones, like you, Jarrett. Every time I turn on the news and see how evil people are, I close my eyes and remember the ones like you who sacrifice all to keep us safe."

"I was gone a lot. I shortchanged you on our marriage." He turned and looked at her. Lacey's throat closed up. She drank more water and began tearing the label off her bottle.

"I wasn't shortchanged on our marriage. I knew I had to share you with the Navy. And the Navy is a demanding mistress. Maybe if I'd had something like this NGO, I could have hung in there after I lost the baby. The baby was my purpose, this tiny little life I carried inside me. My purpose was protecting her, keeping her thriving and alive. And I failed."

He put his hand on her wrist, staying her from peeling off the rest of the label. "I'm sorry I let you down when I left you. I was always focusing on the job and when I was home, I failed to focus on you."

Words she'd longed to hear years ago after she'd miscarried. But she'd grown, and knew he wasn't solely to blame. "We let each other down, Jarrett. We lost each other along the way."

Silence draped between them for a moment as he turned around to stare out the kitchen window. She allowed herself to look her fill of Jarrett.

Jarrett was a big guy, tall and intimidating when you first met him. Every inch of him gleamed with muscle and sinew. Her hungry gaze wandered up his spine to the twin muscles dividing his back and her heart jerked to a halt.

She gently traced the three silvery scars with a finger. They looked like bullet wounds.

He glanced over his shoulder. "I survived."

"Where?"

"Doesn't matter. I spent a month Stateside at the Walter Reed hospital."

"Did anyone look after you?"

A shrug. "My buddies looked after me, and my CO stopped in to visit when he could."

No girlfriend. Jarrett would have mentioned it.

Lacey's stomach tightened. She hadn't been there for him when he recovered, hadn't been there to hold his hand at the hospital, to make him laugh about the lousy food or encourage him when he got restless and wanted to go home because he hated being sick.

Her exploring fingers went to the blue ink swirling around his broad right shoulder. The intricate pattern of curlicues intrigued her. This, too, was new.

"Where did you get this?"

His troubled green gaze met hers. "After a tour of Afghanistan, I headed to Singapore for R&R. Ink shop a buddy recommended. I wanted flames. But he made it too pretty."

The design was beautiful and elegant. "Why flames?"

Jarrett turned around, a hank of dark hair spilling into his face. "Because I wanted a reminder of the hell I'd been through."

"The hell of all the missions you served?"

"The hell of how I felt after you left me, Lace, and the divorce came through." His mouth tensed. "And maybe a reminder, as well, of the hell I'd put you through all those times I left you."

They'd both been there and back. "Hell is a two-way street, Jarrett. You're not solely to blame."

He rubbed a knuckle along her cheek, and the touch, combined with the tenderness in his eyes, made her toes curl. Not mere lust, it was something deeper and more lasting. Connection.

Lacey turned. They'd had connection before, but that bond broke. "I need a shower. I'll meet you downstairs in fifteen and give you directions on where to drive

Fleur. She's going to a friend's house after school. She and Sally have a playdate."

"Lace," he said quietly. "Don't be afraid of me. Of us."

But she'd had too much fear, too many disappointments, to erase them. She ran upstairs.

Glad she had her own private bathroom, Lacey stripped and headed for the boxlike shower. She twisted the spigot to full blast, not caring that she was wasting precious water. Lacey scrubbed her body and soaped her hair. Tears ran down her cheeks, mingling with the water.

No one ever heard you cry in the shower.

When she stepped out of the bathroom, something swung from the spinning ceiling fan. Her bra. A grudging laugh fled her. Trust her ex to do something to make her laugh and chase away the brooding intensity of remembering their past.

Lacey snatched it and dressed in a floral skirt and a white peasant blouse and slipped her bare feet into sandals.

Jarrett waited on the landing outside her room, a smug grin on his face. His dark hair damp, he wore a pair of clean navy blue cargo shorts and a button-down white shirt slightly open at the throat. He looked sexy and impish and her heart skipped a beat.

"Same old prank, Adler. Can't think of anything original?"

"It worked to get your attention all those times when we were married." Heat glinted his gaze. "You look very pretty, Lace."

He leaned closer, his gaze growing intent. She lifted her face. When he pressed his lips against hers, she slid her arms around his neck.

He maneuvered her backward, into her bedroom.

Lacey felt the backs of her knees connect with the mattress and fell onto the bed, still kissing him. Jarrett levered himself atop her, tunneling his fingers through her hair.

"You smell so damn good," he murmured, nibbling at her neck. "Like fresh apples and flowers."

His palm skimmed up her body, cupped her breast. Lacey moaned as he began to knead her breast. She felt hot and hungry and needy.

A door opened downstairs. Instantly, he moved off her, his gaze sharpened. "Stay here."

The old Jarrett, wary and alert. Then a voice called out. "Miss Lacey? You home? I'm back from the market and I'm going to start dinner."

She threw a hand over her forehead and sighed. Jarrett relaxed and shot her a wry grin.

"Lousy timing," he murmured.

Tell me about it. She glanced at the bedside clock. "You'd better go. Fleur's school lets out soon."

Jarrett trailed a finger down her cheek, making her shiver. "Rain check."

Rain check? How about a snowy day in hell check because letting her libido take control was a bad idea. Sex with Jarrett had always been great, incredible, mind-blowing, but it also had been a way for them to bond and connect.

She didn't want or need to bond with her ex-husband. He wasn't a one-night stand who would satisfy her body's sexual needs.

He was a man who could break her heart all over again if she let him get close enough.

Chapter 9

As a SEAL, Jarrett never underestimated the power of training for an op. Or being prepared with the right weaponry. SEALs constantly trained and trained for missions, and their gear was integral to success. But in this sitch, faced with protecting his ex-wife and her daughter, and the deep gut feeling that things could blow and get worse, he needed to be better prepared.

And armed.

After he dropped Fleur off at her friend's house, making sure to meet and greet Sally's mom, and size up the house and their security—much better than Lacey's, complete with a very large German shepherd dog and lots of security cameras—he asked Ace to bring over a gift basket.

The kind of gift basket one did not order through a florist.

Two hours later Ace drove into the compound in

his slick black SUV with the blackened windows. He parked and climbed out.

Grinning, Jarrett stuck out a palm. "My man."

He clapped him on the back, grateful his friend could help him out. Kyle "Ace" Taylor was shorter than him, standing only five feet, ten inches. He wore one of his typical Hawaiian shirts and tan cargo shorts, and his dark blond hair was wavy and streaked, making him look like a surfer. Ace had an athletic, wiry strength like a tightly coiled spring. With his deep blue eyes and movie-star looks, he seemed too pretty to be a warrior.

Until you saw those baby blues narrow as Ace went for the kill. He'd been a sniper for the teams until he'd taken a bullet to the knee and was forced to take mandatory medical leave.

Jarrett had been through Basic Underwater Demolition/ SEAL (BUD/S) with Ace and seeing his friend injured had made him think long and hard about his own options. How long before he was laid up with an injury, or worse?

"Iceman, my friend. I have your little gift basket right here." Ace opened the truck's back door and hoisted out a large black duffel bag. He placed it on the ground, unlocked it and then unzipped.

Relief swept through him as Ace lifted an HK MP7a1 submachine gun out of the bag and handed it to him. The gun was compact, and would allow him to maneuver in tight quarters if necessary. The HK could be fitted with a scope, laser pointer and best of all, a suppressor to reduce both noise and recoil.

"Wasn't sure if you could deliver the goods this fast. I'm impressed." He handed him back the weapon.

"For you—" Ace put a hand over his heart "—I'd do anything. But wait! There's more. If you order now, you get a bonus gift of ammo! Cut through a tin can one moment and slice and dice a tango the next! And a suppressor! Keeps the noise down so the neighbors won't think you're having a party and pout because they're not invited."

"Ace is a handy hardware man," Jarrett drawled, zipping up the duffel bag and locking it. "Sweet."

"Anytime."

Jarrett wished he had his night vision goggles to survey the compound at night for intruders. Sophisticated and expensive, they were an essential for deployment. But smuggling them into St. Marc would get him into very hot water with his CO, not to mention the Navy brass.

"Surveillance?" he asked.

Ace shook his head, causing a hank of hair to fall into his face. He pushed it back with an impatient hand. "Can't get the cameras you need for at least two weeks. And with the capital heating up like a pressure cooker, shipments are slower to clear through customs. Talk about irony. It's easier for me to get this baby on the black market than to order legit security cameras."

Damn. He wanted to wire the compound with proper surveillance, and the right amount of night vision cams, but it would take time to get all the equipment. One of the hazards of island life.

Jarrett clapped Ace's shoulder. "I owe you, man."

Ace's gaze went intense. "You owe me nothing, Iceman. If you didn't haul my butt out of that op in Somalia, my sister would be putting roses on my gravestone instead of cooking me dinner. I can't thank you enough."

Emotion clogged Jarrett's throat. They were brothers in arms, and would always be friends, but it was difficult for him to open up to such quiet admissions.

"Your sister's cooking is so bad you may want to order that gravestone anyway, Ace. Aimee is one fine woman, but she could burn water."

"Hey, do not insult my only living immediate family member, Iceman. She doesn't burn water anymore. She merely scorches it."

"Come into the house and say hello to Lace." Jarrett carried the bag as Ace accompanied him.

Inside, the smells of cooking chili wafted through the air. Ace's nose twitched. "Damn, that smells like really fine chili. I didn't know Lace could cook."

"She can't." Jarrett carefully set the bag down on the sofa. "Rose, her cook, is terrific. Lacey, come say hello to Ace. He did a drive-by."

"Kyle!" Wiping her hands on a checked dish towel, Lacey emerged from the kitchen with a big smile. "So good to see you again. Can you stay for dinner?"

His friend dropped a kiss on her cheek. "Thanks, Lacey, but have to get back to the homestead. Aimee's making a late supper for me. She'll have my head in a bucket if I'm late."

"We have real Texas-style chili Rose is making from a recipe I found on the internet."

A wide grin split his friend's face. Ace fluttered his eyelashes and put his hands to his heart. "I love you. Will you marry me?"

Jarrett told him to do something anatomically impossible and Ace laughed, dancing away from the reach of Jarrett's mock punch.

"Oh wait, you can't marry me. You're already taken," Ace teased and then he stopped, stricken as he realized what he'd said.

"I was," Jarrett said, forcing a smile.

Lacey smiled, but Jarrett sensed his words troubled

her. Yeah, they had been married, and had a good thing, but they let it slip away.

If only they could get it back again.

That night at dinner Rose's six-alarm chili impressed Gene so much that he ate three helpings and declared Rose "an honorary Texan."

Jarrett pushed back his plate and stole another look at Lacey as she talked with Sam. Several times he saw her gaze flick to the sidearms the men carried. Some women might object to the pistols, but Lacey seemed relieved.

That warned him how worried she was about Fleur. He remembered well the days when they'd been married. After coming home from a mission, he'd barely made it through the front door of their house when she ordered him to put away his personal sidearm and lock it up.

Of course she'd also ordered him to get naked, too. That was one order he loved to obey.

Fleur, squeezed between Lacey and Jarrett, had a special chicken and rice dish Rose had prepared for her. She said little. Her hair was done in several pigtails, with bright red bows and barrettes and she wore a red-and-white dress. She looked so sweet and adorable, but her eyes remained solemn as she looked around at the adults.

Worried, Jarrett looked at her plate. She'd barely touched her food. She'd been fine this afternoon when he'd picked her up from her friend's house. Fleur even laughed as he played jump rope with her.

Lace had been great at reassuring Fleur, protecting her from the underlying tension in the compound from the fire last night, but kids were sensitive.

"You're not eating," Jarrett said gently. "What's wrong?"

Fleur shrugged her thin shoulders.

"Anyone bothering you at school?"

A head shake.

"The chicken isn't to your liking?"

"It's okay," she said. Her gaze slid to Sam and to Gene and he saw the fear flickering in the child's face.

Three men at the table. All big guys, perhaps like the father who had killed her mother before the child's terrified eyes.

"You know Gene and Sam are assigned to protect you. They're good guys. You don't have to fear them. They'll make sure you stay safe from the bad men."

"Like you do?"

Jarrett's breath hitched. "Yeah. But if you don't eat that delicious dinner Rose made for you, I can't play jump rope with you tomorrow. Because I only play with children who eat their dinner and grow big and strong."

"I'll never be strong," she whispered. "Some girls at school say I'm too skinny."

Fierce protectiveness came over him at her forlorn expression. "I used to be skinny, too. But I got stronger as I grew older and ate the right food, and you will, too."

Fleur glanced at Sam again, who was built like a linebacker. "I wish I had been strong enough to protect my first mommy."

The lump in Jarrett's throat turned into a baseball. He silently made a promise to do whatever he could to help get her to the States where she could get the psychological help she needed to recover from her past. Lacey was right. Fleur couldn't thrive here on St. Marc. There were too many memories.

How he wished he could find the son of a bitch who

fathered this precious little girl so he could give him a taste of his own medicine. Bastard.

"It wasn't your fault, sweetie."

"I know." She sounded so damn adult it broke his heart all over again. "I have a new mommy and I love her."

"And she loves you very much. She'd do anything for you. She'll always do her best to make sure you have everything you need. She's very special."

Fleur didn't say anything for a minute. And then she looked at him and whispered, "So are you, Jarrett."

Suddenly, he felt her slide her hand into his under the table, as if for reassurance. He'd squeezed it gently, relieved when she began to eat.

When her plate was nearly empty, Jarrett turned the conversation to her school and how the class was preparing for the big recital at the end of the school year in another month. Gene asked Fleur to sing the song she'd been practicing with her classmates. As she sang a song about an old French folktale, Gene's eyes misted over.

He applauded loudest of all when she finished. "Thanks, Fleur. You remind me of my little girl. She's about your age and she loves to sing, too."

Jarrett gave her hand another squeeze as Fleur beamed. "Can you skip rope, Mr. Gene? Jarrett is very good at jumping rope."

Gene grinned. "I bet he is. Not as good as Jarrett here, because I'm not a special warrior like him. I'm not a SEAL."

"What's a SEAL?" she asked.

"It stands for Sea, Air and Land. I'm a special soldier who is good in the water," Jarrett told her.

"Like a fish? We learned about fish last week in

school and how they don't breathe air." She pursed her mouth and made a fish face.

Lacey laughed. "He's a very good swimmer, sweetie. Like a fish. Maybe soon we'll go visit Coco Bay and Holly and Heather. Jarrett can take you to the pool to teach you how to swim."

"I'd be happy to teach your mommy, as well," he said softly, his gaze centered on Lacey.

She looked at him, heat glimmering in her gaze. "Fleur. Time for your bath and then bed. Let's give Jarrett alone time with our guests. I'm sure they want to drink beer and discuss macho stuff."

Lacey nodded at the sideboard near the dining table, where an assortment of glass bottles stood. "I have a great dark rum if you'd like something that puts lots of hair on your chest, Jarrett."

Fleur gave her mother an innocent look. "Do you like hairy chests, Mom?"

As Jarrett laughed, Lacey smiled. She put a hand on Fleur's shoulder and bent down to whisper something in Jarrett's ear. "On one chest I do."

Fleur slid off her chair and said a polite good-night to Sam and Gene. But when she came to Jarrett, she threw her arms around him. He hugged her and watched as Lacey left with her daughter.

He, Gene and Sam went into the living room carrying the beer he'd found in the fridge. Gene popped his open and sighed. "What a sweet kid. I miss my little girl."

"She Stateside?" Jarrett asked.

"She lives with my wife's parents. Her mom died two years ago. Car crash, when I was deployed. With me moving around so much, I couldn't keep her. I try to see her as much as I can." Gene sipped his beer. "And you?"

"Lacey and I have been divorced for five years. It's over between us."

How it pained him to admit that.

"Yeah, didn't look so the way you kept staring at her through dinner," Gene told him.

"Couldn't fool me," Sam drawled.

He didn't want to discuss Lace or his personal life. "Tell me what you found out about the man asking about Fleur."

Gene set down his beer, his cocky grin gone. "Guy's been appearing on and off throughout the past week. Usually just before school is dismissed. He wears dark business suits, expensive and tailored, always with a red checked tie. He looks like an official or a parent, so the locals who set up businesses outside the school or the men who play dominoes think he has a kid in the school. He's short, and he has a scar on his chin."

Sam spoke up. "We did a little checking with the locals. There's a rumor going around that a man is inviting women to his house for interviews about a job working for his business in the capital. They go there for the interview and never return. He's cutting out their hearts to use them in some black magic hoodoo ritual. They call him Big Shot."

Lacey had told him about that horrible rumor. "People like to talk, spread tall tales. Have you seen anything or heard anything else?"

"It could be a rumor," Sam admitted. "Except there's a missing girl. Local named Caroline Beaufort. Last time her family saw her she was wearing a yellow shirt with lace around the collar, black pants. Her nails were painted neon green. We promised we'd keep an eye out for anyone matching that description."

That name… Lacey had mentioned it was a woman

who used to work for her. It worried him. Had someone close to Caroline blamed Lacey for her disappearance?

Lacey had told him villagers in small communities loved to gossip, and any newcomer was subject to scrutiny. Sometimes the locals blamed wealthy denizens for everything from crop failure to their donkeys dying.

He knew black magic wasn't unusual on the island of St. Marc. But this particular story had his instincts on full alert.

Jarrett wanted to run into Fleur's bedroom, wrap both Fleur and Lace in cotton wool and board them on the next plane to DC.

They finished their beer and Jarrett fished out three more from the fridge. Gene was in the middle of telling about parachuting exercises after he and a buddy had drunk too much the night before and "we all ended up puking as the chute jerked us upward like puppets" when Lacey walked into the room.

She grabbed Jarrett's beer and took a swig. "Don't let me stop you," she said with a sweet smile. "You were talking about suffering from the world's worst hangover at twenty thousand feet. I'm sure that earned you a double face palm from your CO. And all the guys you spewed upon on the way down. Boys will be boys."

Jarrett grinned as Gene looked flustered. Oh yeah, Lace had nailed him to the wall. She knew what it was like, being an ex-military wife.

He liked this kind of familiarity, Lace sitting next to him, her warm thigh pressed against his, her taking his beer as if they were still married. Old habits.

He fetched another beer for Lacey and went to take his. Their fingers brushed and their eyes met. Desire glimmered in hers and his body tightened.

Lacey looked at Sam and Gene. "Where are you staying?"

When Sam told her, she looked horrified. "Isn't my father paying you enough? That place is a dump."

Gene gave a lopsided smile. "He is, but the accommodations in town are, ah, limited."

Her gaze flicked to Jarrett. "I have a guesthouse. Five bedrooms, two bathrooms, kitchen and dining area. You can stay there, no charge. It's no luxury hotel, but it's much more comfortable than that flea trap."

Sam glanced at Gene. They nodded. "Thank you," Gene told her. "We'll check out tomorrow and move in, if that's okay with you."

They began a discussion of the various rum drinks on the island, and then Lacey started talking about the best rum she'd ever tasted at a little seaside bar "where the rum erased the taste of the fried conch that had the consistency of a rubber tire."

And then Lacey put a hand on his bare arm. It was casual, like a friend would when telling a story, but it ratcheted up his internal engine all over again.

He leaned forward to ask a question when a scream sounded. High-pitched and filled with terror, it made the hair on his nape salute the air.

Jarrett sprang to his feet, knocking over his beer. "Sam, stay here with Fleur and Lacey," he ordered. "Gene, come with me."

Jarrett raced upstairs and retrieved his sidearm. After flipping on the exterior lights, he went outside, his weapon in hand, Gene following him, his sidearm drawn, as well.

The humid night air wrapped around him like a blanket. The sounds of cicadas in the trees interspersed with a woman's sobs and the excited chatter of several people.

Rose stood outside, wringing her hands. "Oh, sweet Jesus, the poor lady," she cried.

Jarrett took her aside. "What is it?"

But the woman would not say, only continued to sob. Men from the compound and security guards Lacey had hired to patrol the compound stood around talking in high voices.

"Jarrett, the tree." Gene pointed and Jarrett's stomach roiled as he stared.

Suspended from the thick branch of a mango tree by a rope around her feet, the woman hung upside down near the western wall of the compound.

Yellow shirt with lace edging the collar, though now it was stained crimson. Black linen trousers. Her toenails were painted neon green. One white satin ribbon tied around her hair waved gently in the breeze.

Her eyes stared open in frozen shock and horror.

The description fit Caroline Beaufort. Dead, with a large hole in her pretty yellow shirt.

Her heart had been ripped out of her chest.

On the wall near her body were words painted in red, crude letters.

American lady go home or you will end up like this.

Chapter 10

Cold sweat broke out on Lacey's skin as she stared at her former employee hanging from the tree. She'd left Sam watching over Fleur as she'd raced outside to see what caused the hysterical screams.

And now, seeing for herself, hearing Rose's anguished sobs, the excited, stunned chatter of the men, she felt all the blood drain from her. Lacey's breath hitched as Jarrett came over to her.

"Oh God, oh God!" Lacey felt the dizziness push at the edges of her vision. The poor girl…

"Breathe." Jarrett holstered his sidearm and gently pushed her head down, increasing the blood flow to her brain. "Your pulse is too rapid and you could be headed into shock. Stay like that a minute, Lace. I've got you."

"I have to call the police," she said, closing her eyes and bracing her hands on her knees as Jarrett held her shoulders. "But not yet."

Get a grip, get a grip, you can be strong. Oh God, the poor girl!

"Fleur," she managed to say, standing straight, willing herself to gather her lost composure. "I can't let her see this. I have to get her out of here before we call the cops, Jarrett. She's terrified of the police. They took her away when her mother was killed and put her in an orphanage and she didn't speak for two months. But I don't know where to send her!"

She couldn't think, much less focus.

"What about her friend Sally's house? She can have a sleepover."

Fleur had never spent a night away from her since she came to live with Lacey, but it sounded like the only solution. "I can't go with her. The police will want to question me."

"Send Gene. He's her bodyguard now. And he'll make sure she's taken care of, sweetheart. He won't let anything happen to her."

As Sam joined them, Lacey fished out her cell phone, her hands shaking badly. Jarrett took the phone from her, scrolled through her contacts.

"I met Sally's mom this afternoon. Let me make the arrangements. You go sit down for a minute. Sam, get Lace a cold cola. She's in shock and needs the sugar."

Jarrett, quiet, in control and capable.

Fifteen minutes later, Fleur's overnight bag packed, Lacey held her daughter, shielding her face from the terrible sight on the compound wall. She kissed her cheek as she bundled her into Gene's SUV. Gene put her overnight case into the back and climbed into the driver's seat.

Lacey buckled her daughter's seat belt with a steadier

hand. Fleur stared at her with big, solemn eyes and then at Jarrett, who stood next to her.

"Why am I spending the night at Sally's house, Mommy?" Fleur's mouth trembled. "Are you sending me away?"

Lacey's stomach tightened. "Never, sweetie. I promise. You're my little girl now. But Mr. Gene is going to take you to Sally's because there's some grown-up things going on that I have to handle here."

"I can hear the people talking. They're saying a lady got hurt real bad. She's dead."

Lacey closed her eyes a minute, wishing she had a wand to wave away all the bad things that her child had to witness. "Yes, sweetie. And I'm going to be dealing with the local police. The police will want to find who did this terrible thing. I want you to go to Sally's and not think about any of this. Gene will keep you safe. And if you need anything or get worried, call me on the cell phone."

Fleur looked past her at Jarrett. "Will you take care of my mommy, Jarrett? She needs someone to take care of her. The police can be scary. They might take her away like they took me away when my first mommy died."

Jarrett kissed her daughter's cheek. "I will, kiddo. Your mom is staying here with me and she isn't going anywhere. She'll be right here, waiting for you, when you return. You go with Gene, enjoy your time with Sally. Her mom is making hot chocolate for you both, and Sally has her LEGOs all set up for you to make a house."

Fleur nodded. "I love you, Mommy."

Lacey hugged her tight. "I love you, too, sweetie." Then she stepped back, shut the door and watched as Gene drove her daughter out of the compound. The tightness in her chest became a stretched rubber band, until she wanted to scream.

"Make the call," she said dully. "Tell them what Rose found. And tell them to notify the coroner."

Four hours later the police arrested Jean, the man she'd hired to work on the compound.

She had led the police to the gardening shed and they found the buckets of red paint and two wet brushes. Circumstantial evidence, except for one small fact. The shed's walls were bone dry and the brushes wet, along with smears of red paint on his clothing. They found him drinking a bottle of rum in the room she'd kicked him out of earlier that day. He was drunk, but still coherent.

And then he broke down and confessed. Not to the police, but when Jarrett looked him in the eye, rage simmering in his expression as he flexed his powerful fists, Jean caved in.

He admitted to painting the threats. But he swore he did not know who killed poor Caroline. And he went into hysterics, claiming he'd painted the wall before the body hung there.

Jean told the police he'd owed money to a creditor, who told him how to erase the debt. A harmless prank to scare the rich American lady living in the complex. No one would be hurt. He had practiced painting the writing and then painted the threats. He admitted to painting the gate, as well, and hanging the dead chicken. Harmless pranks, he called them.

But he claimed he did not kill Caroline Beaufort. Jean kept crying and protesting he would never hurt anyone.

Innocent pranks. And now a woman was dead.

They took him into custody. And as they led him in handcuffs to the police car, Jean looked straight at Lacey and screamed he was innocent.

She didn't care anymore. All the fight had drained out of her.

Soon as the police left, Lacey collapsed onto the sofa. The cops had questioned everyone on the compound and took photographs. The coroner had discreetly carried away Caroline's dead body in the hearse. A woman had died, perhaps not in her compound, but now her charity would have the pall of the murder hovering over it. A young woman, killed in the prime of her life. And for what?

The police promised to investigate, but she knew how the system worked in this tiny island nation. And other than Jean as a suspect, they had nothing much to go on but rumors. The mysterious Mr. Big Shot, whom locals claimed had charmed Caroline, was a phantom. No one knew where he lived or what he did; indeed, no one even knew if the man existed, for he'd never shown his face in town.

He could have been a myth and Caroline could have been killed by someone else, for cutting out hearts to use in black magic hoodoo rituals was a practice started by a former president of the island, one cop had informed Lacey. President Gerard "Petit Homme" Fournier was a cruel dictator who made his enemies disappear and cut out their hearts, using them for black magic ceremonies to weave terror through the populace and those who opposed his regime. Fortunately, Petit Homme had been overthrown more than three decades ago, but the practice still lingered in the country.

She wondered if she should have moved to the city.

It seemed safer there, even with the protests and burning tires and random gunfire.

She had worked hard to provide a good living for those under her care, and now her compound had become a crime scene. The man she'd hired because he needed a job had betrayed her. All for money.

What if Fleur had seen the body? Would she regress back into the same fugue state she'd been in when Lacey rescued her from the orphanage? Lacey wrapped her arms around herself.

The front door opened and closed. Jarrett came into the living room, his hair tousled, his expression grim. He sat beside her. Saying nothing, he pulled her into his arms.

It felt so good to have him hold her, push back the darkness surrounding her thoughts. He was steady as a rock, an anchor in a turbulent sea. Fisting her hands in his shirt, she buried her face against his rock-hard shoulder.

"The women in the compound are locking their doors for the first time since they moved into their new homes," she mumbled against him. "They're terrified and I don't blame them. Everything I've worked for is crumbling to pieces, Jarrett. But that doesn't matter as much as one thing...that poor girl's death."

Sitting up, she took a deep breath and looked into his solemn face. "When I think about Fleur seeing what happened, and what it could have done to her...and how she could have regressed back to being a terrified little girl sitting next to her mother's body...I think about packing everything and giving up. Turn my back on everything and let the grass take over this damn compound. Turn it back into the abandoned farm it once was. Let them win, whoever is doing this."

He pushed a lock of hair gently from her face. "You're a fighter and you can't quit now."

Lacey sat up straighter, stunned. "You're the one who wanted me to leave."

"I still do. I want you the hell out of here, and Fleur, for your own safety. Find someone else to take charge and run operations. But I don't want you to shut this place down. I saw the faces of those women you're helping. You have done so much already to help them find their own place in the world. They need this NGO. They need what you have accomplished here."

His grip around her tightened. "And I'll be damned if I let them win. We'll find out who is trying to drive you away."

"How? The police think Jean did it."

"Do you?"

Jean couldn't have done that. She'd seen the fear in his eyes when he looked at the dead girl. And though he did have a problem with gambling, and was desperate, she instinctively knew the man wasn't capable of that kind of evil.

"No. The real killer is connected to whoever wants me gone. This is bigger than locals resenting me because I'm a wealthy American who is empowering women. There's some other reason they want me out of here. But I don't know who or why."

She had never felt this sense of helpless anger and hopelessness. Not after she'd lost the baby and their marriage broke up, not even when she'd spent days trying to track down Fleur, going from orphanage to orphanage after the police had removed her from the crime scene. Somehow she'd always managed to pick up the pieces, forge ahead and keep a determined sense of purpose.

Not now. Her purpose had been sabotaged.

Jarrett glanced at the china clock on the living room table. "It's barely past 2300. Why don't you call Helen and see how Fleur is doing? It will make you feel better."

Lacey removed her cell phone from her jeans pocket. She started to dial then stopped. "This afternoon, after you'd told me about Jean, I spent a little time in the gardening shed. I wanted to check out the red paint and see if it was the paint someone had donated."

She flipped through the photos on her phone and showed him the labels on the paint buckets. "And it wasn't. The donated paint was from an overseas company. This paint had labels from a local store. Damn it! I wanted to tell the police and forgot."

Jarrett went still. "Where did it come from?"

"Either Jean bought it or someone smuggled it into the shed. I want to check out the store tomorrow. Maybe the clerk will remember who bought it or have a record. I'm glad I have these photos because the cops took the paint as evidence."

"Good. We'll go first thing in the morning."

"We?"

"You're not going alone," he said quietly.

His determination came as a relief. "All right."

Lacey went outside and called Helen, who told her Fleur was in bed, sleeping in Sally's room. The girls had played a game of LEGOs with Gene, who slept in the guest bedroom near theirs. He wasn't leaving Fleur's side.

When she hung up, she felt grateful for friends like Gene. Her father might be paying him for this assignment, but the man had gone above and beyond duty.

When she returned to the living room, Jarrett was cleaning a weapon. Her heart thudded against her chest.

"That's a machine gun," she said, sitting next to him.

"Submachine gun. Ace brought it over earlier." He set the gun down on the cocktail table. It lay there like a gleaming, lethal black snake, waiting to strike. "I needed reinforcements other than my service pistol. Don't worry. I won't let this baby anywhere near Fleur and I keep my weapons bag locked. But I'll be damned if anyone tries to hurt anyone in this household."

She tried to smile but failed. "I wish you had been around when Caroline was here. Maybe you could have convinced her to work harder so I didn't have to fire her. And then she..."

Words failed her. Lacey wrapped her arms around herself and squeezed her eyes shut, trying to erase the terrible image of the dead woman.

"Hey," he said gently. Jarrett pulled her against his chest and began stroking her hair. "It's going to be okay, Lace. You did your best for her. You couldn't force her to stay here. It was her choice."

It felt so good to be held, to know he was there. She'd remained strong for a long time, but seeing Caroline's body had unglued her. For once she wished she didn't have so many people relying upon her and could run away.

Jarrett pulled away and studied her. "Why don't you go upstairs and get some shut-eye? I'll be there shortly."

Lacey trudged up the stairs and into her bedroom. She couldn't sleep. Maybe a shower would help. But the warm water failed to erase the image of Caroline. Lacey dried off and pulled on a soft cotton sleep shirt and curled into her bed. A tide of cool air drifted through the open windows, along with a chorus of cicadas in the nearby trees.

Heavy footsteps alerted her to Jarrett's presence. She sat up in bed, hugging her knees as the silhouette of his big body filled the frame of her doorway.

"You okay, Lace?" His voice was deep and concerned.

"No." She swallowed hard, knowing the consequences of her next words. "I don't want to be alone. Stay with me."

Maybe this was a bad idea because she didn't want to reunite with Jarrett. He'd broken her heart once before. But he had never mistreated her, and his strong protective streak proved a balm to her weary spirit right now. Jarrett was one of the good guys—honorable and noble, who would never beat a woman or kill her, listening to her screams of pain and fear...

"Lace." He did not move, but his voice deepened. "You sure about this, sweetheart? Because I'm dying here."

Lifting the corner of the sheet, she moved over. "Stay with me, Jarrett. Make the nightmares go away."

Moving silent as a wraith across the floor, he stopped before the bed and tugged his shirt over his head in a one-handed move. The rasp of a zipper sliding down echoed in the room. When he'd fully undressed, he slid into bed with her.

Jarrett's palm was warm as he cupped her face, searching her eyes in the dim light. She rested her cheek against his hand, feeling the heat of his body erase the deep chill seizing her bones. Beard stubble covered his cheeks. He looked a little wild and dangerous, but his gaze filled with tenderness.

"You sure about this?" he repeated.

A hint of vulnerability shaded his tone. She sensed the wired tension in him, not from the night's events, but a deeper, more frenzied sexual need. It had happened when he'd come home from a deployment, all cranked up and craving release.

"Absolutely." Lacey curled her fingers around his wrist. "I'm scared, Jarrett. Scared that when I close my eyes, all I'll see is Caroline and…"

"Don't think of her," he said roughly. "Don't think at all. Just feel."

He kissed her, a gentle, almost sweet kiss. Lacey shut her eyes, concentrating on the sensation of his warm, firm lips feathering over hers, the commanding way he held her, the slight sigh of her own breath as he deepened the kiss and slid his tongue inside.

Beneath the passionate lover had been a considerate man hiding beneath a protective layer of warrior. Jarrett was strong, fiercely loyal, courageous and would fall on his sword before harming her. She missed this, the intensity of passion, and the pleasure.

"I'll try to take it slow. But around you, I'm always going to lose control." His deep whisper sent a delightful shiver coursing down her spine.

He left her mouth, trailed a line of soft, warm kisses down her neck, making her shiver. Her body hummed instinctively to the sultry call of his demand.

A small moan escaped her as he kissed the underside of her ear. Lacey clasped his shoulders, her fingers digging into his skin. She explored the length of his body, dropping a hand between them to his groin. The rigid length of his arousal met her palm. She stroked, enthralled by his desire.

A low growl reverberated through his deep chest. Lacey leaned closer. Fisting a hand through her hair, he crushed his mouth against hers. It was no gentle, teasing kiss, but a man staking his possessive claim. His tongue boldly thrust past her lips, tasting her, exploring the wet cavern of her mouth. Moaning, she writhed, needing more.

He kept at it, exquisite sensual torture, the tension simmering just below the surface. As if his life depended on her.

He nipped her bottom lip then licked it in a lingering caress. She opened her eyes, startled at his hot, intent look. Jarrett gazed at her as if she was the most precious thing on earth. As if nothing else mattered, not his being a SEAL. Only her. The sheer tender longing stirred something deep inside her she thought had died the day the divorce papers were signed. No man since their divorce had ever made her feel like this. She needed this.

They were a man and a woman, with this burning need between them.

Very gently, she kissed the inked tattoo, tracing the pattern with her tongue. Muscles quivered beneath her touch, then he shuddered as she lapped his skin, tasting the salt.

Heat smoldered in his gaze as he turned. Never had anyone looked at her with such fire, such stark craving.

Lacey pulled off her sleep shirt. Her body tingled with arousal, hungering for the contact between them. She was naked, shivering as the cool mountain air blew in through the open window, caressing her breasts.

Beneath the warmth of his gaze tremendous heat suffused her. Lacey arched as Jarrett thumbed her cresting nipples. When he bent his head and took one into his mouth, she clung to him, dizzy with need, her core growing wet and throbbing. He swirled his tongue over the taut peak, then suckled her. She was growing hotter now, a fire stoking inside her as the sweet tension braced her body.

As he kept kissing her breasts, she whimpered, her hips rising and falling off the bed.

"You like this, sweetheart?" he whispered.

"Don't stop."

Jarrett kissed her deeply, his hand drifting over her belly, down to her feminine curls. She made a startled sound, which he soothed with his kisses, as he slid a finger across her wet cleft.

Lacey held on to him as he began playing with her. Slowly he began to pleasure her. He wanted to absorb her, brand her with his mark of passion. She burned the memory of the erotic bliss into her brain.

Because this wasn't destined to last and she wanted this memory to last a long time.

It was consuming, setting her on fire, every inch of her body crying out for something more. Lacey strained toward him as he teased and stroked, his hands sure and skillful. The ache between her legs intensified and she pumped her hips. Every stroke and whorl sucked air from her lungs until she gasped for breath, ready to burst out of her skin. Tension heightened, spiraling her upward. And then the feeling between her legs exploded. Lacey screamed, crying out his name.

Her eyes fluttered as she fell back to the bed, spent and dazed.

Finally, her breathing eased and she lifted her head. A hint of untamed danger lurked in his eyes.

Then he gave a dangerous smile and pushed her thighs wide open. She felt him kiss the inside of her thigh, then he blew a breath on her hot skin. Jarrett opened her legs wider.

He stared at the wet, pink flesh of her center. "You're so beautiful, Lace."

Then he put his mouth on her.

The first touch of his warm tongue made her jerk backward in delighted shock. He slid his tongue between her folds in slow, steady strokes. Stubble on his cheeks slightly abraded her inner thighs. She smelled the hot musk of sex, his aftershave and the night-blooming jasmine drifting in through the open windows.

Lacey cried out, her hands fisted in the sheets, feeling the excitement gathering, the crescendo of sweet tension ready to shatter her once more.

When she screamed his name, he stayed with her until the shudders ceased. Then he looked up with a small smile, wiping his mouth.

"Don't move, sweetheart," he whispered.

Move? Her leaden limbs still trembled from the pleasure he'd delivered. Lacey turned her head and watched him get out of bed, muscles on his ass moving fluidly as he went into his bedroom.

He returned and dropped a few foil packets on the nightstand then ripped one open. Jarrett rolled the condom onto his erection and then joined her.

His heavy weight covered her, pinning her to the bed. Silky hair from his thighs sensually rubbed against her legs as he lay between them. This was the moment, then, when she shed all her cares and thoughts and joined with him.

Needing this closeness, wanting to share herself with him.

Jarrett laced his fingers through hers, his gaze fierce and glittering. Slowly he pushed into her. She wriggled, trying to find ease as he penetrated.

He dropped tiny kisses over her face, soothed her

with a whisper. Then he thrust forward again. Slight pain accompanied the odd fullness. It had been a long time since she'd had sex and she'd forgotten how big he was.

He stayed still, watching her. A drop of sweat rolled off his forehead, splashed upon her like a tear. Lacey became aware of just how much control he exerted, how much this meant to him.

He pulled back and began to stroke inside her. His muscles contracted as he thrust, powerful shoulders flexing and back arching. This was Jarrett, who would lay down his life for her.

The delicious friction was wonderful, the closeness of his body to hers, his tangy scent filling her nostrils. She pumped her hips as he taught her the rhythm, feeling the silky slide of the hair on his legs. He began to move faster, his gaze holding hers as he claimed her with every thrust into her body, with each soft word of reassurance he murmured.

She could fall in love with him all over again. Emotions crowded her chest as she stroked his back. It felt as if he locked her spirit in his, a closeness she'd never experienced. She focused on his expression, the intent pleasure on his face, the intimacy threatening to shatter her even more.

His thrusts became more urgent. Close, so close... she writhed and reached for it, the tension growing until she felt ready to explode.

Screaming his name, she came again, squeezing him tightly as she arched nearly off the bed. Above her Jarrett grunted and then threw his head back with a hoarse shout. Collapsing atop her, he pillowed his head next to hers.

For a few minutes they lay tangled together, the sheets

damp with perspiration, the cool night air sweeping over their bodies. Then he rolled off and held her close, as if fearing to let go.

Jarrett curled his big body next to her slender one, and draped a muscled arm about her waist to anchor her to him. She snuggled against him with a tiny sigh. For a few minutes they remained like that, as Jarrett caressed her damp hair. His deep chest rose and fell with his breaths as she pillowed her head on his muscled shoulder.

"I miss this. Holding you like this," he said quietly.

"You always were a great cuddler," she teased.

But he did not smile. He stared at the ceiling, his gaze distant. "It burned into my memory. Every time I went on an op, I thought of you and the times we'd shared. Yeah, the sex, but this, too. Watching you fall asleep and knowing you were safe in our house. That fueled my purpose when I fought. I was fighting for my country, but also to protect you and any kids we would have. It made it more personal and helped on those nights when I wasn't sure I'd make it out alive."

Touched by the raw honesty in his voice, Lacey lifted her head and caressed his cheek. "Thank you for all you did, Jarrett. I never did thank you. I always took it for granted that you were on watch. Every time you were home, you always made me feel safe. Sometimes I..."

Her voice drifted off. She snuggled back into his arms, disturbed by the thoughts rolling through her head.

Sometimes I miss you so much I wonder if I still love you. I know part of me will always love you and never forget you. No matter what.

As she began to doze off, she heard him whisper in such a faint voice she wasn't sure if the words were real or imaginary, "As long as I'm here, I'll do my best to make sure nothing hurts you or Fleur. You're mine, Lace. No matter what the damn papers say. And I always take care of my own. Always."

Chapter 11

Jarrett awoke in the grayish light of predawn, aware of the soft female body curled up next to him, her silky hair spread over his pillow.

Stealing all the covers. Just like she did when they were married.

He grinned, gently slid his arm away from her slender waist and rolled away, glancing at his impressive morning erection.

Not today, buddy. Let her sleep. Didn't you get enough last night?

Hoo-yah, yeah, they did after both dozing off, then waking again. Three condoms worth, but with Lace it would never be enough. He could make love to her 24/7 and never tire of her sweet, sexy body.

Or those delightful whimpers she made when she was about to come.

Or how she enjoyed stroking her fingers across his

back as she nibbled on his rear end as if he were a gourmet feast.

With a sigh of true regret he'd have to skip out on a morning session with her, Jarrett pressed a gentle kiss against the curve of her smooth backside and slid out of bed. Naked, he padded to his room and dressed in his running clothes.

The air was cool and crisp outside, a welcome relief from the humidity. He set out to run his usual path along the perimeter of the wall. Feet slapping against the earth, he kept his gaze sharpened. At the gate he greeted Marcus, who told him he'd seen nothing unusual during the night.

He hovered by the spot where the body had hung last night. Jarrett squatted down by the grass beneath the mango tree. No blood droplets on the ground or in the grass. She hadn't been killed here, but dumped here. He'd seen enough dead bodies to know Caroline had been dead for more than a day before someone left her here and he'd bet his Trident that it wasn't Jean.

He glanced up at the wall, frowning at the sharp slivers of broken glass. Whoever hoisted Caroline's body over the wall would have to come into contact with the glass and the body itself had shown no signs of postmortem cuts from the glass.

The wall abutted a large stretch of hilly forest that belonged to a farmer who grew corn and beans. But Lacey told him the man had abandoned the farm to live with his son in New York.

Anyone could access the land. He squinted as he looked at the mango tree's long branches. Some extended over the wall.

Jarrett climbed the tree and looked over the wall. Then he climbed down, deeply troubled. There was no way in hell someone could have carted Caroline's body over that wall.

Lace would have to know about this.

By the time Jarrett returned to the house, drenched in sweat, his muscles burning and his heart racing, the sun had begun to peer over the horizon. The smell of frying bacon and eggs greeted him as he went into the house.

He started for the kitchen and ground to a halt in the doorway. Rose sat at the kitchen table, her head buried in her hands, her shoulders shaking.

Rose turned, looking startled. He noticed the dampness tracking her cheeks. "Morning, Mr. Jarrett. I didn't think you'd be up this early."

He joined her at the table. "Rose, what's wrong?"

The housekeeper wiped her eyes with a paper napkin from the holder on the table. "Nothing. I kept thinking of that poor girl. It's gotten bad, bad, bad."

She had found the body, he remembered. Rose told Lacey and the police she had gone to dump peelings into the compost heap near the wall when she saw Caroline Beaufort's corpse.

"Did you hear anything last night, Rose?" It made no sense that no one in the entire complex had seen or hear Jean paint the warning or dump the body.

Rose shook her head, but her gaze flicked away. "It was so horrid. Things are bad, bad, bad here," she said in her singsong accent in French. "I wish Miss Lacey would leave with that precious little girl. I'd hate for anything to happen to her. Miss Lacey has been good to me and many others. Folks are talking and saying she needs to get out now, before worse happens."

He wiped sweat off his face with the edge of his T-shirt. "What folks?"

Her gaze flicked away again.

"Rose, tell me," he urged. "Who's been talking?"

"Just folks around this place," she muttered, twisting her hands. "I have to get to that bacon before it burns."

She fled to the stove and compressed her mouth as she flipped the bacon.

Jarrett went upstairs, wondering about the housekeeper's closed-mouth tightness. He showered and dressed in clean khaki shorts, a Navy T-shirt and sandals and went into Lacey's bedroom. Time to awaken sleeping beauty.

Pulling back the covers on her, he sat on the bed, enjoying watching her sleep. The smell of her floral perfume and the musky scent of sex lingered in the air.

He tickled her rib cage.

Groaning, she pulled the covers tighter.

Jarrett kissed her cheek. "Good morning, sleepyhead. Still not a morning person?"

Opening one eye, she smiled. "Not after all the exercise you gave me last night."

Lacey rolled over, opening her arms. He kissed her, long and deep, and she could feel his arousal.

"I'm actually awake. I woke up after you left. Gene's coming back with Fleur by 0900 and then he and Sam are moving their things into the guesthouse."

He hated giving her this news so early, but better now than when Fleur was around. "I checked out the mango tree where Caroline's body hung. Whoever put the body there last night did so inside the compound."

Briefly he explained about the wall and the broken glass and lack of bloodstains.

Lacey sat up, holding the sheet to her breasts. "It couldn't have been Jean. That sounds much too sophisticated for him, unless he had help."

"Maybe." Jarrett changed the subject. "When do you

want to leave for town? Do we have to drop off Fleur when she comes back home?"

She yawned and stretched. "No school for today because of elections. Everything is pretty much shutting down so people can vote. Even the hardware store isn't opening to the public, but I know the owner, and he promised to open just for us for an hour. I thought after we buy the paint we could all use a break and visit Ace and Aimee at the Coco Bay resort. I have a permanent VIP guest pass to use the spa and the facilities."

Sounded good to him. And he could pull Ace aside, have a private conference and discover if his friend had any news. The hour they had before Fleur returned sounded even better. Jarrett pulled off his T-shirt and began shrugging out of his running shorts.

A slow smile curved her sweet mouth. "What are you doing, Lt. Jarrett Adler? Did I give you orders to get naked?"

"We have an hour. Let's not waste it." He finished undressing and joined her on the bed.

"Aye-aye, sir," she murmured, going into his arms.

They went into town and visited the hardware store, and Lacey asked questions as Jarrett selected two gallons of white paint. He lingered nearby as the owner talked with Lacey. But no one remembered selling red paint in the past month. Business had been slow, the owner told Lacey. No one wanted to do any home improvements. Things were too tense with the elections.

They returned home without incident. An hour later when Gene's SUV pulled into the driveway, they were downstairs in the living room. Gene ushered Fleur into the house and Lacey ran to hug her. She smoothed a hand over her daughter's face.

"Did you sleep okay at Sally's house, pumpkin?"

Fleur nodded. Jarrett was relieved to see the shadows gone from her eyes.

"Gene played LEGOs with us and made a house. He's real good at building, Mommy."

Jarrett shook Gene's hand. "Thanks, man."

"Anytime."

As Lacey brought Fleur into the kitchen, he drew Gene aside. "I have an assignment for you and Sam. Need you to go over the compound inch by inch and see if you can find any evidence that someone stored a body here for a day or so. Question Marcus. Get his records of anyone who's brought a truck into the compound. Caroline Beaufort wasn't hung from the tree by someone who stole over the wall, but someone inside."

He noticed the man looked bleary-eyed. "Get any shut-eye?"

"Nope. Was up all night. Stayed outside their bedroom."

Clapping a hand on the man's shoulder, he told him to get some rest after moving into the new guesthouse.

Jarrett went into the living room and sat next to Fleur. "Your mom thinks it would be a grand idea to run away for the day and have a little mini vacation."

Fleur clapped her hands. "Yay! No school!"

"But you'll have to make up for it tomorrow and do all the homework Mrs. Daily gives you," Lacey warned. "Promise?"

The little girl nodded so hard, her pigtails bounced.

Lacey pointed down the hallway. "Go find your swimsuit and change into your play clothes. And bring Mr. Bunny, too."

Jarrett murmured into her ear as Fleur raced away. "I promise to be a good boy, too. And do all the homework you give me. And I'll let you play with my Mr. Bunny later tonight."

Enjoying her little shiver of pleasure, he went upstairs to pack.

The Coco Bay resort was nestled in a forested hillside near the main road. Jarrett showed the security guard the pass Lacey handed him, and the man opened the front gate. To his disappointment, he found out Aimee and her brother were gone for the day to the capital to get supplies.

The streets were calm with elections taking place, but Aimee wanted to be prepared in case they had to go into siege mode after elections. If the popular democratic candidate won, it was a real possibility.

He guided the black SUV along the curved driveway and parked in the VIP parking lot. The hotel featured outcroppings of white, two-story buildings scattered along several acres. Lushly landscaped, it looked like a tropical oasis, with pink-and-white bougainvillea flowers blossoming amid palm trees.

Lacey took Fleur to the women's dressing rooms to change into their bathing suits while he surveyed the pool deck.

It had a wooden deck with a kidney-shaped pool offering a stunning vista of the turquoise Caribbean Sea. Beneath the scattered shade of coconut palms, guests lounged in the green chairs set on the white sand near the shoreline. Smiling bartenders stationed at a grass hut Tiki bar mixed drinks from a well-stocked bar as waitstaff in turquoise-and-red tropical shirts and white shorts served guests red, orange and green drinks with colorful umbrellas and fruit.

The Coco Bay Resort was a paradise, set far away

from the violence in the capital and the grimness of last night's murder scene.

Several wicker couches with white cushions and throw pillows lined the pool deck near the railing overlooking the beach below. Jarrett found one next to an empty table with chairs and a wide umbrella to shield them from the sun. He set down their bags. The sea seemed smooth as a mirror, no frothy waves, but plenty of people enjoying the warm water.

Lacey and Fleur returned, carrying their backpacks. His gaze caressed his ex-wife, staring at the black bikini that barely covered her very nice rear end, and her generous breasts. She was all curves, smooth skin.

He'd kissed every inch of that luscious, delectable skin last night. And again this morning...

In her one-piece bathing suit with dolphins on it, Fleur jumped up and down, her excitement evident. "I want to go into the ocean."

"Not without me and a life preserver," Lacey warned, setting the backpacks down on the chaise longue.

"I'm too big for a life preserver."

Lacey bent down and tickled her stomach, making Fleur giggle. "You're never too old for a life preserver, daisycakes. Maybe when you learn to swim I'll let you go into the ocean with a raft. But only if an adult is with you."

Impish mischief glinted the girl's gaze as she turned to Jarrett and tugged on his hand. "Will you teach me to swim, Jarrett? Please?"

He melted at the eagerness on her face. "I already planned on it, Fleur. In the pool first, and then when you've learned the basics, we'll go into the ocean."

He turned to Lacey, who unscrewed a bottle of suntan lotion and was about to spread it on her arms.

"Hold off on that. I booked you an hour-long massage," Jarrett told her. "You go relax at the spa, and I'll take care of Fleur."

"But...well...okay."

Longing showed in her eyes. She grabbed a shirt and shrugged into it and donned her sandals.

"You need it. Go," he told her.

He peeled off his T-shirt. He wore his Navy-issued swim trunks. Lacey's gaze swept over his chest, down to his flat torso. Jarrett grinned and flicked his towel at her. "Go. Stop ogling me."

"I can never stop ogling you, Navy Boy," she murmured, heading for the spa.

Jarrett took Fleur to the shallow end and had her sit upon the first step. The water was slightly cool and refreshing.

"First things first, Fleur. I'm going to teach you to blow bubbles." He put his face into the water and showed her.

When he lifted his dripping face, he saw the five-year-old, her arms folded, with a very Lacey look of scorn. "That's for babies! I know how to blow bubbles."

He grinned. "Show me what you know so far."

If he wasn't careful this kid could steal his heart.

An hour later Lacey returned to the poolside, her expression dreamy and her step lighter. She joined them at the pool, sitting on the edge and dangling her feet into the water.

"Mommy! Jarrett taught me how to kick and float on my back! He said I'm a natural in the water."

Lacey slid into the pool and hugged her little girl. "He's a good teacher, daisycakes."

With a special look at him, she winked. "In many things."

Jarrett grinned, remembering what he'd taught her last night. Warmth settled over him as Lacey began showing her how to swim underwater. This was the kind of life he'd imagined for himself: having a family, his lovely Lacey at his side. Relaxing with them on his day off, enjoying the closeness they shared.

Fleur was a sweetheart of a kid, and he was glad to see her being a child instead of so solemn all the time. Sunshine beat down upon his naked shoulders as he splashed water at Lacey and Fleur. They both laughed and squealed, trying to evade him.

Jarrett drifted into a contented daydream; a life with Lacey, waking her up each morning with soft kisses, making love, and at night, helping Fleur with her homework. Then at bedtime, they'd both tuck her in, reading her favorite story.

Then, when their little girl fell asleep, they'd toast each other with wine and make long slow love again before Lacey fell asleep in his arms.

He hoisted Fleur upon his shoulders and played a game of water volleyball with Lacey and four teenagers who'd set up a net near the shallow end.

When they emerged and toweled off, Fleur yawned widely. Ready for a nap.

He led her over to one of the shaded chaise longues, where she promptly fell asleep. Jarrett sat at the table with Lacey, sipping fruit juice. As he asked her questions about the resort, he noticed a man in tennis whites heading for them. Immediately, he tensed, preparing to intercept. And then he saw Lacey's smile.

"Francis!"

Jarrett shot her a questioning look. She flushed and brushed a lock of damp hair away from her face. "We used to date."

"Hey, Lacey!"

As he followed her, his heart sank as he saw her greet the tall, dark-haired man of about thirty. The man carried a tennis racket and had the air of wealth, from his expensive gold Rolex watch to his designer clothing.

Jarrett became very aware he wore Navy-issued swim trunks and his T-shirt was worn and faded.

"Francis!" Lacey hugged the newcomer.

"How are you, darling?" Francis barely looked at him. Too busy twirling his tennis racket. The man was closer to Lacey's age and sported a tan.

"Excellent. Jarrett, this is Francis Monroe. He's on the board of directors for Marlee's Mangoes and his dad and mine are good friends. Dad's recommended to the president that Alastair become the next US Ambassador to St. Marc. Francis, this is Lt. Jarrett Adler of the US Navy."

Francis gave him a diffident look. As Jarrett stuck out his palm, Francis took it in a tight grip. Intentional. Macho man.

"Navy boy," Francis murmured.

Jarrett seized his hand in a very firm grip, watching with satisfaction as the other man winced.

He released his hand. "Nice to meet you." *Tennis boy.*

Francis asked, "Are you here alone, Lacey?"

No, she's here with me.

"Fleur's sleeping over there. You never met my daughter. I'd introduce you, but I don't want to wake her. She gets cranky when she first wakes up."

The other man gave a knowing smile. "Just like you always did at my house, darling." He tweaked her nose and she blushed. "I'm sure she's wonderful, if she belongs to you."

Jarrett's happy little dream of a family life crashed

down to earth. Whom was he fooling? He was a SEAL.
Loved his job, loved keeping his country safe. He would
head home soon as this was over. And then head out
for another mission, another deployment, while Lacey
settled into a long-term relationship, perhaps marrying again. Maybe marrying a rich guy like this Francis, who obviously liked Fleur and circulated in Lacey's
social sphere.

And he'd stay in the teams, growing older until age
forced him to retire or become an instructor. Sit around
at night drinking with the guys, reminiscing about the
good old days of action and adventure so he could avoid
going to his dark, lonely house where no one waited
for him.

No one at all.

Late in the afternoon they headed back home. Though
most of the shops had closed for elections, the main road
back to her compound was busy as they left the town of
La Petite Île.

Dogs wandered alongside the street, noses to the
ground as they looked for scraps. Men carried bags
on their heads as women balanced baskets on their
heads filled with fruit and vegetables. Trucks back-
fired, belching blue smoke. This was the St. Marc she
knew and loved.

Lacey hoped it would stay this way, and there would
be no more violence.

It had been a wonderful day with Jarrett and Fleur.
He'd been friendly and teasing with Fleur, yet stern
when she acted up. He'd make a great dad.

But after she'd seen Francis, her former boyfriend,
Jarrett had said little to her. Maybe it was because Francis kept jabbering, twirling his tennis racket as he pre-

tended interest in her charity and how the adoption of her daughter was proceeding. Or perhaps it was because Francis put a very proprietary hand on her arm, and Jarrett had immediately stiffened.

She'd finally gotten away from Francis with the excuse that she and Jarrett needed to check on Fleur.

Francis wasn't her type. Their relationship hadn't lasted beyond six months. He looked good in tennis clothing, and looked great decked out in dinner clothing, but he was too self-centered and snobbish to pay attention to what her needs were.

Even in bed.

And that little remark about them sleeping together had been pure posturing because of Jarrett. Jarrett, who had spent extra time getting to know her all over again, asking with a quiet murmur, "Like this, sweetheart?" and making sure she had been pleasured before taking his own.

There was no comparison between the two men. Jarrett was a trained warrior, dedicated to protecting his country and keeping civilians safe. Francis barely worked and cared more about his appearance and his trust fund.

Francis was a minnow, and Jarrett was a shark.

She glanced at the backseat where Fleur napped, exhausted from the sunshine and the day's fun. "Do you mind if we make a quick stop along the way? Mrs. Beaufort's home is on the road and I need to express my condolences in person."

Jarrett's jaw tensed. "Is that a good idea for Fleur?"

"She's been to funerals before, Jarrett. And she'll hear talk about what happened. There is only so much I can do to shield her from it."

"You could get her out of this place. Take her the hell out of here, where she won't be exposed to danger."

Anger simmered inside her. "Are you trying to tell me how to raise my daughter?"

"I'm trying to keep both of you alive and safe." Jarrett checked the rearview mirror. "More than your boyfriend would."

Lacey drew in a deep breath. "Francis was my boyfriend. Not anymore. What was I supposed to do, ignore him?"

Jarrett stared at the road and the big truck lumbering in front of them, belching black exhaust. "He acted as if you're still together."

"He puts on a show," she snapped then lowered her voice, not wanting Fleur to wake up and find them fighting. "He's part of the people I socialize with here in St. Marc. We're always going to run into each other."

"Maybe you should pick new friends."

She clamped up, determined not to fight, only speaking to give him directions to Mrs. Beaufort's house.

They turned off the main road onto a dirt road. After a few minutes they came to a small, modest concrete house. Several cars were outside. Jarrett parked the SUV facing the main road.

Another little trait she appreciated. He always ensured that the car would be parked for a quick exit. After being in some tight areas in the slums of St. Marc, she knew the importance of this.

For a moment he sat, drumming his fingers on the steering wheel, looking lost in thought.

"Are you coming?" she nudged him.

Finally, he climbed out.

Fleur had woken up and was slightly cranky, but fell quiet as they walked up to the front door. Clasping her daughter's hand, Lacey knocked, her heart pounding hard as Jarrett stood behind them, his service pistol thankfully tucked out of sight. She saw the lace curtains at the window draw back and a dark face peer out.

The door opened a minute later and Arleen Beaufort, Caroline's mother, greeted them. Her eyes red-rimmed, the woman hugged her.

"Lacey. Thank you, thank you for coming and remembering my Caroline."

Tears welled up in Lacey's eyes as she hugged her back.

She introduced Jarrett, who shook her hand. Arleen reached down and hugged Fleur.

They went into the living room. People were milling about, talking quietly. Arleen pointed to the kitchen. "Fleur, my grandchildren are in there eating milk and cookies. Why don't you join them?"

Fleur looked at Lacey for confirmation. "It's okay, sweetie. Go on."

Arleen led them to the sofa and they sat down. Someone brought over tall glasses of lemonade. As Jarrett thanked the person, Lacey opened her purse.

"This is to pay for funeral expenses," Lacey told her, pressing the check into Arleen's hands. "Caroline was a former employee. Please, let me do this."

For a moment she feared the woman's pride would make her refuse. Then Arleen's thin shoulders sagged. "Thank you, Lacey. Thank you."

Jarrett's expression softened. He reached over, squeezed the woman's hand but his look of respect was aimed at Lacey.

Then fresh tears welled in Arleen's eyes again. "The police won't release the body yet. They say it might be a few days before the coroner…"

"They have to do their job, Arleen, and try to find who did this to your daughter."

Jarrett spoke in a low voice. "Mrs. Beaufort, do you have any idea who might want to hurt your daughter? Did she have a boyfriend, friends who might have been jealous?"

He gathered the woman's hands into his and spoke in a soothing voice, looking directly at her. When he looked at you that way, his expression filled with compassion, his gaze sincere, he connected.

Such a great guy. Not only a warrior dedicated to sacrificing all for his country, but a man who related well with others. That was one of the qualities she'd always admired about Jarrett, and one of the reasons she'd fallen in love with him.

And you're still in love with him. Lacey startled at the thought, and its ring of truth.

"Everyone liked my Caroline. She was popular," Arleen said.

"I know it must be difficult to talk about this. Was she associating with people who were practicing hoodoo?"

The woman shook her head violently. "That's a rumor. An old rumor that people like to spread. My girl would never be around those kind of people. Caroline was a little wild, and she didn't like hard work, but she was a good girl."

"She may have fallen victim to someone who didn't like her," Jarrett said.

"They told me her heart…" The woman stopped and took a deep breath. "Her heart had been cut out of her chest. But not in the style of the old black magic hoodoo. Those who used to do that kind of magic always marked their victims with a pentagram to show the dead person's heart was a gift to the devil. There was no pentagram on my Caroline."

Lacey's stomach roiled and Jarrett's grip on her hand tightened. "Someone wanted this to look like black magic," he guessed.

Arleen blinked at her tears. "It doesn't matter. My little girl is still dead."

Jarrett looked around the room. "Was there anyone she'd gone to visit when she vanished?"

"The man she was seeing. She never told me his name, only that he was very rich. Caroline told me the day before she left here that he was going to take her to his home in the capital and then eventually to the United States. I begged her to see reason. She didn't even have a passport. But she was stubborn, my girl."

"Did any of her friends mention the boyfriend's name, Mrs. Beaufort?"

"She was so secretive about him. But after she vanished… I went through her things and found a photo in her bureau. I'll get it."

Lacey bit her lower lip, trying to reel in her emotions. The mourners, the solemn air in the house and the smiling photos of Caroline lining the dining table, along with the lit candles and the flowers, rattled her composure. And seeing Fleur grow quiet and sad again made her feel guilty. Maybe Jarrett was right. She'd been so happy today, acting and being a normal kid. And now all that had vanished.

Jarrett put a hand on her shoulder and gently squeezed. Lacey covered his hand with her own.

Arleen returned with the photo and handed it to Lacey. "Do you know him?"

The picture was at a black-tie party, the typical kind Lacey had attended many times in her duties as the senator's daughter. Several people mingling near Caroline held cocktails. Her mouth went dry and her heart skipped a beat as she recognized the man laughing with Caroline. Lacey forced herself to speak. "It's hard to tell. The photo is a little blurry. Can I keep this?"

Upon the woman's nod, Lacey slipped the photograph into her purse.

They remained a few minutes and then said their goodbyes. Lacey hugged Arleen again, knowing her world would never be the same. What would happen if she lost Fleur? Her beloved little girl?

When they climbed into the SUV, and Fleur was buckled in, Jarrett's expression remained tense. "You knew who it was."

Lacey nodded as she fumbled with her seat belt. She knew the man in the photograph and judging from Jarrett's reaction, he had recognized him, as well.

The man in the photo standing next to Caroline was Paul Lawrence. Her business partner.

As Jarrett accessed the main road to head home, she cast a worried glance at Fleur. She was asleep again, probably worn out from the long day and the emotion at Arleen Beaufort's home.

"That was very nice of you to give the money to bury her daughter, Lace," he told her quietly. "You have a generous heart."

Generous? She thought of the man in the photo and felt a pinch of guilt. "She needs it. I wish I could have been truthful about the photo, but I didn't want Arleen to know I recognized Paul. I'm going to question him myself before anyone else gets to him, maybe even hurts him because they think he killed Caroline."

"Leave it to me. I'll go."

Her heart skipped a beat. "It'll be dangerous. He'll

be like a cornered animal, Jarrett. And he would never let you in the front door."

Giving her an exasperated look, he shook his head. "Lace, I'm a SEAL. I don't need a front door."

"Jarrett…"

"I don't want you within an inch of that bastard. I don't like him or trust him and now that we know he's somehow associated with Caroline, he's become dangerous. Stay home with Fleur and let me handle this."

She bristled. "He's my business partner."

"And he could be a murderer, Lace." Jarrett shot her a level look.

"He couldn't have killed her. I doubt he was the one seeing her. Paul isn't like that."

"Are you saying that because he's your dad's friend and your business partner?"

Lacey's stomach churned with doubts. Paul had been a ladies' man since his divorce two years ago. What if he had been Caroline's secret boyfriend?

Jarrett's bristled jaw tensed, and the big vein throbbed in his temple. "You're not getting near him, Lace. Let me handle this."

"Not alone. Take Gene or Sam."

He blinked. "I'm better off on my own."

"Huh. That's not what you said all those times you returned from deployment, Lt. Adler. You always stated your teammates were your brothers in arms, and you worked best with them because you were trained to get the job done and they watched your six and you watched theirs."

Silence draped between them for a minute. Then he sighed, so deeply it made his T-shirt tighten over his muscled chest.

"You're right. But I'm going to have to get used to working on my own soon enough."

Lacey gentled her tone. "Why?"

"I don't know what I want to do when I retire, and I don't know if I'll make it another four years to retirement. The ops tempo is getting to me, Lace."

She leaned over, put a hand on his arm. This man had given so much to others, and no matter what troubles they'd had in the past, she knew his quiet dedication to his career and how he'd put his life on the line.

"You can do anything you want, Jarrett. Go back to grad school, become an engineer, an instructor. Find your dream and chase it, Jarrett. You're intelligent and dedicated and operate well under stress. Those are fine qualities any employer would be happy to have."

He gave a wry smile. "Maybe you can hire me."

"I would hire you in a heartbeat, Jarrett," she said softly.

She had faith in him. She only wished he'd had shown the same dedication to their marriage as he had to his career.

As they approached the toll booth on the new highway the government had built, Jarrett nodded at his wallet. "Reach in there and get the money, will you, Lace?"

She opened the wallet and fished out two bills and handed them over. Then as she started to replace the wallet on the center console, it spilled onto the floor.

A photo tucked among the credit cards caught her eye. Shock filled her as she pulled it out and stared at the folded, laminated photo.

The sonogram of the baby she'd miscarried.

How long had he carried this? As Jarrett pulled up to the toll booth and handed over the cash, Lacey traced the lines of the baby's form with a trembling finger. Memories gushed back like a tidal wave.

Waiting until he had pulled out of the toll booth, Lacey showed him the photo. Jarrett glanced at it and swore quietly. He pulled into the parking lot of a tire business, parked and stared at the paper. He glanced over one shoulder at the sleeping Fleur, and the sorrow in his expression made her heart ache.

"You didn't forget her," she whispered, and she knew he would understand what she meant.

"How could I, Lace? She was my daughter. We created her, our little girl. I had dreams about her, dreams about holding her, playing with her, teaching her how to talk, hell."

Taking a deep breath, he looked away, his jaw tense as rock. "I even thought about when she'd grow older and date. And how I'd lecture her, and the boys, and tell them if they didn't open the car door for our daughter, didn't show her the respect a man always shows to a lady, they were gone."

She smiled despite the gathering dampness in her own eyes. "I'd be surprised you would let her date at all."

"Oh, I would. And chaperone with an assault weapon." His mouth twitched as if he smiled, but it was a brief smile. "When I got the call from you that day, all I could think was how damn scared I was, and how terrified you must be. And pacing the hospital hallways, praying you were okay, praying the baby would make it and this was just a scare, it was hell. I've been through missions where I wasn't certain if we'd make it out alive, where the guys all joked about Hershey squirts in our jockeys when the intel we got was bad and a buttload of tangos would be firing at us, and nothing compared to the fear

I felt when I heard you were bleeding heavily and being rushed to the hospital."

He looked down at his hands. Big, capable hands. "That little girl inside you meant everything to me. It was a family we were starting. A little girl with your sweet smile, your laugh and your sunny personality. It was a new start for me. The day you told me you were pregnant, I felt I could live again."

Lacey's heart skipped a beat. "What do you mean?"

He glanced at her. "Remember that op that went south in Afghanistan?"

"The one where the helicopter went down?"

He nodded. "I was there, Lace. The guys who were killed in the helo crash were part of the QRF sent to extract us."

At her puzzled frown, he added, "Quick Reaction Force. Peter was on that helo. My swim buddy from BUD/S."

She remembered the awful crash, and how quiet Jarrett had been when he'd gotten home, refusing to talk about anything. They had gone to Peter's funeral and she'd seen Jarrett pay his respects to Peter's parents. Of course she'd know Peter and Jarrett were close, but each time she'd tried to coax him into talking about it, asking if he was okay, he'd rebuffed her questions, saying he was fine.

Everything was a-okay.

And it was not.

"Pete was a hell of a warrior. We were teammates. He was part of the QRF sent to save my ass, and he died. I came home, safe and sound, and he came home in a body bag." He took a deep breath.

"Pete died out there in the desert, and he was on that helo to save me. And I survived. Every mission I took after that, I told myself, 'This one's for you, Pete.' It was my way of dealing with the guilt of being a survivor."

"Jarrett, you never told me." She placed a hand on his arm.

"How could I? I had vowed silence to the code of the teams, but more than that, I vowed to never burden you with my work, with what I have to deal with all the time."

Jarrett flexed his scarred fingers. "Some people think because we're Navy SEALs we feel no fear. That's pure BS, Lace. We feel fear. We're human. It's how you push past the fear to get the job done that matters. But no one ever taught me how to deal with the guilt of being the one who didn't come home in a body bag, everyone weeping over my goddamn coffin."

Her stomach felt like ground glass. She blinked past the burning tears.

"And then you told me you were pregnant and I felt I'd been granted a second chance. This was why I was chosen to live and not die in my twenties like Pete. The day you lost the baby, I lost part of myself. That's the real reason I took that mission after you miscarried, Lace. It wasn't to escape you. It was to escape myself, to convince myself that I could still make a difference, to make it up for the time when Pete died a hero, trying to save my ass from an op that went wrong."

Suddenly, the insight struck her. She saw Jarrett, always pushing himself to work harder, faster, be stronger and more courageous. Pushing himself because taking those missions meant he was out there, doing the job he'd trained for, doing it to honor his fallen comrades.

And she'd thought, because he had never told her, that he did it for the adrenaline rush, to experience the thrill of adventure.

He ground his jaw and sweat popped out on his fore-head. "I could never erase the guilt for his death. Deep inside I blamed myself even though logically I knew that he accepted the responsibility for doing his job, as we all do."

She squeezed his arm. "You were his mission leader, his friend. He was a professional, like you. He knew what he was getting into, just as you did during all those combat missions you undertook, Jarrett. He was a loyal, good friend and so were you. Wouldn't you have done the same had your positions been reversed?"

For a long moment he said nothing. Then he sighed deeply. "Yeah. I'd have done anything for him and my teammates. And they'd do the same for me. It's what makes us SEALs. The training, the physical toughness and sharpness and concentration you need on an op, that's critical. But it's knowing they're behind you one hundred percent that counts the most. My brothers in arms."

Lacey leaned close and opened her arms. She cradled him against her as he buried his head into her shoulders. For a few moments she hugged him, her palm flat against his chest, feeling his heart thud a steady beat beneath her palm. Then he pulled away.

As he started to reach for the keys to start the engine, she put a hand on his wrist. "Wait. Thank you for sharing with me."

She took a deep breath, knowing she could tell him the secret she'd kept since founding her NGO. "You asked me back in the city why I named my NGO Marlee's Mangoes."

Dropping his hand, Jarrett watched her. "Marlee is an unusual name for a charity in a French-speaking country."

She bit her lower lip. "Yes, but it was a perfect name for a little girl born in the States. I never told you, but that was the name I had picked out the day I found out we were going to have a baby girl."

He closed his eyes. "Damn."

"I called my NGO that because the charity gave me a reason to keep pushing on after I lost Marlee. And it was my way of making her live on, keeping her memory alive with something good and right and hopeful."

Moisture coated his eyes when he opened them. "It's a good name," he said, his voice husky. "I like it. I wish you'd have told me, Lace. Because I'd have done something, too. I didn't want to forget her any more than you did."

"We were both wrong," she whispered. "So wrong all these years."

Maybe it wasn't too late to start again.

Chapter 12

Two days passed without incident. The entire country had turned tense with the news a new president had been elected. The mood had been cautiously jubilant among the women in the mango factory who had voted for the popular candidate, a man who promised to help the lower classes.

Jarrett found out that while he'd been gone, Sam and Gene had discovered something interesting on the day Caroline's body was found.

Gene told Jarrett he'd checked with Marcus, the security guard. There had been a delivery of supplies to the mango factory that day. The supplies were delivered to the back entrance of the factory, and a storage room accessible to only Lacey and Collette.

Only two other vehicles entered the compound that day. One was an SUV belonging to Lacey. The driver had parked it and then left, leaving the compound to catch a bus. The other was a black SUV belonging to Paul Lawrence. Jarrett went over the time logs with Marcus, the security guard. Paul had entered the compound around 1 p.m. to meet with Lacey. His SUV left at 3:30.

The man had gone to the mango factory to talk with Marie, the employee he was helping out. But why would he hang around until after the factory shut down and the women went home for the day?

Jarrett didn't immediately tell Lacey. She was still at Fleur's school with Sam, having a conversation with the principal about having Sam remain on the school grounds to watch over her daughter during the day. It was a good time to investigate further.

While Gene texted Sam to tell him what they'd found, Jarrett went into the kitchen. Rose was pulling croissants out of the oven.

"Rose, are there any deep freezers in the mango factory?"

She placed the flaky treats on a piece of foil. "Miss Lacey bought two last year to store grouper she buys from the local fishermen. Why?"

"I need to see them."

Jarrett caught a glimpse of fear in her eyes. "Miss Lacey keeps that room locked tight. All the deliveries for the compound are stored there. She doesn't want anyone in there, Mr. Jarrett."

"Are the freezers filled now?" he asked.

"No, but I can't just give you the key. I'll get into trouble."

"I'm the one who's doing this, Rose. Not you. There's nothing to be scared of."

But the woman kept shaking her head. He leaned against the counter. Ever since Caroline's body had been discovered, Rose had been a wreck. Granted, it was nerve-racking to know a murder victim had been dumped on the property, but instinct warned Rose was upset for another reason.

"Everything okay, Rose?"

She fussed with the croissants. "I keep thinking about that poor lady. That's all. I wish Miss Lacey would take Fleur far away from here and leave."

"Even though you'd lose your job?"

"Some jobs ain't worth your life."

She looked up and the sweat beading her forehead was not from the heat of the oven. The woman was terrified.

Jarrett went to her. "Rose, I'm here and Gene and Sam are staying here, as well. We're going to find out who did this, and who's trying to run Lacey out of here. We'll keep you safe."

But Rose kept shaking her head.

"Tell you what I'm going to do. I'm going to take all these keys with me and one of them will open the back room and the freezers."

He went to the key rack on the kitchen wall and sorted through the keys, keeping one eye on Rose, who watched him. When he came upon a set of keys on a chain with a carved wooden sandal, he heard her intake of breath.

Got it.

Jarrett pocketed the keys. "Now you won't get into trouble because you didn't give me the key. Are these the only set of keys to the back room and the freezers?"

She nodded.

Minutes later he and Gene walked to the mango factory. The sweet, syrupy scent of ripe fruit hit his nostrils as he walked inside. There were fewer women slicing and bottling fruit today.

He asked one of them where Collette was and she pointed to a small office with a window. The manager was talking on the phone, her back to the assembly room.

"Does she ever work here late, after the building is locked?" he asked.

The woman shook her head. "Miss Lacey was firm about that. She wants everyone gone by three so they can go home and spend time with their children and families."

He glanced at the office again. It would be polite to tell Collette what they were doing, but Jarrett didn't want polite. He wanted answers.

They made their way to the back storage room and Jarrett unlocked it and flipped on the light switch. Two large deep freezers used to store supplies lined the wall. Rose said both were empty and locked. Using the key Rose had given him, he opened the first. It was empty.

The second one was empty, as well. But there were a few tiny droplets of crimson on the bottom.

"Fish blood?" Gene asked.

No way to tell without a lab to analyze it. Jarrett leaned down and scanned the freezer. As he started to close the lid, a flash of yellow caught his eye. He lowered the lid.

"Help me move this away from the wall," he told Gene.

When they did, he lifted the lid and told Gene to hold it upward. Then Jarrett bent down and pulled a scrap of yellow lace from one of the hinges.

Caroline had left them a message.

"Damn," Gene said. "Someone dumped the body in here until they hung it from the mango tree."

"And he must have had the key to unlock the building and the freezer," Jarrett mused.

Gene lowered the lid as Jarrett tucked the scrap into his pocket. Without DNA testing, they couldn't be certain the lace scrap belonged to Caroline, but it was looking more certain that Lawrence was guilty.

"What are you doing in here? This room is supposed to be locked."

Collette stood in the doorway, holding the ever-present clipboard and pencil. She glowered until they straightened up.

Then she was all smiles. "Oh, excuse me, Mr. Jarrett. I thought someone was messing around in here. Miss Lacey is very strict about keeping this room off-limits to the workers."

"I plan to lock up again when we leave." Jarrett leaned against the wall, arms folded. "Has anyone been in here over the past two days?"

The woman stared straight at him. "No. Why?"

"No fish, no meat stored here?"

"Not for a while." She tapped her pencil against the clipboard. "Oh, wait. Mr. Lawrence was here recently. He talked with Marie a little while to see how she was doing and then he asked to get into the storage room. He wanted to remove the fish he'd stored here when he went on a deep-sea trip with his friends. Miss Lacey lets him borrow the deep freezer from time to time."

How convenient. "How long have you worked here, Collette?"

The woman's gaze sharpened. "About eight months now, Mr. Jarrett. Miss Lacey needed help keeping the women organized and productive. Excuse me. Have to go do my job now."

The woman certainly seemed dedicated to her job.

He put the lace scrap into his pocket, wishing he had access to a lab. But with the country growing restless as election results were tallied, he wasn't even certain he could find someone to test for DNA. After calling the police about the case, he found out there was one lone detective investigating the murder, and that detective had been called away on road patrol because of the rising tensions.

Terrific.

Jarrett spent the next two hours catching up on emails and work. His CO had sent an email, asking how he was doing, meaning, have you gotten your act together yet? We need you back, sharp and alert, now that you've had time to decompress.

He nearly laughed at that. Decompress? Relax? How could he even lower his guard when someone was trying to run Lacey off her compound? He'd forged a new connection with his ex-wife, one he didn't want to break. And if he left her now, it would snap like a matchstick, for he'd be doing the exact same thing that caused her to seek a divorce—abandoning her when she needed him the most.

Deciding he needed to burn off energy, he went for a short drive in one of the compound's trucks, checking out the route to Fleur's school, investigating the back roads Marcus had told him about. It was always good to know options.

When he returned he found Lacey in her office, working on the computer. She glanced up. "Perfect timing. I need someone to help me put labels on the envelopes and then stuff them. I'm doing a fund-raising letter to donors in the States and need to send these out through the courier service today for my dad to mail. Have a seat."

Jarrett sat at the small table and began to peel off labels and stick them on envelopes.

"How did you hire Collette?" he asked.

"Paul recommended her. She used to be a manager in his factory, but when he cut back on staff two years ago, she left for the States. She returned because she missed her family." Lacey gathered papers from the printer. "Why?"

"Is she competent?"

"She's smart, increased our production by fifty percent simply by organizing the women in shifts that suited their schedules, giving them flexible hours and paying them by the amount of jars they produce, not the hours they work."

Jarrett helped her insert the letters into business envelopes and put labels on them. "What happens if you leave here, Lace? Does the charity shut down?"

Lacey shook her head. "I made sure that would never happen. My long-term goal isn't staying here, Jarrett. It was to begin a foundation that would eventually be run by people in St. Marc. I wanted to give these women a head start and then eventually turn it over to a board of directors in St. Marc who would keep it going."

"And Paul Lawrence is on that board? Who else?"

"I'm the president. Paul is the vice president. Then there's Francis who is the treasurer, Collette, my friend Helen and her husband, George, and Rose. I put Rose on the board because the mango marmalade is her recipe, and she represents quality control. But I'll have to find new board members soon because Helen and George are moving to Paris the end of the year."

She pushed back her hair. "I want business people from St. Marc who will be dedicated to our long-term goal of empowering women as well as helping to raise funds for operational expenses. I do have a 501c3 tax status in the States for the purpose of fund-raising. I'd always be involved in raising money and doing special events and mailings."

He stacked the envelopes and gave her a long, thoughtful look. "And what if something happens to you and you return to the States? Who takes over then?"

"Paul would be the president of the board, but Collette would remain as the manager to keep operations running until they voted on finding a replacement for me."

Paul again. He didn't like this connection. Jarrett stayed her hand. "Look at me, Lace."

She turned, her eyes so blue in her face, her expression troubled. "You found something out about Caroline's murder."

"Paul Lawrence may be involved. Your security guard said his SUV was at the mango factory long after the factory had closed. Collette said he was getting fish from the deep freezer."

"I let him store fish there. That's nothing unusual."

"But this is." He pulled the scrap of fabric from his pocket. "I believe Paul dumped Caroline's body there in the deep freezer until it could be moved later, when everyone had gone home."

Lacey took the fabric and turned it over. Her shoulders slumped. "Ever since his divorce, Paul has been a player. He's not much to look at, but he has money and he's charming. But I've never known him to turn violent. Even if he was Caroline's mysterious phantom lover, why would he kill her? Even if she was pregnant and pressuring him to marry her, he could have just dumped her. That happens all the time in St. Marc. Half the women who come to me for help are unwed mothers."

"Maybe she knew something and threatened to expose it," Jarrett said.

He'd bank on Caroline's murder tying in with the reason behind the threats Lacey had received and the pressure for her to leave the compound and return to the States.

"Has Lawrence asked you about returning to DC? Hinted you should go back for your own good?"

She sighed. "I thought it was because he worried for my safety. Now I think it's because he's the one who's been leaving all the threats. If I returned to the States, he could control Marlee's Mangoes."

"Why would he want that?"

"Because it's starting to make money, and if he controlled that money he could pay off his debtors. We're losing money again on the coffee exports. I've been so involved with my charity that I let him run things at the coffee factory, but got word that he was considering layoffs. He kept delaying me from seeing the profit and loss statements, and finally I went to the accountant. I don't know what he's involved in, Jarrett, but it's not good. I think he has a gambling problem."

"I'll do a little digging and find out." Jarrett kissed her cheek and then the corner of her mouth. Damn, her skin was soft and sweet and tasted fine. He wanted to take it further, lead her back to the bedroom and make long, slow love to her. "I don't want you anywhere near him, Lace. I'll go later to talk with him."

Lacey looked so upset, he wanted to cheer her. But his first job was ensuring her safety. "I have to pick

Fleur up from school soon. Sam has to leave the school early to get Gene. They're going to the capital to get the security cameras and buy a lot of food and supplies just in case. There are reports the newly elected president may not get into power. Seems like everyone is running to the grocery."

The situation had the makings of a coup, and he didn't like it. "I'll pick her up. Stay here, focus on your work."

Work would help distract her. He knew how she felt, everything crumbling to pieces around her, and needing to hold on to something solid and good.

Chapter 13

Fleur was in a good mood when he met her at school. She chattered about her day, playing jump rope at recess, and showed him the drawing of the bird she'd done in class.

Jarrett hugged her and then helped her into the SUV, making sure she was buckled in. As he pulled out of the school yard, he was glad to see her so animated. This past week he had grown fond of the little girl, and she was beginning to mean a lot to him.

Not only because she was Lacey's daughter, but because she was a tough, spirited kid who had been through hell. And she had a survivor's spirit.

Traffic crawled as Jarrett drove. He navigated past a slow-moving caravan of donkeys laden with woven baskets. A few men and women hawked wares along the roadside, but the market wasn't as crowded as it had been the previous day. Jarrett kept his gaze sharpened.

Vendors sat beneath faded beach umbrellas as they sold bright yellow bananas, tasty-looking mangoes, packs of gum, sweets or fried chicken on the sidewalk.

It was too easy to lose oneself in the frantic explosion of noise, smells and color, but he'd learned to train himself to spot lurking threats hidden by a cacophony of human activity. The banana vendor with the wide straw hat who seemed to be haggling with a customer over his wares could have a pistol tucked beneath his faded T-shirt. The weary-looking farmer nudging his mule past the line of vehicles stuck in traffic might use that machete as a weapon.

He always remained on guard. It was ingrained into his nature. Paranoid, his ex-father-in-law once called him. Well, hell yeah, with good reason. Lacey's old man had never served in a country where insurgents planted IEDs in the road, or an innocent-looking child lobbed a grenade at you as if it was a softball. Cold sweat trickled down his neck as he scanned the market. All his instincts tingled.

Never one to ignore that little tingle, for it had saved him many times, he hung back as the traffic inched forward like a caterpillar. Gave himself enough room to cut out and not be blocked in. The truck in back of him honked impatiently, but Jarrett ignored it.

Finally, the traffic began to move forward, and the bus in front of him belched black smoke. The truck behind him pulled out and passed him on the left, almost clipping a car coming from the opposite direction.

Fleur pointed. "Look, Uncle Jarrett! Mamma says drivers like that are cray cray."

A half smile touched his mouth, but it dropped. Now that the truck no longer blocked his rearview and side mirrors, he saw the bike.

Not just a bike, nor a typical scooter seen around the island. This was a sleek black crotch rocket coming up fast behind him on his right, weaving through the traffic like a sewing needle piercing fabric. All his instincts roared to the surface. Black helmets hid the faces of the riders.

And then Jarrett saw the passenger on the bike reach into his leather jacket. The motorcycle sped up on the right. Sunlight glinted on the metal the passenger held, the barrel gleaming wickedly in the bright sunlight.

Damn it!

He unhitched her seat belt with his thumb and pushed Fleur down roughly to the seat. "Stay down," he roared in French.

The passenger fired, and a hail of bullets pierced the back window. Glass showered the backseat. Fleur screamed and climbed off the seat, squeezing herself onto the floor. Jarrett gunned the engine, but the SUV wasn't built for speed. Still, he had to outmaneuver them. A narrow lane was about one hundred feet to his left, but it was blocked with market stalls and vendors.

His mind kicked into automatic, even as the assassin fired the assault weapon again. He barely heard the glass shattering in the front window, felt the stinging kiss of the bullet as it scraped his right pec. He jerked the wheel hard right, hoping to ram the assailant, but the biker braked, skidded and then maneuvered around the side, still firing. By now people were screaming, abandoning their wares and running everywhere like a mass of ants streaming from an anthill.

He reversed with one hand, pulled his sidearm free with the other and fired at the bike's driver. Three quick pops and he heard a scream as the bike tore forward. Jarrett shot again, and the biker lost control, skidded sideways on the loose gravel and crashed into a stall filled with bright orange mangoes.

Thank you, sweet Jesus, for mangoes.

Jarrett gunned the engine, found a side street and plowed through it, crashing into now-empty market stalls. He tore down another street, then onto a dirt road leading to the main road. As he reached the main highway, he glanced left once and saw the traffic jam at the marketplace, but the road was clear ahead of him.

Speeding toward Lacey's home, he glanced down at Fleur crouched there, head buried in her arms, blood covering her yellow checked dress.

"Are you hurt? Fleur! Answer me," he roared.

The only sound was a small whimper.

He didn't dare stop and check her wound until they reached home. When he pulled in front of the gate, Marcus saw him and yanked the gate open. Jarrett sped through as Marcus closed the steel gate. He parked, unhitched his seat belt and bent over Fleur.

"Fleur, sweetheart, it's okay now," he crooned. "Are you hurt? Let me see, please, honey…"

Marcus opened the passenger door but Jarrett was already out of the vehicle, racing around the side and scooping the terrified little girl into his arms, very gently brushing away the bits of small broken glass from her body. He heard alarmed shouts and Lacey's voice.

Jarrett placed Fleur on the ground and examined her dress and the blood. He cradled her face in his big hands, alarmed at how quiet she'd grown. But she appeared unhurt. He breathed a small sigh of relief that the SUV had windows made from safety glass. And then Lacey was at his side. He was amazed at her cool calmness. She didn't scream or grow hysterical, but picked up her daughter and thoroughly examined her.

Relief showed on her face as she lifted her gaze to Jarrett. "She's shaken up, but not injured." Then her eyes widened. "Jarrett, it's your blood on her dress. You got shot!"

He clapped a hand to his chest, wondering why it came back stained red. The coppery scent of blood slammed into his nostrils as a brief bout of dizziness hit him. "Bullet only grazed me. I'm fine."

"You're not fine." Still cradling her daughter, Lacey began issuing orders to the women who had followed her. "Get clean bandages and the first-aid kit."

She went to take his arm, and he shrugged her off. He was a SEAL, damn it, not an invalid. And he'd failed to keep her daughter safe from all harm. Lace had trusted him with the most precious thing in her life, and he'd botched it. Should have shown up earlier, made arrangements to pick her up sooner and take a different route. But he had not.

Fleur wrapped her arms around Lacey, clinging to her like a limpet. He made it into the dining room before another bout of dizziness hit him. Jarrett sank into a chair.

"You're losing blood." Lacey set Fleur down, opened the carved sideboard and withdrew an elegantly embroidered linen table setting. He started to protest, but she silenced him with one of her signature looks. She folded the place mat into a square and pressed it to his chest wound.

He took it from her and applied pressure.

"I'm ruining your fancy place mat," he said, hating how helpless he felt.

"I'll buy more."

Lacey sat beside him as the woman brought in bandages and the first-aid kit, but Fleur hooked her arms firmly about Lacey's neck, as if the little girl was drowning. Jarrett winced, not from pain, but the terror still lingering in the child's eyes.

"Sweetheart, I have to let you down for a minute so I can help Jarrett. He's hurt. Sit down at the table. I'll be right here."

Rose came into the room and went to take Fleur's hand. "I'll get her changed and clean her up, Miss Lacey."

"No," Fleur whimpered. "Please, no. I need to stay with Mommy. Mommy!"

His chest tightened and his breath hitched. No longer was Fleur the normal, talkative child who'd chattered about her day. She had regressed back to when she'd lost her birth mother to her father's brutal violence.

Lacey shook her head. She bent down and hugged her daughter. "I'm right here, baby. I'm not leaving you. But I need to take care of Jarrett."

Rose's gaze darted to Lacey and she twisted her hands.

"Rose, get Mr. Bunny and Fleur's storybook, please. The one I've been using to teach her to read in French," Lacey ordered.

The woman stood there, staring.

"Now," Lacey snapped.

Then his ex-wife turned to her daughter and said in the gentlest voice he'd ever heard, "Sweetie, I am going to tend to Uncle Jarrett now. He's kind of scared because he got hurt."

Jarrett lifted his eyebrows, wondering where she was going with this.

"He needs your help to keep his mind off his injury, okay?" Lacey took the book and the bunny rabbit as Rose returned to the table. "I want you to hold Mr.

Bunny in your lap and read aloud to Uncle Jarrett from your storybook so you can show him how much you've progressed with reading."

Jarrett nodded in understanding. By giving Fleur a diversion, the little girl wouldn't see how injured he was.

Hugging her stuffed animal, Fleur opened the book and began to read aloud in French. Lacey tore open his shirt and winced. He glanced down at the narrow groove scraping through his right pec and the blood streaming from it.

"It's just a flesh wound," he muttered in English as she began to clean it.

"And you've lost blood, Lt. Jarrett Adler. Quiet while I fix this."

The stinging pain burned, but he'd had worse. Jarrett laced his fingers around her wrist as she began to clean his wound. "I'm sorry I let this happen," he said quietly in English.

Her lower lip wobbled, but the stubborn line he knew well formed between her silky brows. "Don't be ridiculous. Because of you, she's alive," she whispered in the same language.

The peroxide stung like a bitch as Lacey cleaned his injury. Then she dressed the wound as expertly as any hospital corpsman would.

"Where did you get the medical training?"

Lace capped the bottle of peroxide and wiped her perspiring forehead with the back of one hand. She disposed of the bloodied gauze and returned to the table to pack the kit.

"I have to be self-sufficient. I spent two months volunteering at a local clinic when I moved here. I figured if anything happened, I could at least care for myself."

She blinked rapidly. "Although I never figured on anyone I knew getting shot. Stay here."

She went into the adjoining kitchen and returned with a sports drink and uncapped the bottle, handing it to him. "You've lost blood and need to replace fluids."

"I'll be fine." He drank until draining the entire bottle and then turned to Fleur. "Thank you, Fleur. That really helped take my mind off getting fixed up. You read really well."

But the child still had the same blank stare as when he'd pulled her from the car. It would take a long time, and professional help, to get her past her trauma. Jarrett glanced at Lacey, who bit her lip. She offered a bright smile to Fleur.

"Sweetheart, why don't you get changed and cleaned up and take a nap before dinner?"

Fleur looked at Jarrett. "Are you going to die?"

Good God. Ignoring the pain in his chest, both from the bullet wound and the emotional tightness of the question, he squeezed Fleur's hand. "No, honey. I'm a big ole tough grizzly bear and I'm sticking around, I promise. You can count on that."

She gave a little nod and clutched her bunny harder with one hand and the book in the other as Lacey led her away. Jarrett sat again, burying his face into his hands.

Christ, what a goat fluster. And Lacey was not going to like what he had to do...

Fishing his cell out from his pocket, he called Gene.

They had been at a popular grocery store frequented by the wealthy and ex-pats, when several army vehicles had rolled by, headed south. Rumor had it the army was taking over the local radio stations and shooting journalists.

Gene and Sam had left, seeking refuge with a

friendly French ex-pat who had a well-guarded house. Their American accents made them moving targets.

Damn. He told them to sit tight, explained what happened. They would return at 2200 to the compound, when everything quieted.

Minutes later Lacey returned. He looked up into her troubled face as she examined the bandage. His wound had not resumed bleeding, fortunately.

"You should go to a hospital and get an IV, but I wouldn't take you to a hospital around here. The closest hospital is out of commission. And it's too dangerous and you're too exposed."

Suspicion filled him. "What's going on, Lacey? I called Gene and Sam and they told me the St. Marc army is shooting journalists at radio stations."

Jarrett leaned closer. "Spill it, Lace. Why? What did you hear?"

Raising her gaze to the ceiling, she heaved a deep sigh. "There's been a military coup. It happened an hour ago. General Georges Montana has seized control of the government and refuses to allow incoming President Salles to assume power. The national palace fell under control of the army."

That was why the market had been half-deserted. This changed everything.

"Tell me exactly what happened. Was it a protest against the government and you got caught in the cross fire?" she asked, looking hopeful.

Jarrett understood. A direct attack was far worse than random violence.

He told her everything that had happened and destroyed that hope. Opening her eyes, she gathered his hands into hers and her fingers trembled violently. "Thank you for saving Fleur."

Guilt pierced him. "She could have been badly hurt."

He did not say the words hovering there. *She could have been killed.*

"But she wasn't, because you were there. If I had been driving…" Lacey bit her lip.

"Hey." He pulled his hands free and slid a palm around the nape of her neck. "You weren't. She's safe for now."

Her blue eyes glistening with tears, Lacey shook her head. "They were after my little girl. Why, Jarrett? Because I'm American and our country wants St. Marc to have a democratically elected government? Because I'm trying to help battered women who've been to hell and back?"

"I don't know. But I'm damn going to find out who's behind this. I believe your partner is involved. He may have killed Caroline, moved her body to the deep freezer after the building was closed and locked and everyone went home. And if something happens to Fleur, there's no impediment to your returning to the States." He ground his jaw. "And then he could get all the money from your charity to pay his creditors."

"Is Paul that desperate he'd kill a child?" she whispered. "What's he involved in, Jarrett? Who could do such a thing? He's my father's good friend."

A fierce protectiveness arose inside Jarrett. He hated to see how her shoulders slumped in defeat and wanted to draw her close, hold her and never let go.

"I've tried to get in touch with him all day. But his phone keeps going to voice mail. I'll try later. Right now I have to go see my daughter."

As she rose, Jarrett grabbed her hand. She was not going to like this, but he had no choice. "Lace, we have to talk."

Wariness filled her expression. "Now?"

"Now, before it gets worse and I can't get you out of here. If the military takes over the airport, it'll be too dangerous and you might not be able to leave. You can't protect her here. I can do everything I can…" The guilt pierced him again and he had to take a deep breath to push it aside. "But she's a target and she's too vulnerable to remain here."

"I'll hire more security. I'll keep her here, at home. She can study with me…"

Hearing the desperation in her voice, he felt his stomach pitch and roil. He softened his tone. "Can you really keep her safe here, now that you know someone wanted her dead? I doubt they were gunning for me. They targeted Fleur. Why, I don't know, but I do know I want you and Fleur to leave here today."

"No! I'm not leaving!"

"Then you have to send her away for her own good and yours."

A fat tear rolled down her cheek. "How can I? She's my daughter. I made a promise to her the day I signed the adoption papers, even before that. I swore to Fleur I would always be there to keep her safe."

Lacey scrubbed her face with an angry fist. "I can't even get the paperwork expedited to get her to my parents' house in Washington. Everything is shut down. I can't leave her, Jarrett."

He'd already thought of that. "Stay with Ace and Aimee. The security at the Coco Bay resort is top-notch. You and Fleur will be safe and protected for the time being. Ace will guard you with his life."

Watching the doubt on her face, he felt a tentative relief. Maybe she'd listen to reason and get the hell out of here. He knew how important her work was, but damn it, she was a sitting duck. And this place was too wide open, too vulnerable to attack now that there wasn't an operational government in place.

Forget the dangers from the military coup. The greater danger was closer to home, because whoever had peppered the SUV with bullets this afternoon was planning an outright assassination. Someone who didn't hesitate to murder a child wouldn't let a mere eight-foot wall with broken glass bottles defray him.

On his missions, Jarrett had always been prepped. Training was integral to being a SEAL. They trained for every possibility, always had a Plan B and even a Plan C in place in case Plan A went FUBAR. But here he felt like he was fighting blindfolded, with his hands tied behind his back. He didn't know who the enemy was, and it frustrated the hell out of him.

"Let me think about it. I want to give Fleur time to rest, and you need to rest, as well, or you'll open that wound."

He placed a hand over the bandage. The stinging pain had eased somewhat. Hell, this was nothing compared to the time he'd taken a bullet to the shoulder. But it was worse because it happened here, and the gunmen were aiming at Lacey's daughter. Fresh anger filled him. The sooner Lace got out with her daughter, the better, for then he could set a trap and wait for the son of a bitch to show his ugly face.

And give him a little surprise, courtesy of a 9 mm bullet.

He went upstairs to rest and immediately fell asleep. Jarrett woke instantly about two hours later when someone knocked at the door.

He rolled off the bed, grabbed his sidearm and raced

downstairs. He met Lacey coming down the hallway. She glanced at the gun in his hand.

Normally, she would have made a joke about his odd way of greeting a door-to-door solicitor, but after today's events, she said nothing. Lacey walked with him to the living room. She peered out the window and heaved a deep sigh filled with obvious relief.

"Put the gun away. It's Collette and the women who live on the compound."

He holstered his weapon but did not drop his guard as she opened the door. Collette stood on the front porch, a steaming casserole dish in hands covered by thick blue oven mitts.

"May we come inside?" her manager asked.

As Lacey stepped aside, the women and Collette filed into the kitchen. All the women carried in dishes, from big bowls of rice and beans to coconut cream pie. Jarrett's stomach rumbled, reminding him he'd forgotten to eat lunch.

As they set the items down, Collette placed the casserole on the table and removed the oven mitts.

Her expression was filled with sympathy. "I am so sorry, Lacey, for what happened today with Fleur. I told the women you could use a friend, and dinner, and everyone pitched in at the kitchen to make you something."

There was enough food to feed all of his SEAL team. Lacey hugged her.

"It is the least we can do," Collette added. She gestured to Marie, the nervous woman who had been flustered when Jarrett approached. "Marie even made her famous rice and beans dish."

"Miss Lacey, if not for you, I would be on the street right now," said Marie.

Lacey blinked hard as Marie took her hands. Jarrett stared down at the woman's hands, weathered from hard work, dark as coffee, the fingers long and elegant.

"You saved me, Miss Lacey. You saved me from the worst person in the world—myself. Because you taught me that I'm worth something and I shouldn't return to my man because all he had to give me was more pain," Marie told her.

Each woman came up and kissed her on both cheeks and then nodded at Jarrett. Collette hugged her again before she left. At the door the woman turned with an apologetic look for Jarrett.

"I'm sorry I was curt with you, Mr. Jarrett. It's been very tense at the factory. With the unrest on the streets, and with what has happened here, the women are scared they will lose their jobs and their homes. They have no place else to go, and having a stranger around, especially a man, asking questions and being around their workplace, is intimidating."

"I understand." But he didn't offer any friendly overtures or welcoming gestures. Jarrett didn't trust easily. Especially after what happened today.

He nodded goodbye to the women. As Lacey closed the door and leaned against it, he saw the fatigue rimming her pretty blue eyes mix with something stronger.

Steely determination.

She wasn't going to leave, he realized.

"Lace, you should start to pack for Aimee's place," he told her.

"No." She looked around the room. "This is my home now, and my charity, and these women are under my care. Maybe they had a choice before things started falling apart with the government, but they don't now. Two other charities who could have helped them, would have given them money and a place to live, have pulled out."

Stretching out her hands, she stared at them. "I look at women like Marie who need Marlee's Mangoes. What will happen if I leave here and the place closes down?"

Jarrett said nothing, only continued to gaze at her.

"I can't abandon them with the country disintegrating like this. Collette will leave and the place will fall apart. These women believe in me, and they trust me. Who will take care of them if I leave? If I leave…"

Her voice broke. "I'll be a failure, just like before."

He gentled his voice. "There's a difference between failing and knowing when to resort to plan B, Lace. You can return later."

"By then it will be too late. But I can't send my little girl away."

"You must." Jarrett winced as he leaned forward to cup her cheek, needing to touch her, knowing this was going to crush her. "Because someone doesn't want to scare you out of here anymore, Lace. Someone wants to dispose of Fleur and they believe she is the only reason you're still here and not returning to the States."

Lacey shook her head. "I need to check on Fleur. She was asleep a little while ago, but I'm sure she's awake now."

He locked the front door, gave Lacey a few minutes then went into her daughter's bedroom. Fleur sat on her bed, dressed in clean pajamas. Staring at the wall, she rocked back and forth, her arms around her stomach as Lacey sat beside her.

Her mouth wobbled as he joined her on Fleur's narrow bed. "She won't talk. She won't stop doing this, Jarrett. And I don't know how to help her."

Fleur hadn't been physically wounded, but the violence had shattered her emotionally. Jarrett's throat tightened. He rested a hand on her thin shoulder. "Hey, daisycakes," he said, using her mother's nickname, "can you look at me a minute?"

Saying nothing, she lifted her head. Jarrett gritted his teeth. In her large, dark eyes was the same blankness, devoid of all emotion, he'd witnessed in other children while overseas. Victims of violence who had seen far too much in their young years, they had retreated far inside themselves for protection.

And so had Fleur.

It would take a lot to pull her out of her safe space. And the first step was making her feel secure. Not here. Fleur squeezed her eyes shut, as if shutting away the world.

He spoke in a soothing, low tone in French. "Fleur, I'm sorry about the bad men who tried to hurt you today. I promise you, I'll do everything in my power to keep this from happening again. But it may mean you have to leave your mom so you can be safe."

No response.

"Fleur, sweetheart, I don't want to send you away," Lacey said softly. "You're my special angel, my daisy-cakes. It's you and me, kiddo, against the world."

No response, just the shut eyes and the rocking.

Lacey put her arms around her daughter, but Fleur did not respond. Then Lacey slowly got up, tucked her into bed and pulled up the covers. Fleur stared at the ceiling.

She went out of the room as Jarrett followed. Her gaze was dull with pain as she closed the door.

"Call Ace. Find out how soon he can get here to take Fleur." Her voice cracked. "I can't do anything for my little girl anymore. I can't protect her, Jarrett."

He pulled her into his arms. For a minute she remained there as he stroked her hair, trying to comfort her. But then she jerked away and her expression became as wounded and blank as her daughter's.

As she fled toward her room, Jarrett felt the old guilt and grief surface. He'd left her after they'd lost their baby, that tiny little life that had been growing inside her. He'd failed to be there when she needed him most.

And now he'd failed her again and she was losing her daughter because he couldn't keep Fleur safe.

Chapter 14

Lacey had thought her heart would break the day she lost her baby years ago. She remembered it so well, the panic clogging her throat as she kept bleeding out, the desperate prayers as the ambulance rushed her to the hospital…

And the pain lacing her heart far worse than the physical pain.

She thought nothing could ever equal the emotional trauma of her miscarriage and subsequent divorce.

How wrong she was.

When Ace and his sister pulled into the compound in a sleek black Montero two hours later, her heart squeezed tight. With every ounce of her strength, she summoned an encouraging smile for Fleur as she walked her outside. Fleur clutched her stuffed rabbit as if it was a life preserver.

A cool breeze rustled through the coconut palms and

the bright pink bougainvillea. The jasmine bush she'd planted last year was blooming, sending a delicate fragrance floating on the wind. It was a lovely day, but it should be raining.

Because she was abandoning her little girl, whom she'd promised to never leave.

Lacey hugged Aimee and shook Ace's hand. Ace took Fleur's suitcase from Jarrett and put it in the trunk. The two men stood quietly talking as Lacey struggled to rein in her composure. Fleur must not see how shattered she was, for this was difficult enough for both of them.

Squatting down, she looked at her daughter, the fear swimming amid the blankness in her eyes, the tension in her thin body. So thin, despite the protein she'd fed Fleur over the past year. Lacey gently gripped her arms.

"Just for a little while, sweetheart. You're going away with Mr. Ace and Miss Aimee so you can be safe. No more bad men on motorcycles shooting. There's the pool you can play in, and lots of toys…"

Fleur looked down, refusing to meet her gaze. "But you won't be there."

Her voice cracked. "I know. I have to stay here and help the women because they don't have anyone else to help them. Things are getting bad and we don't know what will happen. And I need you to be in a place where you'll be safe. Be good and do everything Mr. Ace and Miss Aimee tell you. And play nice with Holly and Heather, okay?"

Fleur nodded but would not look at her.

Aimee squatted down with her. "Hey, Fleur, you're going to have a real good time with us. Holly and Heather are looking forward to playing with you. And they're very eager to see Mr. Bunny and hear how well you can read in French."

Lacey hugged Fleur fiercely, but she remained stiff. Sweat trickled down Lacey's spine as her daughter pulled away. Pulled away from her, as if she didn't want Lacey in her life anymore because she knew, even at five years old, that adults could hurt her.

Jarrett went to Fleur and bent down to her eye level. "If you get scared in the night, or you need to talk to someone other than Mr. Bunny, tell Miss Aimee and she'll call me and your mom. At any time."

Fleur gave a little nod and then climbed into the backseat. Lacey could not move, could not breathe. She felt as if someone had compressed all the air out of her lungs. If she moved, she would start sobbing and never stop. Hold it together, just a little longer.

Ace glanced at her then nodded at Jarrett. "I'll call you later."

And then he and Aimee were in the big Montero, pulling away, Fleur staring out the window, her palms flat against the glass.

Soon as the SUV cleared the gate, Lacey staggered over to the front stoop, sat and buried her face into her hands.

Jarrett sat next to her, holding her tight against his chest as she sobbed. She cried for everything that had been building inside her for the past few weeks, for her little girl's stricken pain, for the women who had no other options but to remain at Marlee's Mangoes and for her own shattered marriage with Jarrett.

For Fleur's mom, who had never wanted to leave her daughter, either, but who lost her life at the hands of a brutal killer.

Saying nothing, he held her, stroking her hair, letting her cry it out. Finally, she raised her head and gave him a lopsided smile.

"Your shirt's all wet and your bandage probably is, too."

"Screw the bandage." He framed her face with large, gentle hands. "You're going to get through this, Lace. She's safe with them and I'm here with you. I'm not leaving, understand? I'm sticking around."

They went inside as she found a tissue to blow her nose and wipe her tears. Jarrett found two bottles of water and then muttered, "Screw it."

He went into the dining room and the liquor cabinet and then returned to the kitchen with her bottle of dark rum. After pouring two shots, he handed her a glass.

She gulped it down, relishing the slow burn. Drinking wouldn't numb her pain, but it helped her to fight off the deep chill settling into her bones.

Jarrett tossed back his shot and looked at the kitchen. "Where's Rose?"

"I gave her the night off. I didn't want her around for Fleur's departure and with the coup d'état, she's worried about her family. I had planned to cook before Collette and the others brought all that food."

Arching a dark brow, he considered. "Damn, had I known that I would have lined up the fire extinguishers and bought another bottle of rum to wash down the taste of your cooking."

Lacey hiccupped. "I'm not that bad."

"True. I've had worse. Bugs and worms in the jungle on an op. Actually, the mealworms were much tastier than your cooking."

She smiled, for this was a familiar tease and she recognized what he was trying to do, distract her from the pain of Fleur's departure. "If you don't want to eat all the food the women brought over, you can cook, Lt. Adler."

"Trying to make me earn my room and board, woman?" He winked as she pulled Collette's chicken casserole from the refrigerator.

Soon they had dinner on the table, the casserole heated and sitting on a metal trivet. Jarrett had found a bottle of fine French wine and poured two glasses for them both. Fierce and protective, Jarrett had a tough outer shell and yet within that steely core lay a vulnerability she had only glimpsed in their marriage.

Maybe if he had shown her that side of himself when they were still married, she would have stuck it out. But Lacey knew she was different now from the naive girl who had sought out a divorce. The world wasn't as black-and-white as she'd envisioned, and people were much more complex.

Like Jarrett. One had to coax out the layers and peel them back, like an onion, to find the true treasure within. And back then she had been too wounded to even try.

Jarrett glanced at her plate and her untouched food. "Eat, Lacey. You need your strength."

"I can't."

"You're still upset about Fleur."

"I wasn't thinking about her," she admitted. "I was thinking about us. What we had when we were married. And how you had it all, and I didn't."

His gaze shuttered. "What do you mean?"

The rum had made her melancholy. "What we almost had. A family. A child to give me purpose. Your life had purpose. You were Navy, a SEAL, fighting for your country, to keep us all safe. You were so damn dedicated. And I had no purpose."

The guarded look dropped as he folded his muscled

arms across his chest. "Why didn't you ever talk to me,
Lace? Tell me how you felt."

"I never said anything because I knew the nature
of your work, Jarrett, and how you had to focus on
the job. I never wanted you to deploy and worry about
me. I never complained, never wanted to let you know
because you had enough on your shoulders. But I had
nothing to occupy my time."

"The job with your dad. What about that? Wasn't
that occupying your time?"

"It was online. I seldom interacted with anyone. And
the other SEAL wives, they had children and activities
that kept them busy." Her mouth turned down. Maybe
it was time he learned the truth she'd hidden.

"They didn't include me in their circles, anyway. Oh,
they were friendly enough and supportive, but when it
came to social activities, stuff like lunch with the 'girls,'
they didn't include me. Maybe because they were wary
of the big senator's daughter, the senator who wasn't
one to readily fund the military. My life when you were
gone was empty. I wanted a baby to fill it. A baby who
looked like you, had your grin and that little dimple in
your cheek when you smile. A little person to hold and
hug and be a reminder of you…"

Her voice cracked. "In case you came home in a
coffin. Every time you left, I was terrified you'd never
return."

Jarrett looked stricken. "You never said anything."

She sniffed, nearly laughing at the reason why. "My
dad was the one who warned me to not be a clinging,
whiny Navy wife."

"Your father? The almighty Senator Stewart, who
hated my guts because I stole away his little girl?"

"He didn't hate you." Lacey sighed, wishing she

could turn back the clock. So many regrets. "He was damn angry that we eloped without saying anything, and he thought I was far too young. But after the deed was done, he told me I had to buck up and be a good Navy wife and you were a warrior fighting for our country, and you needed to have a clear mind and not think about problems at home when you deployed."

"Damn," he said softly.

"This is why my NGO is so important. It gives me purpose, a feeling I'm making a real contribution to making the world a better place, just as you are. All I have is Marlee's Mangoes to give women a new life, so I could give myself a new life."

"You never seemed like the kind of woman who indulged in self-pity." He reached across the table and took her hand, his fingers stroking against her skin. "You were strong and self-sufficient. Like you are now. And you have a kind heart."

The words loaned her strength she didn't feel. Lacey picked up her fork and began eating. Maybe she'd made some bad decisions in life, but she'd done so for the right reasons.

When they finished dinner and washed the dishes, Jarrett turned. He bent his head down and his kiss was soft and tender, not the passion-drugged kiss of the other night. It was almost as sweet as the first time he'd ever kissed her, when he'd taken her to the elegant steak house and then kissed her in his truck. Tentative, as if he feared hurting her. Respectful, and yet layered with simmering passion.

Then he took her hand and led her upstairs to his room. His lovemaking chased away all the bad thoughts and nightmarish images, and replaced the pain with sheer pleasure.

Chapter 15

At 2300, Jarrett put Operation Sneak 'N' Peek into action.

Sam and Gene had returned to the compound. The capital was tense, with military vehicles forming roadblocks on the main road. They had made it out only because Sam had greased a few palms with the cash Lacey had given him for the security cameras.

Dressed in black long-sleeved shirts and trousers, dark greasepaint over their faces, he and Sam planned their visit to Paul Lawrence's house. And if Lawrence happened to be home, well, the man would wake up to a nice little session of Q&A, answers provided courtesy of Jarrett's Sig Sauer. Gene would remain behind with the now-sleeping Lacey and guard the house.

Spreading out on the dining room table the map of St. Marc that showed the location of Paul Lawrence's house, he circled the target with a red pen. Several photos Lacey had taken of a cocktail party at Lawrence's house were also strewn over the table.

"We'll park a distance away and go through the woods to the perimeter. Lacey told me Lawrence did have cameras around the property that'll have to be disabled. No dogs. Razor wire fence."

"Snip, snip," Sam said.

"The house has a wraparound balcony and French doors in the guest bedroom where Lacey stayed once. Best point of access. Gene, did you find anything out about his staff?"

"Lawrence had a cook, a maid and a butler, but not anymore. His wife is also gone. She divorced him two years ago and went to live in Paris."

He couldn't do this alone. He needed a team.

Teamwork. It's what made the SEALs strong and successful in many missions. Jarrett had served hundreds of combat missions and had been deployed to Iraq and Afghanistan several times. He had enough fruit salad on his chest to show his valor. But all those medals meant nothing compared to the welfare of his teammates.

As they prepared their weapons, Sam whistled at the sight of the HK MP7a1 submachine gun. "Sweet. You use that baby on the teams?"

Jarrett nodded and sighed. "Man, I'm gonna miss the adrenaline thrill when I leave the teams."

"Thinking about retiring?" Sam asked.

Jarrett checked his pistol. "Yeah. The ops tempo is grinding away at me."

It killed my marriage, too. Hell, I can't blame the job, it was me, as well.

"The stress of constantly being deployed or away from home. I understand." Gene shook his head. "One reason I left the military. Still, I miss the action and the excitement. We thought about forming our own security company, but guarding paunchy executives as they travel overseas or arrogant diplomats isn't the same."

Sam nodded. "Maybe if we had a company that had another purpose, and made us feel like we did when we were in the military, that would suffice. But it would have to be a damn good purpose. One reason we took Stewart's assignment. Protecting that sweet little girl, checking her six as she's in school, that makes it worthwhile. Not standing guard while some braggart diplomat circulates at cocktail parties and social functions."

A security firm with purpose. Not mercenaries, hired out for a contract to make money, but something deeper and more fulfilling.

Something to think about.

Jarrett nodded. "Let's roll."

He and Sam climbed into Sam's SUV and headed south.

Parking a half mile away on a side street, they hoisted the packs over their shoulders and went through the woods.

But when they reached the eight-foot-tall stone wall ringing Lawrence's property, the razor wire had been cut and the housing to the security camera had been smashed. Someone had already been here.

Vandals maybe. But Jarrett had a strong feeling it was not.

They made it to the second-story balcony and Jarrett tested the French doors. They opened easily.

The guest bedroom was a blizzard of ripped pillows, an overturned mattress and china figurines smashed on the plush carpeting. All the bureau drawers were pulled out and on the floor.

They went through the rest of the house. Chairs were overturned, drawers opened and furniture ripped open.

In the master bedroom Jarrett went to one of the cushions and saw a white powdery dust. Dread filled him as he stroked his finger across it and then tasted a tiny sample. His tongue immediately went numb.

"Sweet hellfire, that's pure gold."

Lawrence's little problem wasn't gambling, but cocaine. No wonder profits from the coffee business had dried up. They went straight to Lawrence's nose.

"St. Marc used to be a haven for smuggling. They'd drop shipments from planes into the mountains and then smuggle them to Florida. I have a feeling the military coup is backed up by heavy drug money. The former regime running this island once allowed a plane from Colombia to land on the national highway to deliver a load of coke." Sam investigated an overturned drawer. "I'd say this is where your wife's business partner ran into his cash problem."

She's not my wife. Words died on his tongue. The bigger issue was waving an enormous red flag in his face. Was Lawrence aiming to drive Lacey away because he'd wanted to take over Lacey's mango business?

It didn't make sense. Even if the charity was operating in the red, the money wouldn't be enough to suffice.

"He's hiding if he owes that much money." Sam looked around.

Jarrett went into the master suite closet. All of Lawrence's clothing was gone. The man had packed and left. But where did he go?

The downstairs was also chaotic. In the kitchen the refrigerator had been opened and the contents emptied. Milk soured on the floor. Jarrett sidestepped the mess and saw the corner of a white envelope sticking out be-

tween the refrigerator and cabinets. He drew it out and
blew off the dust.

Sam leaned close and frowned at the shaky hand-
writing with Lacey's name on it. Whoever tore up the
house must have missed this.

Jarrett pulled his bandanna over the lower half of
his face then slit open the envelope with a knife. After
the anthrax scares in DC, he always took precautions.
Inside was a crisp sheet of elegant ecru stationery, but
the note penned upon the paper was written in a shaky
hand in French. He read aloud.

"Lacey, get out of St. Marc while you can. Things
are heating up and I'm in real trouble. I got involved in
a risky business venture and I'm over my head because
I owe a lot to the wrong people. I'm sorry. I never meant
to hurt you or your daughter. Paul."

It was almost as good as a spoken confession. Yet a
tingle raced down his spine. It seemed too pat.

"Looks like Lawrence killed Caroline and was the
one trying to scare away Lacey," Sam said.

"Maybe." Jarrett tucked the envelope into his pocket.

When they returned to Lacey's house, Jarrett called
Ace on his secure cell and told him what they'd found.
"How are things? Fleur okay?"

"She's fine but it's not good, Ice. The President of the
United States is trying to negotiate with General Montana to get him to step aside and end this coup peace-
fully before our guys storm the castle." A pause on the
other end. "You and I may be called back in."

Damn. "How are the negotiations?"

"Cautious, from what I hear." Another deep pause.
"Senator Stewart has POTUS's ear on this. He's pushing
for military intervention. Thought you should know."

A chill raced down his spine. He hated knowing

Lacey's dad was involved in any of this, because as long as Senator Stewart's daughter resided on St. Marc soil, she remained vulnerable.

And a different kind of target. What if some happy military honcho decided to take her hostage?

"What are the chances of a full-scale invasion?" It was a huge risk, sending in US forces.

"The current US ambassador to St. Marc is delaying his retirement. He's in DC, trying to get the POTUS to negotiate instead of invade. He doesn't want St. Marc to become a US-occupied territory."

And the possibility was very real. Jarrett shoved a hand through his hair. He had to stand ready if he was called. But that meant leaving Lacey here, alone.

Just like he had when she'd lost the baby.

For the next two days Jarrett remained vigilant listening to the radio reports and shoring up the compound. He constantly patrolled, this time carrying the assault rifle he'd stored in his weapons duffel. While he remained with Lacey, Gene and Sam went out during the day to gather information on the streets, and try to find out any intel on Paul Lawrence's disappearance.

Grateful for his presence, Lacey listened to the radio, as well, trying not to fret that the situation was growing progressively worse in the capital. She called her worried father and assured him she was safe and all was fine.

Many Americans had already left the island and Fleur's school had canceled classes. But she was relieved to hear Fleur had loosened up a little and was preoccupied with playing with Aimee's twins.

Rose remained with her family, having obtained permission from Lacey. In light of the circumstances, she knew how worried her housekeeper was about her aging mother and father, so she gave her an advance on her paycheck and told her to take five days off.

Lacey set aside groceries at the guesthouse for Gene and Sam, and then stockpiled food for herself and Jarrett and the women in the compound. Most of the women who lived outside the compound hadn't shown up for work. She didn't blame them, for tensions were growing and there were more roadblocks set out by citizens angered that their new president wasn't yet in power.

She worked with the women on the compound to stock the mango salsa and marmalade. Collette had telephoned, apologizing for not showing up for work, as well, for she wanted to sit tight with her family. Half the town was in siege mentality.

She and Jarrett fell into an easy rhythm with each other and their daily routine, much like the kind they shared during their marriage. Yet this was better and more comfortable than their marriage because it lacked the previous tension. She realized why as she went over the accounts for Marlee's Mangoes.

When she and Jarrett had been married, she relied upon their relationship and her role as a wife to feel complete. Now she had achieved that on her own. They had made love constantly, and each time she lay in his arms afterward, wondering what she'd do when he left. He'd ingrained himself into her heart again, and it would be damn hard to cut him loose.

The third day after the coup d'état began, she woke early, showered in the downstairs bathroom and prepared a breakfast of fresh mangoes and oatmeal. Lacey heard humming from the upstairs bathroom and went to investigate.

A white towel slung around his lean waist, Jarrett

stood at the bathroom mirror, scraping the bristles off his lean cheeks with a razor. Steam misted the air, and droplets of water slicked his tight washboard abs. Her mouth watered. Forget breakfast. Here was a much more tempting sight. The man was all sleek muscle and sinew.

He gave terrific back rubs.

And great front rubs, too, she recalled with a delicious shiver.

As he finished, wiping his face with a towel, she entered the bathroom. He turned, his green gaze glinting as he caught her expression.

"Breakfast is ready downstairs. But I'm hungry for something else."

Lacey undressed and dropped her clothing on the bathroom floor. As he started to speak, she put a finger to his mouth. Then her fingers caught the edge of the towel and yanked.

Jarrett stood nude before her, bared to all his glory. And oh, so glorious. He was half-erect. She knelt on the bathroom mat and took him in her hand.

"Lace." His voice went husky.

"Hush. My mamma told me to never talk with my mouth full." She licked the rounded head, swirling her tongue as if he was the most delicious chocolate ice cream. Jarrett leaned against the sink and groaned.

Taking him full into her mouth, she watched him, eyes closed in ecstasy, one hand gripping the sink, the other hand fisted in her hair. She loved doing this, loved seeing this big, bad SEAL in her power, knowing how she could pleasure him.

Lacey dragged her nails over his skin, enjoying the slightly salty taste of him and hearing his grunts of pleasure, and how he remained absolutely still, letting her set the pace. And then he tensed and with a loud moan, he climaxed.

Satisfaction filled her as she stood, wiping her mouth. Eyes closed, he leaned against the sink, panting. Then his eyes flew open.

"Turnabout is fair, Lace," he muttered.

Squealing, she fled the bathroom, but he picked her up and slung her over one shoulder. Jarrett marched over to the bed and dumped her there. He took the belt from her robe and tied her wrists together. Naked, she wriggled on the bed, her skin tight with delicious anticipation. Then worry shaded his expression as he paused.

"You okay with this?"

Her heart turned over. Jarrett was always considerate, worried he might hurt her with his considerable strength. Lacey waggled her fingers. "I'm a big girl, sailor. I can take whatever you dish out."

Sensual heat turned his gaze dark. "I can dish out a lot, sweetheart. Prepare for a full frontal assault."

He looped the belt around the headboard, stretching her arms above her head, but with enough slack on the belt to make her comfortable. Jarrett's gaze darkened as he leaned over her.

"I could have used zip ties, but you know how to break free from those."

"Because you taught me." Lacey licked her lips. "What are you planning to do with me?"

"I'm going to be so deep inside you you'll feel me every time you walk, and you'll remember me for days." Jarrett took a pillow and gently placed it under her hips. "But first, I need breakfast, too."

She studied the bristles shadowing his jaw, muscles rippling beneath his flawless skin, the hard curve of his shoulder, the muscled contour of his long limbs.

A pulse jumped madly at his throat. He smelled of sex and long, dark nights spent tangled in passion.

Expression fierce with intent, Jarrett knelt between her outstretched thighs. His gaze gleamed with appreciation as he studied her.

He slid down her body, kissing her belly, laving his tongue inside the indent of her navel. The sweep of his tongue felt like wet, rough velvet. Then he settled between her thighs.

"Relax," he murmured.

He parted her soaked folds and then dipped his head. A hot stroke of wet velvet between her legs. The first lick of his wicked tongue made her gasp. And then she started to moan. Each seductive sweep over her folds had her writhing, helpless to resist the carnal pleasure. When he swept his tongue over her center, she cried out.

Then he bit very lightly.

She screamed.

He suckled and licked, coaxing out the rich scent of her own salty arousal.

Jarrett slid a finger inside her, very slowly, testing her inner passage. He lifted his head. Fire danced inside his irises, turning them dark as sin. Lacey squirmed, desperately needing his mouth again.

"Oh yeah," he said softly. "You're almost ready for me, sweetheart. I'm going to drive hard and fast into you until you beg me to stop. Or not stop."

The sweep of his tongue once more, licking and suckling her as he slid a second finger inside her, stretching her open.

Lacey arched back, her body taut at the ropes holding her prisoner. Moisture wept from her as his fingers moved deep into her passage. Pleasure built higher and higher. A loud sob wrenched from her throat as he found a spot and stroked. She screamed.

"Yes," he murmured with satisfaction.

Jarrett pressed down. Hot pleasure exploded in her loins. The orgasm wrung tears from her eyes, her inner tissues squeezing him tightly as she writhed.

"Good girl," he crooned.

She watched, eyes heavy-lidded as he brought his fingers to his mouth, licked them slowly. "I think you're ready for me now."

A smile curved his mouth. "Let's try for two."

"Please," she begged, her hips pumping. Desire became a relentless master, driving her to wild excess as he continued to pleasure her.

"Look at me, Lace."

When her eyes remained closed, his voice became a whiplash of command. "Look."

Lacey opened her eyes and stared at him. His expression intent, he looked almost savage, but deep in his eyes she saw the Jarrett she'd fallen in love with, the man who made her feel beautiful and unique and special.

Sweat dotted his forehead. He kept pleasuring her, his fingers working magic.

Frustration bit her. On the edge of an orgasm, she pushed against his hand.

"Tell me. Do you want to come?" he commanded.

"Yes," she sobbed. "Please. Make me come."

Her body grew taut as a bowstring; she looked upward. He pressed on her sensitive knot of nerves and the tension shattered her into shards. Her mouth parted with a scream of his name.

Shuddering, she collapsed back onto the mattress. After a moment she opened her eyes and saw him kneeling between her legs, his thickness rising from a nest of dark hair. He bent his head.

"Give me your mouth," he commanded.

Lacey parted her lips, tasted her musky arousal on his mouth. He cupped the back of her head, holding her steady for his possession as his tongue thrust inside.

Then Jarrett pressed soft kisses across her belly and breasts, splaying his hands across her rib cage. Touching her, tasting her as if she was indeed beautiful. Lacey began regaining a sense of power as he worshipped her with his mouth. Cupping her breasts, he kneaded them, flicking the hardened nipples with his thumbs. He encased one taut nipple with his mouth and suckled her, licking the peak.

He settled atop her, supporting his weight with his hands. His chest hairs rubbed over her sensitive nipples like a brush of silk. The rounded edge of him pushed into her. Swollen from her climaxes, she wasn't certain she could take him.

His thick erection slid into her slowly. His smoldering gaze locked with hers.

When he withdrew, waiting, his gaze locked to hers, Lacey pumped her hips.

"Don't stop." She barely recognized the sultry purr of her voice.

Jarrett smiled darkly and obliged her.

His thick length filled her. Jarrett rested his forehead against hers, a bead of sweat dropping onto her cheek and splashing down like a teardrop.

He groaned and began thrusting in long, slow strokes. Blood thundered in her ears, rushed to her loins. Her limbs quaked wildly beneath the steady, hard thrusts.

Emotions flowed out of her. Lacey closed her eyes, the words spilling from her lips.

232   *Navy SEAL Seduction*

"Jarrett, oh, love me, please. Love me."

Wonder parted her lips. She opened her eyes to see him gazing fiercely at her as he surged into her.

"Yes," she sobbed, writhing.

"You are beautiful, Lacey," he whispered, brushing his mouth against hers. "My beautiful Lace."

With a low groan, he thrust harder. His hips hammered into her, hard male flesh smacking against her soft yielding femaleness. Lacey arched, desperate to touch him, but her arms were restrained by her bonds. Her hips bucked as he rode her hard and fast. A scream rose from her throat.

Pleasure so intense she couldn't bear it built to a shattering crescendo. A scream tore from her throat as her hips jerked convulsively; Jarrett rode her throughout without mercy as he gripped her hips. Tossing back his head, he groaned, his big body shuddering as he released his seed. Jarrett collapsed atop her, his breath thundering into her ear. Slowly, as if resenting leaving her, he pulled out of the tight clasp of her body.

Trembling, she lay on the sweat-soaked sheets, feeling him untie her bonds. Then he joined her on the bed and gathered her close, murmuring softly to her.

There in the security of his strong arms, she felt all her cares slip away.

If only they could stay like this forever.

But she knew reality would set in soon enough.

Chapter 16

They heard reports after breakfast of the growing chaos in the city. The St. Marc Army was barely keeping order, and there were bursts of fire from automatic weapons. Several people had been killed in the violence, including two prominent radio journalists who publicly called for the return of the elected president.

Lacey called Fleur twice. All was quiet at the Coco Bay Resort, but most of the guests had checked out. More worrisome was the news that supplies were dwindling and gas, needed to run the generators, was in short supply in town. Jarrett could see the fear in Lacey's eyes as she worked in her office.

Was her little girl safe after all? What would happen to her?

Late that afternoon he got the call he'd expected and dreaded. His CO, Captain Callahoun, was ordering him to Paix Beach, where a Zodiac would pick up him and

Ace at 0200 half a mile north of the Coco Bay resort. He was to bring Lacey to the Coco Bay with him and any other Americans living in Lacey's compound. No details yet. He'd be briefed upon his arrival.

Judging from Callahoun's grim tone, Jarrett guessed the senator had pulled strings and was arranging to evacuate his daughter. But what about Fleur? She wasn't a US citizen. The papers necessary for her immigration had been stalled with the growing chaos in St. Marc.

He was going to have to abandon Lacey. Again.

Jarrett had a quiet, private conference with Sam and Gene and then prepared to tell Lacey over dinner. His stomach tightened. The job came first. Always did, but this time he was leaving her in an unstable country with violence erupting around the corner and a murderer on the loose. Gene and Sam hadn't heard anything regarding the whereabouts of Paul Lawrence. The intel they'd gathered had referenced the mounting violence spilling over from the city to pockets of the quiet countryside. Factions of the populace who wanted the military out and their newly elected president in power were clashing with the pro-military.

Gene and Sam understood he couldn't say why he had to leave.

He hoped Lacey would understand, as well.

The power had gone out earlier, and to save on gas, Lacey opted for dinner by candlelight. Two tall rose tapers cast flickering shadows over the elegant white linen tablecloth and the bone china plates. Jarrett poured her a glass of white wine, but settled on bottled water for himself. The delicate floral scent of her perfume teased his senses, reminding him of last night's fierce love-making and how he'd fallen asleep, Lacey in his arms.

He was going to miss her, and this time it hurt even

worse because he remembered well what he'd lost the first time he'd left her.

Halfway through eating the chicken she'd warmed, Lacey looked at his empty wineglass. "You're not drinking."

Then suspicion filled her expression. "Jarrett, what's going on?"

An opening line if he needed one. He carefully set down his fork. "Lace, I have orders to leave. My CO called this afternoon."

"You're leaving me?"

Candlelight did not mask the wounded expression on her face. Steeling himself, he reached over to clasp her hand. "I've been called back. But you're going with me and Sam and Gene to Coco Bay."

"Why?"

"I can't say."

"Oh, right. It's classified. But this involves me." She went still and her gaze flipped down to his sidearm. "There's only one reason they'd call you away from your leave, Jarrett. They're worried that the situation in St. Marc is growing more unstable."

"I don't even *have* the details yet, Lace. They're very tight-lipped. But my CO is adamant that you're coming with me to Coco Bay."

"I can't leave here. This is my project, my people. Who will help these women?" Lacey looked around, her mouth wobbling. But no tears shone in her blue eyes. "If there is military action, they'll be sitting ducks. And what about the murderer? What if he returns?"

He had already planned for that. "Marcus and the other security guards promise to maintain order. I paid them an advance on their salaries."

But his reassurances failed. "I can't leave these people, Jarrett. I made a promise."

"You have no choice. You're going to leave if I have to carry you over my shoulder." Taking a deep breath, he said the words he knew she'd dislike. "This isn't an option. I'm under direct orders to escort you to Coco Bay."

"No."

"Yes."

She searched his face, and her body tensed. "Something's going to happen. What? The Navy wouldn't recall you unless…"

Paling, she shook her head. "They wouldn't."

"I can't tell you. You know that, Lace."

"Of course. The secrecy that goes with a mission, with being a Navy SEAL. I don't need to get it from you. All I have to do is pick up the phone and call my father."

He gave her a level look. "He won't tell you, either. All he'll say is to go with me tonight to the Coco Bay Resort. Pack lightly."

"Damn. Damn." She slammed a fist down on the table and the delicate wineglasses shook. "I can't do this."

Couldn't listen to her, couldn't bring himself to see how she was coming close to tears. Nice dinner. A heaping of guilt, accompanied by a large side dish of regret. His temper began to fray. Hell, he had a job to do. No distractions.

Focus on the mission. Her. Jarrett retreated to combat-ready mode and glanced at his watch. "You have an hour to pack. We're leaving at 1900."

"You're a bastard, Jarrett Adler." The words stung,

but far worse was the look on her face. Gone was any of the faith and trust she'd placed in him.

And he couldn't blame her.

"It's my job," he said grimly, standing and clearing off his plate. Hell, he had no appetite left now.

He wondered if he ever would again, for each time he remembered the hurt and betrayal etched on her face like a carved relief on a marble statue.

In the end, Lacey capitulated. She knew Jarrett had no choice. He was only obeying orders. Still, she resented not having control. The women in her compound had understood and quietly wished her well, but the fear in their eyes had been shattering.

They felt deserted, and rightly so.

She also called Collette and told her that she was leaving for a few days. No reason to alarm the woman.

The only good thing was anticipating seeing her daughter. But when they arrived at the sturdy steel gate at Coco Bay, alarm filled her.

No security guards stood in the booth outside the gate. Sitting in the back of his rented Montero, squeezed next to Sam, Lacey watched the former spec ops soldier slide out his pistol from the holster on his belt.

Jarrett honked. The gate remained closed.

Then he fished out his cell phone and called Ace.

A few minutes later the gate opened, and Jarrett drove through. He parked just inside the gate and rolled down his window to greet Ace, who was coming down the drive shouldering a lethal-looking automatic weapon.

"Where's your security?" Jarrett asked.

Ace's jaw tensed. "They all quit. Park before the main building and I'll meet you there."

When they parked and got out, Aimee came outside, her dark brown hair gathered in a French braid, worry stamping her pretty features. She hugged Lacey. Lacey introduced Sam and Gene as Aimee's brother jogged up the drive.

"What's the deal?" Jarrett frowned. "I don't like leaving the women here unprotected."

"I can take care of myself," Lacey protested.

He flicked a glance at her. "In this unstable environment?"

Ace held his weapon with a practiced grip. "Guards were too worried about the military taking over this place as a staging ground. Hotels like this have been targets in the past. It's the one place the military knows they can have access to food, water, a swimming pool."

"And liquor," Aimee chimed in. "I have a new security detail arriving tomorrow morning. I'm paying them double and they're professionals. Jarrett, please tell my big brother that his marching around with that gun isn't going to deter a tank."

"I'd put the odds on Ace, not the tank." Jarrett glanced at Sam and Gene. "You guys help with the luggage. Aimee, I know Lace will want to see Fleur."

"The girls are asleep. I'll take you right away. Kyle, will you show them where to put the suitcases and where their rooms are?"

Gripping her backpack stuffed with her laptop and files, Lacey followed Aimee into the resort. The normally busy marble lobby was quiet, with a clerk on duty behind the registration desk. The distant hum of a large generator was the only noise.

Aimee led her up the carved wooden staircase to the third floor and headed down the hallway. "We cut unnecessary things, like the canned music, to save on gas powering the generator. Who knows when the power will be restored? We've been without electric for two days."

"It's like that all over," Lacey agreed.

"I'm sorry you can't have a guest cottage, but this floor is all family suites, so you should be comfortable. They're large, have living rooms and separate kitchens, and a fully stocked mini bar. We've moved to this floor with the girls, so you'll be here with us. We all have rooms next to each other. Ace insisted. Easy escape down the fire exit and being on the third floor buys time in case of trouble."

"Do you expect trouble?"

Another shrug. "I'm not. I've lived here long enough."

But worry shaded her eyes. Aimee walked down the hallway and using an old-fashioned metal key, opened a door and flipped on a light.

The turquoise-and-white room was cool and soothing to the eye, with the kitchenette off to the right and chairs lined up to the counter, a dining table opposite the kitchen flowing into the living room. Drapes had been pulled to shut out the light. Aimee crossed the living room and opened the door.

Inside the master bedroom, three little girls curled up on the king-size bed. Two ten-year-old twins with fair skin and a scattering of freckles across their noses, sandwiching a much darker-skinned child who slept in a tight fetal position.

Fleur.

Tears burned her throat as Lacey crossed the room and gazed down at her daughter. For a few minutes she simply stood there, watching her sleep. So tiny and frail, and yet Fleur had a steely core, a survivor spirit that had endured so much in five years.

"She's been sleeping like that ever since her arrival," Aimee whispered. "The girls have been very protective of her. They say she's their little sister."

"Thank you."

Not wanting to disturb their rest, Lacey turned and went out the door. Aimee closed the door quietly behind her.

"My bedroom is next to theirs in this suite, but if you want Fleur to stay with you tomorrow..."

"If she's comfortable here, please leave her. Maybe I can crash on the sofa. She's already had enough disruption." It hurt to say those words, but she knew she had to do what was best for her little girl.

Her friend gave a knowing look. "No need. I put you in the suite next to this one. Jarrett's in the room next to yours. You're a good mom, Lacey. She has real special needs, and you've been challenged, I know."

"Does it ever get easier?"

Aimee sighed. "No. But there is wine."

She winked and Lacey smiled.

The room Aimee had given her had a connecting door. Her luggage had already been carted into the room, but she didn't unpack. Instead, she headed for the mini bar. Aimee found two wineglasses and soon they were curled up on the sofa, talking about the events in St. Marc.

And then Aimee dropped a bombshell on her. "The real reason Jarrett wants you here is because I believe we're being evacuated out of here. And we're not returning until everything is over."

The wineglass shook visibly in her hand. Lacey set it down before she spilled the Chardonnay. "Jarrett told me he's leaving tonight."

"So is Kyle. He's been tight-lipped, but I can tell.

They're recalling him back to active duty. Tonight. And I don't think he'll be back unless it's to invade."

Sweat dampened her brow as she gripped her hands tightly together. "What makes you think so?"

"Last night I saw him prowling around the beach, making some sort of notations. When I questioned him, he claimed to be doing a trash check. But our cleaning crew rakes over the beach every morning."

"What do you think he was doing?"

Aimee sipped her wine before answering. "I believe he was assessing the shore for an invasion and the Navy wants him to take part. But before the doo doo hits the fan, we'll be out of here. Whether we like it or not. Kyle warned me to prepare to leave and turn management over to someone else."

Lacey stared at her friend. "And what if you don't want to go?"

"I doubt I'll have a choice." Aimee pushed back a stray lock of dark hair that had escaped the French braid. "I've been thinking about leaving, anyway. Dale's been gone two years now and it's time. Return to the States, get a job and go back to school, get my business degree. I guess this is a little sooner than I'd planned."

Maybe Aimee didn't have a choice, but she certainly wasn't leaving. "What if they force me to leave without Fleur? She's not a US citizen and her paperwork still hasn't come through."

Aimee gave her hand a reassuring pat. "Jarrett would never allow that to happen. He'd find a way, even if he had to smuggle Fleur on board one of those rubber raiding boats they use."

If only she had the kind of faith her friend possessed. But she was a senator's daughter and knew the politics of Washington.

After saying good-night and thanking Aimee, she retired to her room and unpacked, figuring she would settle in. The bed looked soft and inviting.

Just a few minutes.

When she next opened her eyes, the clock on the bedside table read 1 a.m. Lacey yawned and sat up. Realizing she had never spoken to Jarrett since arriving, she decided to knock on his door.

Her clothing rumpled, she raked a hand through her hair. She thought about changing, maybe applying some makeup and then laughed. Every time she'd been here before, she had never left her suite without looking perfectly groomed. But these were different circumstances.

Jarrett's door was slightly cracked open. She went inside. Maybe she could surprise him, climb into bed with him for a snuggle, and that would lead to something else. At least to feel his strong arms surround her, hear his deep voice quietly assure her that everything would be okay.

The soft golden glow of lamplight came from his suite. Lacey quietly walked inside and then ground to an abrupt halt.

Dressed entirely in black, Jarrett sat at the dining table, smearing black greasepaint on his face. A wicked straight knife hung on his belt, near his sidearm. He looked dangerous—the kind of quiet lethalness you would not want to encounter in the night.

Ace was next to him, dressed the same, his normally cheerful grin gone, his face darkened. Dread filled her. He looked up, his body tensing.

"You really are leaving and returning to the Navy. And you're not coming back." It hurt to say the words aloud.

"I'm sorry, Lace. I stopped by to see you, but you

were sleeping." He stood, stretching well over six feet and suddenly he seemed as remote as the moon. Inaccessible, an operator who moved in far different circles than she did.

She felt herself mentally shrink into a tiny ball, curled up tight much as Fleur had been sleeping on the bed. At the table, Ace watched her with a guarded look then nodded.

"Iceman, meet me in my room in ten."

Then Aimee's brother slipped out, leaving her alone with Jarrett.

Hugging herself, she stared at him. "So this is it. I'd kiss you goodbye, but I don't want to get greasepaint all over me."

The lighthearted tone masked her grief and the questions she didn't dare ask. *Will I ever see you again? Are they sending you someplace dangerous again? Will I hear about you from a phone call or on the news?*

Will I finally get the dead letter you always write before you deploy?

He crossed the room, seeming taller than ever, more bulky with muscle and much more serious. This was Jarrett, who had made her feel such exquisite passion, who had bonded with her, had seen inside her heart.

This was a stranger, but one with the power to break her heart.

"I'm scared," she whispered.

"Sweetheart." Reaching out, he cupped her cheek with his left, clean hand, thumbing her skin in a tender caress. "I don't want to leave you, but I must. Do everything Aimee tells you."

"They're going to send transport for us."

At his silence, she knew her instinct had been right.

"They're going to evacuate us from here and stage an invasion."

"You'll be safe," he said softly. "I promise, with all my heart."

I promise I'll always be there for you. Yet it had been a shattered vow. He dropped his hand.

"Don't make vows you can't keep, Lt. Adler."

"Lace…" He started to reach for her, but she stepped back.

"Goodbye, Jarrett."

She fled out the door, not bothering to look back.

Chapter 17

Inside the captain's stateroom on board the USS *Tornado* the next morning, Jarrett stared at his CO, his emotions swirling like the patrol boat's namesake. They had been debriefed, and his head spun. He had tried not to think of the hurt on Lacey's face when she'd left him, the way her body had pulled in tight, as if trying to draw herself into a tight shell.

Must focus on the job at hand.

The Zodiac had brought them to the patrol boat sitting offshore, where a full-scale US military operation stood by to be launched. He, Ace, Captain Luke Callahoun and Rear Admiral Kurt Walters sat at the conference table.

The USS *Tornado* was a compact patrol boat perfect for staging a coastal invasion. With its machine guns, automatic cannons and Stinger antiaircraft missiles, it was a deadly blip off the coast of St. Marc. Nine

SEALs from his team stood ready to detach and invade from the *Tornado.* Another SEAL team was on board the USS *Jack Smart.* And along with eight Army Spec Ops teams, there were marines and eight warships off shore conducting battle exercises near the harbor of the capital.

All that firepower and Lacey was still on the island. Damn it.

"The president has decided to not wait for Congressional approval of an invasion." Admiral Walters looked neutral as he relayed the news. "Despite the constant, ah, urgings of Ambassador Rossin, POTUS is convinced an invasion is the only way to restore democracy."

"Our goal is to protect US citizens who insist on staying on St. Marc, as well as keep order during the invasion as we kick General Montana's ass out and restore power to the newly elected president," Callahoun said.

Admiral Walters pointed to the strategic map displayed on the computer screen on the wall. "Operation Restore Freedom plans for simultaneous entry in several key areas around the island. We don't want to engage unless necessary. The USS *Jack Smart* will be the launching craft for spec ops forces, joined by the USS *Donald Fischer.* We have 20,000 troops standing ready to invade, and then when power is restored to President Salles, a peacekeeping force of 4,000 UN soldiers will take over."

"Has State urged all US citizens to leave St. Marc?" Jarrett tried to keep his restlessness in check. "Are our guys sending a transport?"

"No. POTUS is still hoping for a diplomatic solution, and Ambassador Rossin is working around the clock with State to convince Montana to stand down. Most US citizens have already departed on commercial aircraft."

Captain Callahoun leaned forward. "Senator Stewart has specifically requested the evac of his daughter and Ace's sister and her family. No military intervention. We don't want locals to know and alert the St. Marc Army, so the senator has made arrangements to charter a yacht to transport the civilians. They're to report to the marina at Paix Beach at 1300."

His CO kept his gaze centered on Jarrett. "Miss Stewart and her party will board the USNS *Comfort* and remain there until arrangements are made to transport them safely back to the States."

Jarrett's head spun. At least Lace would be evacuated, and the *Comfort* was a Navy hospital ship, not a combat vessel. But he worried about Fleur.

"What about Fleur? Lacey's adopted daughter?"

"She will be allowed to join her mother. Senator Stewart is working out the last-minute arrangements for her passport and entry papers," his CO told him.

Relief filled him. The diplomats at State could figure out the logistics. At least if Lacey had her daughter, she might be coaxed into leaving.

His CO looked at Ace. "You're still on medical leave, but you'll be providing our preinvasion teams with intel necessary for recon. You know the area better than anyone else."

Ace ground his jaw and stared stonily at their CO. "I'm good to go, sir."

"No, and that's an order, Chief Petty Officer." Callahoun softened his voice. "I need you at full capacity."

Ace gave a brief nod, but Jarrett sensed the defiance in his friend. He knew Ace's stubborn streak.

He only hoped his ex-wife's famous stubborn streak

would not surface when she was ordered to board the *Comfort*.

When the meeting was over, Jarrett pulled out his cell. He went on deck to call Lacey. Wind whipped his clothing, and the breeze was refreshing, but did not cool the sweat on his brow.

Lacey answered on the first ring.

"You're being evaced tomorrow," he told her.

"My father told me. We have to board the yacht at one o'clock. For a deep-sea fishing cruise." Her scornful sniff carried through the phone, loud and clear. "We're leaving while everyone else, all our friends, remain here. And what's going to happen to them, Jarrett? Will they get caught in the cross fire?"

"Get on that boat, Lace. That's all I can tell you." He softened his voice. "Fleur needs her mom. She needs you to be safe and alive."

"She'll be on the boat."

Worry needled him. "Promise me, Lacey. Promise me you'll be there with her."

Promise me you'll be in a safe place so I can do my job. Promise me we can see each other again and regain what we lost.

Promise you won't hate me for leaving you again…

A heavy sigh. "I promise."

Out of the corner of his eye he saw two of his SEAL teammates approach. Then a tiny whisper came over the phone, so faint he almost missed it for the wind and the chatter of his teammates mugging it up.

"I love you, Jarrett," she whispered. "Even if I never see you again, I know this much is true."

He gripped the phone tightly, his heart constricting. "Love you, too, beautiful."

Thumbing off the connection, he stood motionless

for a moment. His SEAL teammates, Cooper and Scott, jostled him.

"I loooo-ve you," Cooper sang out.

He grabbed Scott's arm and fluttered his eyelashes. "You're so boo-ti-ful, I could die."

Jarrett gave the ghost of a smile and told them to do something anatomically impossible. Then he studied Coop, relieved to see his buddy looking more relaxed, the shadows gone from his eyes. Last month they had lost Max, a Belgian Malinois dog who had been conducting recon on a mission. Coop had formed a deep attachment with Max, growing almost as close to the dog as his handler had. Max was killed flushing out a tango, and took a bullet that surely would have hit Coop.

"Hey, Coop. Good to see you again." Jarrett nodded at him.

"Same here, LT."

These guys were his buddies, his friends. His family.

Not Lacey. They were no longer together, and he wasn't sure if they ever would be again after this.

He stared at the coastline. Lights glowed sporadically along the shore, but mostly it was dark, for the electricity was still not working.

He could only hope and pray Lacey would board the yacht tomorrow that would start her journey safely home.

Because by tomorrow night, if they got the green light to go, he wasn't sure she could make it home at all.

Jarrett spent the next day prepping and going over the plans with his team. They would approach the shoreline at Paix Beach at 0200 and secure the hotel, for intel said the army was headed there in the morning to commandeer it as a command post.

He hoped to hell Lacey would meet that yacht.

And then late afternoon, adrenaline pumping, they got the news the invasion had been canceled, thanks to a last minute intervention. General Montana had resigned and left the country, but US forces would remain on the ground to ensure a peaceful takeover of power by the democratically elected president of St. Marc.

His team was itching for action, not to stand down, but Jarrett felt nothing but relief. He awaited further orders, while Ace made a call to his sister. He tried calling Lacey, but her cell went to voice mail.

Not a big deal. Cell service on the yacht must be sketchy. Once on board the *Comfort*, he could reach her.

Then at 1700, Ace got a call from a frantic Aimee. She and the twins and Fleur were safe on board the *Comfort*. But Lacey had not been with them.

Jarrett took the phone from Ace. "Aimee? What the hell happened?"

He tried to keep cool, keep his voice calm. Panic wouldn't help.

Ace's sister sounded close to tears. "I'm so sorry, Jarrett. I tried to get her to go with us, but she insisted she had to return to her home because Rose had called in a panic and said she needed money. Price gouging is happening all over St. Marc and without that money, the women at Marlee's Mangoes will go hungry. Lace said she would take my bow rider from the marina and catch up with us. We waited and waited and delayed the trip to the *Comfort*, but she never showed up. I called her cell and it goes to voice mail. I don't know where she is!"

Aimee burst into tears and began to sob.

His heart pounded a crazy beat, but he forced his mind to focus. "Did she go alone back to the compound?

Aimee? I need you to tell me everything. Think! Who is there with you?"

Finally, she gulped audibly. "Sam and Fleur. Lacey wouldn't let anyone go with her, but Gene tailed her back to the compound. I tried calling him but no answer on his phone, either."

Relief filled him. The man was good. "Put Sam on the line. Now."

Sam spoke quietly, his tone grim. "Sir. I'm sorry, I wanted to go with Gene, but I felt responsible for getting Aimee and her children and Fleur to the *Comfort*. I'm headed back to the compound now for Gene."

"No. Stay there with Aimee and the girls. I need you there. I'll send word soon as I can."

He hung up, feeling the cold sweat trickle down his backside. Ace narrowed his eyes. "Son of a bitch. Someone has them both."

"Maybe. I'm headed back."

"Word is we're shipping back to the States, Ice." His friend's gaze remained steady. "You gonna go AWOL, I suggest you do it now. I'm with you."

"No. She's my responsibility."

He headed toward the bridge, but before he got there, he ran into Callahoun. His CO rubbed his jaw and looked weary.

"I just got off the phone with Senator Stewart. He's tried to call his daughter and there's no answer. He puts the blame on you and he's making waves in DC."

Jarrett clenched his teeth. "It is my fault, sir, for not overseeing her evac."

"You were under orders to report for duty. I'm giving you a direct order now, Ice." The captain's gaze flicked to Ace, who had followed. "Return to Miss Stewart's house. Find her and bring her to the *Comfort*. This is a black op, off the books. Understand? I have no clearance on this mission."

He nodded, his chest tight. If anything happened to them, they would receive no help. No official records.

"I understand, sir. I'm on my own."

Callahoun smiled grimly. "No, you're not. The entire squad is going with you."

An hour later the sleek black combat boat dropped off Jarrett, Cooper and Ace a few miles from Lacey's compound. They found a vehicle near the road and Ace hot-wired it.

When they arrived at the compound, it was deserted. No security. No trace of the women, or Rose. Lacey's house had been wrecked, looking much like Paul Lawrence's had. Inside the mango factory, everything had been smashed. It looked like looters had caused the destruction.

He knew it was not.

Jarrett heard a low moan come from the storage room and raced toward it. He opened the deep freezers. In the first one lay a woman. Rose, her eyes wide open in an expression of fear and pain. Jarrett felt her pulse.

"She's gone."

Damn it. In the second one, a man lay there, curled on his side. Blood streamed from his head.

Gene. Badly hurt, but still alive.

They gently lifted him out, mindful of the head wound, and laid him on the floor. Ace began triage as Coop opened his bag and removed the emergency medical supplies they'd brought.

Gene opened his eyes and gasped. "Easy," Jarrett said soothingly. "What happened?"

"Followed Lacey...here. Eavesdropped outside...it

was a trap. Bastards used Rose...as bait. They killed Rose and took Lacey..." He coughed.

"His left lung's punctured, Ice." Ace began treating him. "Miracle he's still alive."

But was Lacey? "Talk fast, Gene. Where did they take her? Who?"

"Two men. White. Late 30s. Yacht... The *Crimson Jewel*. Headed to Panama. Lacey's with them. I tried... tried saving her, but they shot me." He smiled weakly, his skin pale. "Takes more than a bullet to keep me down."

"Good man."

Taking out his cell, Jarrett called his CO. He needed help. It was time to call the support of his team behind him.

He only prayed they wouldn't be too late to save her.

Chapter 18

Her head hurt and her throat was dry. Lacey struggled to open her gluey eyelids and remember what happened. And then everything rushed back.

She had arrived back at the compound, and Rose had looked at her, apologizing.

"I had no choice, Miss Lacey. They were going to kill my folks."

And then pain exploded in her head, leaving only darkness.

The gentle sway of the ground beneath her warned she was no longer on land. Lacey raised her hands and realized they were secured with zip ties. Her head felt like a watermelon. Beneath her was a teakwood floor. Lacey heard a motor churning and voices. With caution, she raised her head.

She lay in a lounge with a long sectional sofa. Lamps glowed on tables next to the sofas. Large glass windows were covered with white shades. A set of stairs was off to her right.

Two men sat at a nearby table, assault rifles hanging from their shoulders. They were playing cards. One wore a dark business suit with a red checked tie and had a visible scar on his chin. He fit the description of the man who'd hung around outside Fleur's school, asking about her.

Judging from the hum of the engines and the slap of water, she was on an oceanbound yacht.

She watched the men, engrossed in their game. After trying to move her feet, and realizing they were bound by zip ties, she tested the plastic ties around her wrists. Lacey lay still and tried to stay calm.

The men were arguing in Spanish about killing her and dumping her body into the ocean. They said the timing had to be right, but *El Jefe*, their boss, wanted it to be perfect.

Terror clogged her throat, but she tried to keep her wits about her. Trussed like a chicken, her arms and legs bound with zip ties. She had a little secret these thugs didn't know.

Jarrett had taught her how to escape zip ties. He'd done it for "fun" one day after she'd bet him she could tie him up and incapacitate him.

Footsteps sounded on the stairs. She looked up and her heart sank.

Mr. Augustin.

The man went to the thugs playing cards. "You fools. She's awake. Stop talking. Don't you realize this woman can hear everything?"

The dark-haired man laughed. "It doesn't matter. *El Jefe* says she will sleep soon in the ocean."

More footsteps on the stairs. Lacey closed her eyes, trying to keep her body from shaking.

And then she heard Augustin say in a quiet voice, "Yes, *El Jefe*."

She opened her eyes to see the arms dealer give the newcomer a respectful nod before he ran up the stairs again.

Lacey stared helplessly as her captor sat on the sofa with a smug smile.

"Hello, Lacey. I suppose this means I'm no longer officially in your employment."

Her captor laughed. Collette. The manager of Marlee's Mangoes.

The woman who was going to kill her.

She's alive. She has to be alive.

On board the *Tornado*, radar had picked up a blip about ten miles out from the southeast coast of St. Marc. It had to be the yacht Gene had mentioned. The yacht was now stationary.

Now he and his team of four other SEALs were going follow the blip and board the yacht.

Gene was on board the *Comfort* in surgery. It wasn't known if the man would make it. He had a collapsed lung, where the bullet had pierced it, and internal injuries. But the guy was tough and chances were good.

A half-moon hung in the sky like a lemon wedge, scattered clouds blocking the light. He'd prefer complete darkness, but no choice. With gloved hands, he clutched his HK MP5SD as the Zodiac sped toward the yacht.

Wind whipped at his face as he kept his eyes on the target. He pulled his AN/PVS-7 device and put it on his head, and then flipped on the NVD goggles, turning everything putrid green. Now he could clearly see the outline of the sleek yacht, bobbing in the choppy waters.

She had to still be alive. Had to be.

Focus. Do your job.

On his left, Ace used the GPS and studied the dial. He rapped Jarrett's hand, gave the thumbs-up. Jarrett nodded.

Let's do this.

Jarrett took a deep breath, trying to ease the worry from his mind. Always in the past, he'd pushed aside the fear, replacing it with focus and drive. But now fear had crept along the edges of his mind like little gray blobs, because this was Lace.

His woman.

His love.

All those years without her had proved one thing. He didn't want to give her up, not to divorce and now, not to death.

"We'll get her, Iceman," Coop promised. "We'll find her and bring her home. No worries."

He centered his breathing and mentally went over a checklist for all his equipment. The worry became a grinding little thing in his mind, but he pushed it aside. *I'll worry later.*

She has to be alive.

Lacey knew she was going to die. She saw it in Collette's eyes amid the same smugness always present with her former manager. Once she had interpreted the smugness as confidence Collette could teach other women.

Now she saw it for its true nature—an arrogance and sociopathic indifference to all other concerns but Collette's own.

Her manager sat on the sofa with a smug smile. "You nearly cost me a large sum, Lacey Stewart. But soon, all that will be resolved."

She managed to speak through her cracked, dry lips. "Why are you doing this? Money? Don't I pay you enough?"

The woman laughed. "You might say. Your puny salary could never buy everything I have earned on my own. You know me as Collette. My associates refer to me by my real name—Corine. Or C.A. Batista, matriarch of the Mendoza drug cartel in Guatemala."

Lacey's stomach churned. What the hell had she done? And why was this woman intent on killing her?

"You were the one who tried to kill my daughter?"

Her throat was parched and her lips cracked. It was hard to speak. Harder still to keep the terror at bay and keep from panicking.

"I wanted you out of the country. It almost worked." Collette scoffed. "And then everything seemed to fall into place, except that fool Montana resigned and left the country. Had he remained, and you had left for the States, I would have assumed control of your charity. That's no longer an option.'

"Why do you want my charity?" *Keep her talking, stall for time. Get answers, be aware of your surroundings.* It was what Jarrett would have done.

"I don't care about your stupid charity. I care about your land. I had a very sweet deal worked out with the former owner. I paid him a healthy amount each month for using his land. He asked no questions and never came onto the property. But he died and before I could purchase it outright, his son sold it to you. The do-gooder from America who wished to form a charity."

"Were you the one who killed Caroline?" Lacey demanded.

Collette's gaze flicked away. "Paul warned me to be subtle. But his foolish, feeble attempts to scare you away weren't working. The dead chickens, the painted threats done by that imbecile you hired as a gardener. The dead body on the mango tree seemed a perfect way to cast suspicion on you and make you leave. And still, you remained. Paul was a fool. He grew too fond of my product, and I had to do something."

Her father's friend, her business partner, was in on this, as well. Was there anyone surrounding her she could have trusted?

Jarrett. She prayed he knew she was missing.

"What did you do with Rose?"

"You don't have to worry about her any longer. She was terrified I would follow through on my threat to execute her parents. Rose was quite an asset in helping me smuggle Caroline Beaufort's body onto the compound and hanging it from the tree and giving access to my men when they started the fire. All of that should have chased you away. But it didn't."

Poor Rose. The housekeeper had betrayed her, as well, but she paid with her life.

"With you missing, I will take charge and no one will question my authority." Collette smiled. "I will convince your father that you would want Marlee's Mangoes to continue. It will be your legacy. The houses you wished to be built on the land will never be built. It is impossible. That land where you wanted to build houses hides my lab and the cocaine I hid there for the past four years."

The woman was insane. She could see it now, in her eyes, and the light she'd mistaken for zeal. It was power

Collette craved. In an odd way, she found herself respecting Collette. To work for nearly a year in a low-level management position for a charity, all to conceal her true objective, took enormous cunning and patience.

Then she looked right at Collette and felt a slow-burning rage.

The woman headed one of the largest drug cartels outside Colombia. And all this time she had hidden cocaine right underneath Lacey's nose.

Collette wasn't patient or clever. She was greedy and power-hungry. Maybe it gave her a thrill to pretend to be managing the mango operation while she plotted on how to take down Lacey's charity and ruin everything. Collette didn't care about the women's lives, her own country. She only cared about herself and her drug empire.

"You present a little problem. If we kill you and dump you into the ocean for the sharks, with the ocean currents you might never be found, and I need your father to claim your body so you can officially be declared dead. But we can't keep you here for long. I have a business to run."

A cruel smile touched her mouth. "I need a way for them to find you…after you're dead. Bow rider won't fully sink. They'll find the wreckage with your body."

She beckoned to one of the men. Shouldering his assault weapon, he came over. Collette took a pistol from the holster attached to his waist.

Jarrett had a pistol like that, she thought in rising terror.

"Bring her outside. I don't want to stain the floor."

The man picked up Lacey and flung her none too gently over one shoulder. He climbed down to a bow rider boat bobbing in the ocean.

The boat was taking on water, fast. The man dumped her onto the starboard aft bench as Collette followed.

She recognized the elegant keychain dangling from the starter with the initials PL.

She wasn't alone. In the faint glow of the yacht's running lights she saw a man sitting near the helm. Dressed in a pair of dark knit slacks and a white shirt, he stared sightlessly at the sky, a round hole neatly piercing his skull. The dead man was her business partner. Paul.

From the yacht's deck, Collette laughed.

"Paul was so worried about you," Collette called out. "He wanted out and was no longer an asset and begged me to spare you. Now when they find your body and the note we left at your house, they'll blame him. The both of you went on a little night ride and it was a murder-suicide."

As Collette raised the pistol, Lacey jerked her body around, praying the woman would miss her heart. The gun fired. Pain exploded like a firecracker. She slumped downward, knowing if Collette saw she'd failed to hit vital organs she'd finish the job.

Playing dead in the darkness offered her only chance. If Collette thought she was dead, the woman might leave, buying her time to make her escape. Lacey did not move, trying to keep her breathing as quiet as possible. The white-hot burning in her body and fear made her want to scream, but she did not move.

You've got a chance. You can make it.

"Stupid spoiled American girl. Why couldn't you have stayed in your own damn country?"

Through the red fog of pain burning in her shoulder, she watched her former business manager climb the ladder back onto the yacht. And then the yacht sped off, the giant wake crashing into the bow rider.

Blood streamed down her arm and over her chest. She couldn't focus. Lacey labored to breathe.

And then she envisioned Jarrett's stern face, his scowl, as he yelled at her. "Don't give up. I'm a SEAL. I never give up the fight."

You can do this, she heard his deep voice in her head. *Save yourself.*

With every last ounce of strength, she raised her hands above her head and slammed them downward. Pain exploded in her chest like a hammer. Lacey screamed, but the zip ties broke. She hobbled to the helm. The engine did not start. She fiddled with the radio, before realizing the housing was destroyed.

Hopping to the bow, she tossed off the seat cushions from the benches, and lifted the lid of the hidden storage compartment. She'd been on this boat before. Paul was anal as hell about his boat and always made sure the life vests were stored here, along the EPIRB, the Emergency Position Indicating Radio Beacon.

Collette had planned this too well, but perhaps in her enormous arrogance, the woman forgot. And she didn't know Paul and his anal-retentive streak.

A sob rose in her throat.

No life vests. The EPIRB was dead. She found Paul's rusty fishing knife and sawed at the zip ties on her ankles. After freeing her legs, she kept searching through the compartment. Her fingers scraped over something silky. She pulled it out and found three flags. The flag of St. Marc, a US flag and a pirate flag. No first aid kit. Only a small fishing cooler, empty and stinking of bait fish.

But hidden by all of them, tucked into the corner... She nearly wept. A flare gun. Lacey picked it up and checked the chamber. Empty.

But she knew something Collette did not. Lacey wrapped her wounded shoulder with the US flag and cinched it tight to slow the bleeding. She went aft, passing Paul's body, trying to keep her mind clear, her breathing centered. Jarrett had been in worse scrapes. He wouldn't fall to pieces like a wussy girl and break down.

Paul had this bow rider specially designed. There was additional storage under the starboard cushion. Lacey tore off the cushion and lifted the lid.

"Thank you, thank you," she whispered.

Nestled among two towels and a colorful bathing suit was a small box. She opened it and saw two flare cartridges. Water had already poured into the aft section, and the boat listed starboard. The towels were soaked. Water had seeped into the plastic packaging. It might not fire.

With trembling fingers, she ripped open the package. But the first cartridge was damp. It would not fire.

She examined the second cartridge. Damp as well, but maybe…she loaded the gun, aware of the salt water sloshing around her ankles and the waves pounding against the hull. Mixed in with the smell of seawater was the pungent stench of gasoline. They were going down fast.

She aimed the gun skyward and dressed the trigger. The gun did not fire.

Her shoulders sagged. What was the use? She was going to die out here, on Paul's boat. No one knew she was here. Rose had told Jarrett that she took the SUV and left for Ace's house to see Fleur. By the time he discovered the deception, she'd be dead.

Never give up.

One more cartridge remained. It was also damp, perhaps not as much as the first two. Water sloshed around her ankles now. Lacey loaded the gun and pointed it upward. Oh, please...

She pulled the trigger and the gun fired. The recoil startled her and she fell backward, onto her ass. But the pain didn't matter as she watched the flare sail upward, cutting a red trail through the night, like a star leading home.

It soared ten feet and then fell to the sea.

Not high enough. Who could see it at that height? She refused to let her mind sink into despondency. There were boaters around. Maybe one had spotted it.

Collapsing back against the seat, in the sinking boat she prayed someone would see it and render aid.

Maybe she could bail out. She searched around for a bucket, anything to bail out the boat. Hope faded as she found a fist-sized hole in the aft section.

No use bailing out. The bow rider was going down, and she was going with it. Lacey grabbed a seat cushion and clung to it as the water lapped at her ankles.

She looked up at the sky, at the waxing sliver of a moon gleaming down upon the sea. Salt water trickled down her cheeks. Jarrett was out there, somewhere, maybe worried about her or wondering why she'd abandoned everything.

Her shirt was soaked with blood and she was losing consciousness. Lacey forced herself to keep awake as the boat continued to slip deeper into the water. Surely someone would find her.

She began to shiver violently.

And then a wave rolled toward her, and she fought it, but her arms were too tired. She let go of the cushion. It floated away, bobbing in the water.

No, please...

She swallowed a mouthful of water and coughed. She simply could not hold on any longer.

I'm so sorry, Fleur. I'm sorry, Jarrett. I'm sorry I didn't give us the chance to become a couple again, a family.

Dimly she heard something in the distance. It seemed a long way off. The last thought she had as the grayness pushed at the edges of her vision and her lungs screamed for air was a wistful hope that Jarrett had come for her after all.

Chapter 19

The SEALs had pinpointed the position of the suspect yacht headed south. In the Zodiac, Coop, Deke and Ace crouched down alongside Jarrett, all wearing their wet suits and combat gear. They were armed and prepared to board soon as they caught up.

Ace shouted to him above the sound of the waves. "We're losing them."

But Jarrett's instincts tingled. Yeah, they'd lose the yacht, but he suspected Lacey wasn't on it.

Dark as ink out on the ocean. His NVGs were first-rate but he spotted nothing with them. They headed south, following the yacht.

Instincts fully charged now, he removed his NVGs to improve his peripheral vision. He scanned the horizon. And then he saw a red flare burst into the air about ten feet, then nosetail straight into the water.

Lacey.

"Follow that flare," Jarrett ordered.

"Ice, we'll lose the yacht," Coop protested.

"Do it. Crank it up."

Coop turned the Zodiac around. Brine splashed in his face, but he barely felt it, for the chill in his bones was making him numb.

They reached the spot where the flare was fired. Jarrett's blood turned to ice as they came upon a bow rider flipped upside down.

There was a body floating in the ocean. Deke shone a light on the body.

Long blond hair.

No. No.

Jarrett tossed down his weapon, jumped into the water and swam toward her. He lifted her head up and towed her toward the Zodiac.

As the other SEALs lifted her on board, they began emergency resuscitation. He climbed onboard, his heart racing, his mind frantic. Blood streamed from a wound under the American flag she'd wrapped around her shoulder.

She was dead.

Calm down. You can save her.

Jarrett took over the mouth-to-mouth from Coop, leaving Ace for the chest compressions. The glowsticks Deke held showed Lacey's skin bluish and pale. No breaths.

She had given up. His Lacey, the one who had always fought, who'd nagged and pestered him to keep pushing on, to reach past the superficial and grab the brass ring because she believed in him.

She had given up. And it killed him to see her hopeless, lost and empty.

"No." He grabbed her shoulders, feeling the fragile bones and soft skin. Pale. She was so damn pale. "I won't let you do this, Lace. You're not giving up. God-damn it, I'm not giving up."

He bent over and continued giving her mouth-to-mouth as Ace resumed chest compressions. *Calm, stay calm. Must focus. C'mon, Lace, breathe, damn it, breathe. You have so much to live for. Fleur. Your dad, the charity you worked so hard to build up and all those women you taught to fight back.*

Me.

Please, Lace.

Jarrett breathed into her mouth. Then he sat back. And heard the sweetest sound on earth.

Lacey, coughing and gasping. Alive.

"Whoa, there she goes. Thank you, sweet Jesus," Ace said, sliding off her.

Gently, Jarrett turned her over onto her side as she began to vomit up seawater. He rubbed her back, his lungs expanding with air as he breathed out a huge sigh.

Never again. He didn't care what he had to do.

He was never giving her up. Ever.

I should be dead. But I hurt too much.

Slowly, she opened her eyes. Lacey's head ached and her legs burned, and she felt a deep throbbing in her ankles and hands.

She smelled metal, disinfectant and the slight tang of Jarrett's spicy cologne on her pillow. Carefully she moved her head to the right. She was lying upon a cot or bed of some sort, in a dorm-style room filled with empty hospital beds. Lacey looked down. She wore a hospital gown, partly pulled over her shoulder and chest, which sported a large white bandage.

A tube snaked out of her right hand, and a cuff was

on her left arm. Blood pressure cuff, she realized as she struggled to sit up. Ow. Her body felt as if someone had jackhammered it with a concrete chipper.

A man sat on a stool near her bed, thumbing through a book. He glanced up and dropped the book. Dressed in black cammies and a black T-shirt, he had close-cropped dark hair and a well-toned, athletic look.

"Thank God. You're awake." The sailor smiled at her and glanced at the tube snaking out of her left wrist. "I'm Chief Petty Officer Scott Weaver, from Team 15, US Navy SEALs, better known as Deke. I'm the corpsman who did triage on you."

He beckoned to a woman in blue scrubs, and she came scurrying over.

Lacey tried to gather her bearings as the woman checked the machine by her bedside.

"I'm Lieutenant junior grade Nancy Jones, a Navy nurse. You're on the Navy hospital ship USNS *Comfort*."

Nurse Jones made a notation on the laptop she carried. "You've been unconscious for a full day, Ms. Stewart. It was touch and go to see if you would make it through surgery because you lost a lot of blood, but you had plenty of volunteers willing to donate for a transfusion."

"An entire team of them," Scott interjected. "It's part beer, part piss and vinegar."

Nurse Jones rolled her eyes. "SEALs," she murmured.

"Water," she whispered, her mouth dry and her lips cracked.

Scott brought over a sippy cup and helped her to drink. The water was warm, but she'd never tasted better.

Her body felt as if someone had hammered it with

iron, but her head wasn't as muzzy. Still, sitting up had drained her. She lay back.

"How did I get here?" she asked.

"The *Comfort* has been conducting disaster relief exercises in the Caribbean," Scott told her. "It was faster than medevacing you to Miami. We heloed you over. You were in bad shape, Lacey. Almost as bad as Gene."

"Gene? What happened to him?"

"Ice said he tailed you to the compound and Collette's guys shot him when he tried to rescue you after they knocked you out cold. He was here for a while, but they medevaced him to Miami. He's going to be fine. Ice is arranging for all his medical care to be put on his tab."

"Jarrett," she said. "Is he here?"

Does he care? Or did he think that I ran off and left him?

She closed her eyes again to hide the tears brimming in them, and then heard Scott's voice echoing over an intercom system. "Lt. Jarrett Adler, report to sick bay. Your patient is awake. Hoo-yah!"

Lacey opened her eyes again, blinking fast. Scott returned. "That'll get his attention."

"He has more important things to do."

Nurse Jones frowned. "Lt. Adler is the SEAL who rescued you." She looked up. "Your father is here."

Senator Stewart, flanked by a tall, gray-haired man in navy cammies with a commander's insignia, and a suit with an earpiece, came to her bedside. Her dad, pulled away from DC. She felt confused and ashamed for interrupting his work.

"Ten minutes," Nurse Jones warned.

"Lacey, oh, thank God you're okay." Her dad reached for her hand.

"Dad," she whispered, reaching out. "I'm sorry."

He squeezed her hand. "Sorry for what, honey? I'm so happy you're awake. You're going to be just fine."

"I screwed up." She blinked hard, trying not to cry. "Fleur? Is she okay? Where is she?"

"She's here. Officially. She has her papers."

"I can take her to the States?" Now the tears did run unchecked down her cheeks.

Her father's brow furrowed as he reached for a tissue on the bedside table and handed it to her. "Don't cry, honey. I know you wanted this to happen sooner..."

She wiped her face and blew her nose. Dad. She loved him, but at times, he was clueless. "No, it's okay. She's safe now. She's safe."

That was what mattered most. Her little girl was going to finally live the life Lacey wanted for her, and get the help she needed, and not have to worry about the *bad men*.

He kissed her cheek. "I have to go now and meet Alastair Monroe." He flashed one of his famous smiles. "He wanted a personal tour of the *Comfort*, along with Francis. Alastair will make an excellent ambassador. He's quite the politician, steamrolling over everyone, shaking hands and making friends. He wants Francis to work with him in diplomatic relations. Francis has charm, but that boy is like a locomotive running over the ladies. *Choo choo*."

Something keep nagging her, tickling the back of her mind like a feather. But she couldn't remember what.

"Are you going to be okay there, Dad?"

"Of course. The island is safe and protests have died down because of the UN patrols they sent in. You rest."

He turned and left, and her mind clicked over everything, but the pain drugs pumping into her arm made it difficult to concentrate.

"Hey, Iceman! She's awake," Scott said.

And then Jarrett was by her bedside, his green gaze filled with relief and tenderness. He wore the same Navy T-shirt as Scott, and Navy cammies. He crouched down by her bedside. "Lace."

He kissed her cheek, and warmth filled her. She reached up and traced the stubble shadowing his hard jaw. She had never seen anything better than his handsome face, the smudges of exhaustion around his eyes. "I love you. I love you so much," she told him.

He blinked and his gaze grew guarded. Jarrett stepped back and gestured and she saw four other men dressed in blue T-shirts and camouflage pants. She blushed as she realized what she'd said in front of them. Obviously they were his teammates and she'd gone all gushy. Not appropriate.

Especially since she was no longer his wife, no longer had any claim on him.

As they gathered around the bed, she became awed at the impressive display of muscles, strength and quiet determination.

"Lace, these are the guys who helped rescue you. Team 15. You already met Deke. This is Snake, Dino, Spuds and Coop."

She felt half-naked and exposed, but pushed past that to focus on their faces. They had saved her life. "Thank you. If not for all of you, I'd be flotsam in the Atlantic by now."

"Ma'am. Glad you're doing good." This from Coop, a tall SEAL with piercing blue eyes, close-cropped black hair and a scar slicing through his lower jaw.

"Coop donated a pint of his blood," Scott told her.

"Yeah, but Iceman saved you with mouth-to-mouth," Coop interjected.

"He wouldn't let Ace do the mouth-to-mouth, only the chest compressions," Spuds told her.

She glanced at Jarrett, whose jaw tensed so hard it seemed ready to crack.

"We all wanted to donate blood, but only Coop was a match," Deke said.

She offered a half smile, suddenly weary. "What about Rose?"

"She's dead," Jarrett said gently. "Your father is arranging for the burial, and to take care of her elderly parents. I'm sorry, Lace."

He pulled up a stool and stroked her fingers as the men said goodbye and left. "You picked a fine piece of property to start a charity, Miss Lacey. The CIA has been after Collette for a long time. They found steps leading to a tunnel and an underground bunker hidden in a cave. Wall supports, a generator and a sump pump to pump out water. The tunnel runs for forty feet before accessing the cave. There's a huge cache of cocaine, street value of over $300 mil, weapons and a lab."

He kissed her fingers. "You don't do anything by half measure. Rest here. I'll be right back. Someone is dying to see you."

Lacey closed her eyes and heard a soft voice called out in French, "Mama."

Fleur. Fighting fatigue and the morphine, she opened her eyes and struggled to sit. Wearing bright pink shorts and a flowered shirt, her daughter came into the ICU, riding piggyback on Jarrett. He sported a huge grin, and Fleur looked relieved but solemn as he set her down.

"Sweetheart. I'm fine." She hastened to assure her

daughter she was going to be okay. "I'm here now and I'm going to get better."

"Let her rest, Fleur." Jarrett tried to tug her away, but Fleur laced her little fingers around the railings of Lacey's hospital bed and refused to let go.

"She'll be okay here. Please, let her stay," Lacey told Jarrett.

He considered then dragged over a big recliner and plopped Fleur in it. He fished out a cell phone and tucked it into her shorts pocket. "You stay right here with your mom. If you need me, press the number 1 on the phone. I have business to do, but I'll check on you in a couple of hours. I have to meet with your grandpa and a few others."

Lacey smiled as he kissed her goodbye. "I thought I was your number one," she told him.

He winked. "You were, until this flower came along."

Jarrett tickled Fleur's ribs, making her laugh, and then he left.

The ICU was fairly deserted. She was the only patient. Gradually she dozed off.

Her nurse brought in a tray of soup and a sandwich. She tasted it. Ice cold. A few minutes later the nurse brought it back steaming hot. Too hot now. Lacey lacked any appetite. Pushing it aside, she decided to save it for Fleur.

As Fleur closed her eyes, Lacey did, as well.

A few minutes later she heard a noise and her instincts tingled. Lacey opened her eyes. Clad in a dark suit, with a bright red tie and a starched white shirt, Francis stood near her bed. But his clothing wasn't what startled her nor his presence.

In his hands he held a pistol, pointed directly at her

daughter. Trembling, she opened her mouth to scream as she fumbled for the nurse call button.

"Don't, Lacey. Or I will shoot her." Pale-faced, Francis looked crazed, his eyes wild.

Fleur's eyes opened. She stared at Francis, terror etching her face. *"Chou Chou,"* she whispered.

The knowledge hit Lacey like a slap in the face. *Chou Chou.* The one man Fleur feared more than any other.

"Oh, dear God," Lacey whispered. "It was you. You're Fleur's father. You killed Jackie."

The gun trembled in his hands. "She wouldn't shut up. Just wouldn't shut up, just like Caroline. Wanted to marry me. The bitch was trying to blackmail me into giving her money."

"It's called child support," she rasped. "Francis, why did you kill her?"

Lacey reached for her daughter's hand and pulled Fleur close. Pretending to hug her, she fished into the pocket of her shorts and then flipped on the phone and pressed the number one, leaving the connection open, praying Jarrett could hear.

Francis laughed, a high-pitched, maniacal sound. "Caroline, Jackie. All the same. Bitches. Like my mother, who left my father to screw another man. They think they can trap you with sex. Caroline was pregnant. She threatened to expose me, tell my dad. He can't risk that kind of scandal. I had to do it, Lacey. I had to do it. And then I told Paul, and Paul promised he'd clean up the mess. He offered to hide the body. He was always helping me. He always scored for me, got me the best stuff. He knew people who had kilos of it."

Francis's trust fund went straight to his nose. She'd always thought his boundless energy came from high spirits. Now she knew better.

He kept talking, babbling about Caroline and how he did love her, but she was so demanding; they were all demanding.

"I tried to get rid of her, Lacey. That little bastard of Jackie's." His wild gaze whipped over to Fleur, who had crept out of the lounge chair and stood by her bedside. "We could have had a go at it if not for her. She saw me. She knew. I hired two men Paul recommended. But that bastard Navy Boy of yours dodged the bullets."

Fleur whimpered. Lacey inched closer to the bedside table and the steaming hot soup. Closer.

Francis raised the pistol. "I'm sorry, Lacey. She has to die. Don't you understand? My dad can't afford a scandal."

Now!

Picking up the mug of hot soup, Lacey threw it in his face. "Run, Fleur," she yelled.

Francis screamed, clawing at his face as Fleur raced away. Lacey rolled out of bed and hit the floor, trying to crawl away. She felt a brief pain as the IV popped free of her hand and tried to get up, but she was too weak.

Horrified, she saw Francis swing the gun toward her daughter, running to escape the ICU.

"You little bitch!" Francis screamed. "I'll kill you."

And then she looked up and saw two size twelve combat boots and heard the lethal pop of a Sig Sauer firing.

Francis collapsed onto the linoleum floor before her eyes, his face frozen in a mask of shock.

"No one messes with my woman, Tennis Boy. Or my little girl," Jarrett said in a deep voice. "No one."

He went to Francis, checked his neck and then raced over to Lacey.

Others now ran into the ICU, but she only had eyes for Jarrett.

"Fleur?" she whispered.

"She's fine. She runs pretty damn fast. Zigs and zags, making her a harder target." Jarrett brushed back her hair. "Her mom taught her well."

His gaze narrowed and he swore quietly as he took in her bleeding hand where the IV had pulled free. He lifted her into his arms and carried her to another bed and set her down.

"Damn woman, I leave you alone for a few minutes and look what happens," he said in a mock sigh. "What am I going to have to do to keep you out of trouble?"

Smiling, she touched his face. "Marry me."

Epilogue

The wedding promised to be the social event of the season. Nearly 800 people had been invited, many of them politicians and Navy brass. No press, but the media would get the official wedding photos of the bride and groom. The president had been invited, and had to decline but hinted he "might" swing by the reception to wish them luck and share a glass of Dom Perignon.

A far cry from their first wedding, when she and Jarrett had eloped to Las Vegas.

The scandal and shock of Francis's death had rippled through DC like a tidal wave. Alastair Monroe had gone to Paris after the funeral, retreating from public life. Her father had been the most stunned of all.

But Alexander Stewart was enormously grateful for Jarrett, his future son-in-law.

It's going to be okay. The chant reverberated through her mind as she checked her appearance in the mirror at the bride's room in back of the cathedral. Fleur, bedecked in a sleeveless white long gown, a replica of her mom's, a circlet of red roses in her hair, practically bounced up and down with excitement.

It was Fleur who insisted on expediting the wedding. She'd already started calling Jarrett "Daddy" from the day of Lacey's hospital release. Jarrett pulled out the half-carat diamond ring, got down on one knee and proposed. Not to Lacey, but to Fleur, asking permission to "marry your mom."

Fleur said yes immediately, nearly as quickly as Lacey had.

Being a senator's daughter pulled strings and they hired the best wedding planner to stage this elaborate event in only four months. Lacey had hoped for a quiet, small wedding, but her parents insisted on this. Dad had "wanted to show off my new son-in-law."

He'd never been more proud of Jarrett. Her father was a silent partner in Jarrett's new business. Jarrett had completed his last spec ops mission. In six months he would resign and enter civilian life as he fully assumed charge of Project Security Operations Specialties, Project SOS for short. The agency offered protection to corporate executives and civilians, and taught self-defense techniques and gun training. Sam and Gene were already officially employed, and Jarrett planned to bring on additional hires, like Ace, who intended to retire at the end of the year.

She had appointed another board of directors of Marlee's Mangoes in St. Marc and a new president. Her new charity, Hope for Marlee, was based in the United States. The NGO aided battered women in distress and helped to find them new hope and new lives.

Lacey smoothed down the lace on her dress, checked her veil. Her bouquet of red roses and baby's breath had white lilies, as well. The formal ceremony had her tied in knots, but Jarrett had been beside her all the time. Every time she fretted and expressed the desire to run away to Vegas, he'd flash her a wide smile and then pull her into his arms, murmuring, "It's going to be all right."

Those words were usually followed by a wink, and then Jarrett pulling her into the nearest private room for a bout of quick sex that erased all her fears and made her forget about the wedding. Last week when she'd nearly gone into tears after hearing her dress might not be ready in time, she had been at her parents house in DC having lunch with the entire wedding party. Jarrett mouthed across the table, "It's going to be all right," and then winked. He had quietly excused himself, dragged Lacey into the big upstairs bathroom and locked the door. They had returned twenty minutes later, Jarrett all smooth professionalism, but his hair slightly rumpled. Lacey couldn't help the dreamy smile on her face.

Trying to summon the same smile now, she took a deep breath and stepped into the vestibule with her dad.

As the bridesmaids in their red satin floor-length gowns proceeded down the aisle, and Fleur tossed the red rose petals down the white carpet, Lacey stared at the altar.

Six Navy SEALs stood next to Jarrett in full white dress uniforms. "Our ice cream suits," Jarrett had joked. The same squad that had rescued her from the sinking bow runner now stood ready to witness their leader remarry her. Rows of "fruit salad," the medals they had earned, marched across their uniforms. Above the medals was pinned the Budweiser, the gold Navy SEAL trident.

Her bridesmaids, all cousins and friends, had nearly swooned when they found out they would be escorted by Navy SEALs.

As best man, Ace would be paired with her matron of honor, his sister, Aimee.

The men looked distinguished and handsome in their dazzling white uniforms, and the church was packed with notable guests, many of whom were strangers to her. A bout of nervousness seized Lacey. She tried to smile, but her face felt frozen. All these people staring at her! As a politician's daughter, she was accustomed to social events, but not one where she was the center of so much intense speculation. Lacey wondered if she looked good enough. The bullet wound was hidden by her dress, but the surgery had left a scar on her arm that remained visible. At first she wanted the sleeveless dress because it was lovely, with the yards of satin and white lace, and the high collar that would match the one on Jarrett's uniform. And she'd seen the sleeveless dress as a symbol of her future and her refusal to hide life's scars.

But now with nearly 800 guests looking at her, she had a moment of doubt. Lacey almost wished she had insisted on carrying out her plans to elope. And then she saw Jarrett. Tall, proud and handsome in his white uniform, the soft overhead lighting shining down upon his dark head, he had eyes only for her. He did not look at her dress, nor her flowers or her scarred bare arm.

Jarrett looked right into her eyes.

The music swelled as she walked down the aisle. As she drew closer, Lt. Jarrett Adler mouthed, "It's going to be all right." Then his crooked grin widened as he pointed to the vestry on the right and winked.

And then she smiled and knew everything was going to be all right.

* * * * *

Don't miss the next thrilling installment of
SOS AGENCY, *an exciting new miniseries by* New York Times *bestselling author Bonnie Vanak, coming in early 2017 from Harlequin Romantic Suspense!*

And check out these other titles by Bonnie Vanak, available now from Harlequin Nocturne:

DEMON WOLF
PHANTOM WOLF
THE COVERT WOLF

REQUEST YOUR FREE BOOKS!
2 FREE NOVELS PLUS 2 FREE GIFTS!

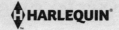

ROMANTIC suspense

Sparked by danger, fueled by passion

Her voice sounded oddly hollow. "Something wrong?"
he asked, doubling back.

Mirabella turned the monitor so he could see the
screen more readily. The anonymous email sender was
back. He glanced at the time stamp and saw the email had
been sent out early this morning. It was the first thing she
had seen when she'd opened her computer.

"What new bridegroom is getting away with murder?"
the first line read. "Better be careful and watch your back,
Mirabella, or you might be next on his list."

Anger spiked within him. Zane bit back a number of
choice words. Cursing at the sender, or at her computer,
would accomplish exactly nothing. He needed to take
some kind of effective action, not merely rail impotently
at shadows.

Zane put his hand on her shoulder in a protective
gesture.

"Don't be afraid, Belle. I'm going to track this infantile scum down. I won't let him get to you."

He meant physically, but she took it to mean mentally. "He's already gotten to me, but I'm not afraid," she fired back. "I'm angry. This jerk has no right to try to say what he's saying, to try to poison people's minds against us." Her eyes flashed as she turned toward Zane. "What the hell is his game?"

Her normally porcelain cheeks were flushed with suppressed fury. He'd never seen her look so angry—nor so desirable. Instead of becoming incensed, which he knew was what this anonymous vermin was after, Zane felt himself becoming aroused. By Mirabella.

Now wasn't the time, he upbraided himself.

It was *never* going to be the time, he reminded himself in the next moment. He'd married her to save her reputation, to squelch the hurtful, damaging rumors. Stringing up the person saying all those caustic things about them, about *her*, did not lead to the "and they all lived happily ever after" ending he was after—even if it might prove to be immensely satisfying on a very primal level.

Nothing wrong with a little primal once in a while, Zane caught himself thinking as his thoughts returned to last night.

Don't miss
THE PREGNANT COLTON BRIDE
by USA TODAY *bestselling author Marie Ferrarella,*
available August 2016 wherever
Harlequin® Romantic Suspense
books and ebooks are sold.

www.Harlequin.com

HRSEXP0716